Debtor's Daughter

Wicked Sons Book 11

By Emma V. Leech

Published by Emma V. Leech.

Copyright Emma V. Leech 2025©

Editing Services Magpie Literary Services

Cover Art: Victoria Cooper

ISBN No: 978-2-487015-51-7

About Me!

I started this incredible journey way back in 2010 with The Key to Erebus but didn't summon the courage to hit publish until October 2012. For anyone who's done it, you'll know publishing your first title is a terribly scary thing! I still get butterflies on the morning a new title releases, but the terror has subsided at least. Now I just live in dread of the day my daughters are old enough to read them.

The horror! (On both sides I suspect.)

2017 marked the year that I made my first foray into Historical Romance and the world of the Regency Romance, and my word what a year! I was delighted by the response to this series and can't wait to add more titles. Paranormal Romance readers need not despair, however, as there is much more to come there too. Writing has become an addiction and as soon as one book is over, I'm hugely excited to start the next so you can expect plenty more in the future.

As many of my works reflect, I am greatly influenced by the beautiful French countryside in which I live. I've been here in the Southwest since 1998, though I was born and raised in England. My three gorgeous girls are all bilingual and my husband Pat, myself, and our four cats consider ourselves very fortunate to have made such a lovely place our home.

KEEP READING TO DISCOVER MY OTHER BOOKS!

Other Works by Emma V. Leech

Wicked Sons

Wicked Sons Series

Daring Daughters

Daring Daughters Series

Girls Who Dare

Girls Who Dare Series

Rogues & Gentlemen

Rogues & Gentlemen Series

The Regency Romance Mysteries

The Regency Romance Mysteries Series

The French Vampire Legend

The French Vampire Legend Series

The French Fae Legend

<u>The French Fae Legend Series</u>

<u>Stand Alone</u>
<u>The Book Lover</u> (a paranormal novella)
<u>The Girl is Not for Christmas</u> (Regency Romance)

Audio Books

Don't have time to read but still need your romance fix? The wait is over…

By popular demand, get many of your favourite Emma V Leech Regency Romance books on audio as performed by the incomparable Philip Battley and Gerard Marzilli. Several titles available and more added each month!

Find them at your favourite audiobook retailer!

Acknowledgements

Thanks, of course, to my wonderful editor Kezia Cole with Magpie Literary Services

To Victoria Cooper for all your hard work, amazing artwork and above all your unending patience!!! Thank you so much. You are amazing!

To my BFF, PA, personal cheerleader and bringer of chocolate, Varsi Appel, for moral support, confidence boosting and for reading my work more times than I have. I love you loads!

A huge thank you to all of my beta readers and cheering section! You guys are the best!

I'm always so happy to hear from you so do email or message me :)

emmavleech@orange.fr

To my husband Pat and my family ... For always being proud of me.

Table of Contents

Family Trees

HOUSE OF ROTHBORN
To Bed the Baron

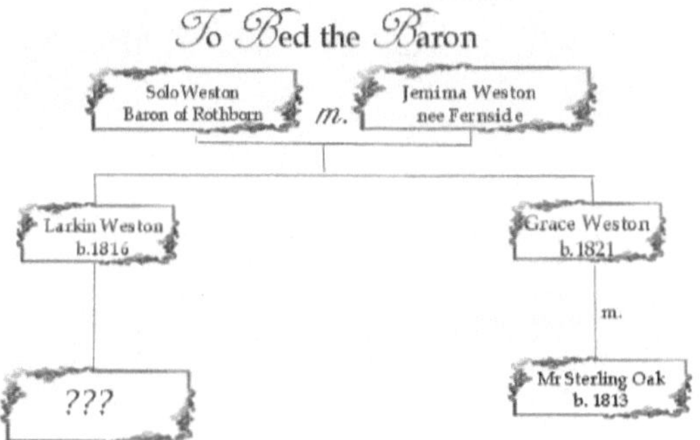

HOUSE OF BEDWIN
To Dare a Duke

Emma V Leech

HOUSE OF HUNT
To Steal a Kiss

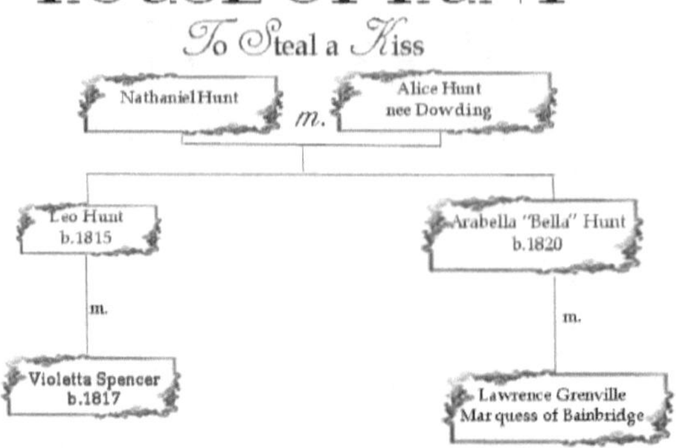

HOUSE OF CAVENDISH
To Break the Rules

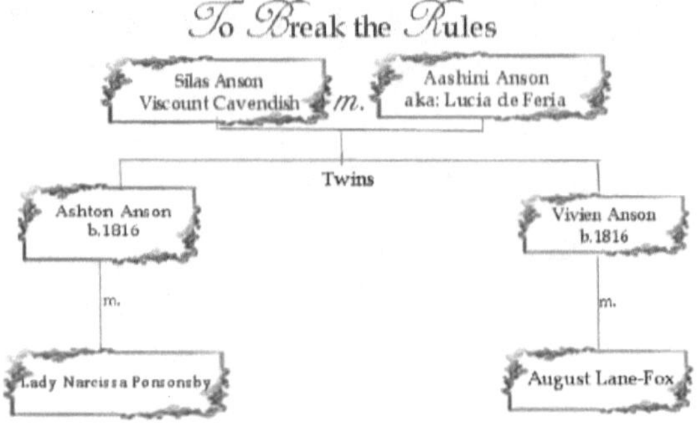

HOUSE OF TREVICK

To Follow her Heart

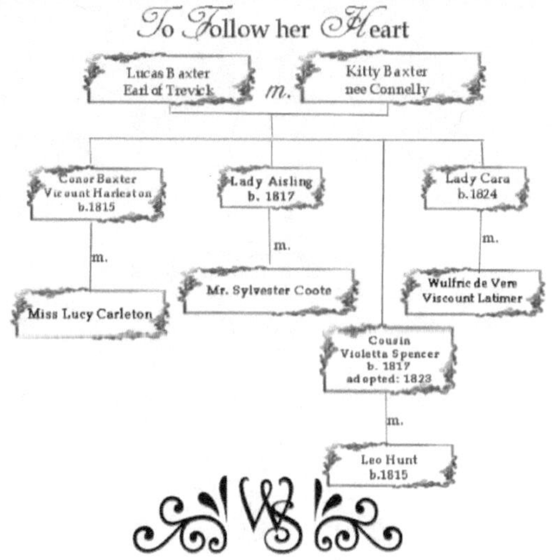

HOUSE OF ST CLAIR

To Wager with Love

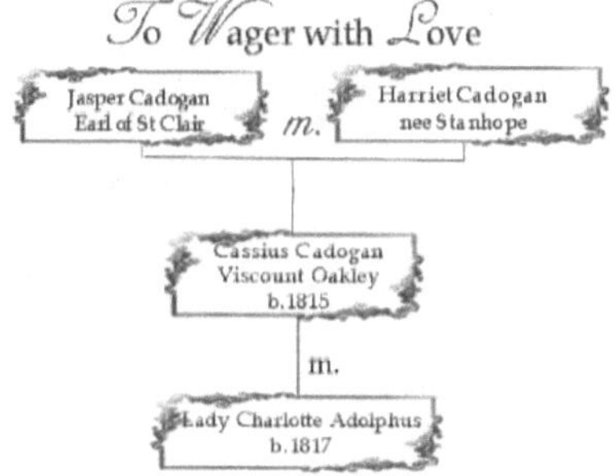

HOUSE OF CADOGAN
To Dance with a Devil

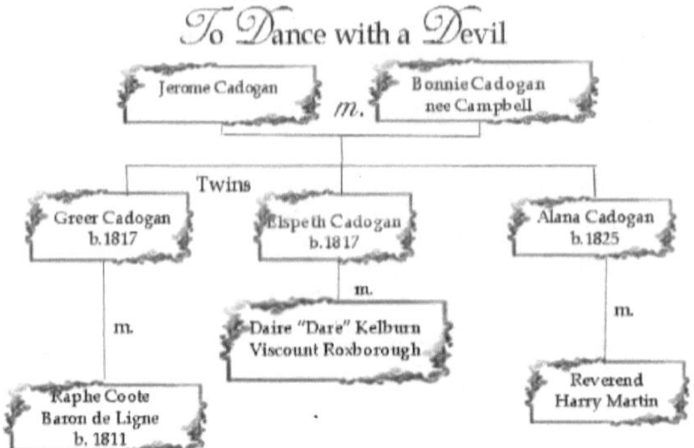

HOUSE OF MORVEN
To Winter at Wildsyde

HOUSE OF DE BEAUVOIR
To Experiment with Desire

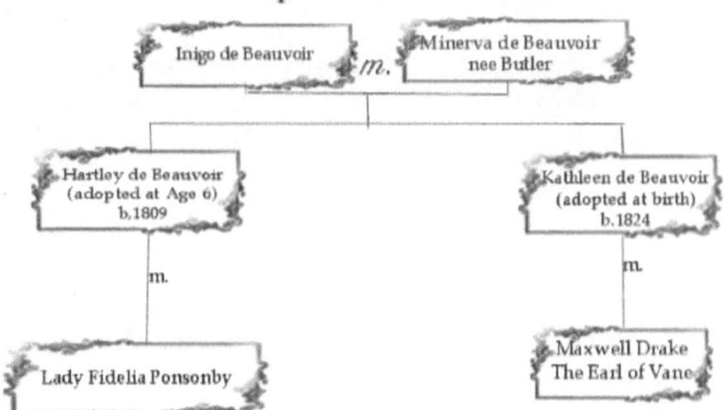

HOUSE OF KNIGHT
To Ride with the Knight

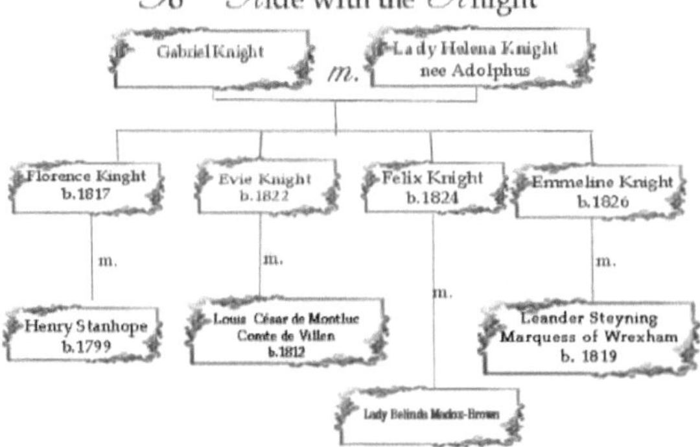

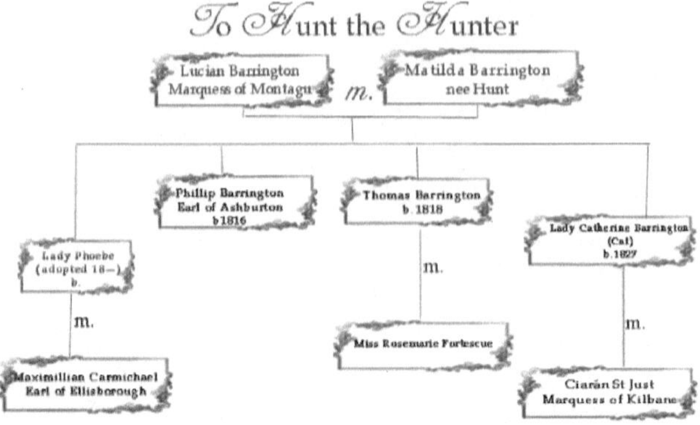
HOUSE OF MONTAGU
To Hunt the Hunter
Lucian Barrington
Marquess of Montagu
m.
Matilda Barrington
nee Hunt
Phillip Barrington
Earl of Ashburton
b.1816
Thomas Barrington
b.1818
Lady Catherine Barrington
(Cat)
b.1827
Lady Phoebe
(adopted 18—)
b.
m.
m.
Miss Rosemarie Fortescue
m.
Maximillian Carmichael
Earl of Ellisborough
Ciarán St Just
Marquess of Kilbane

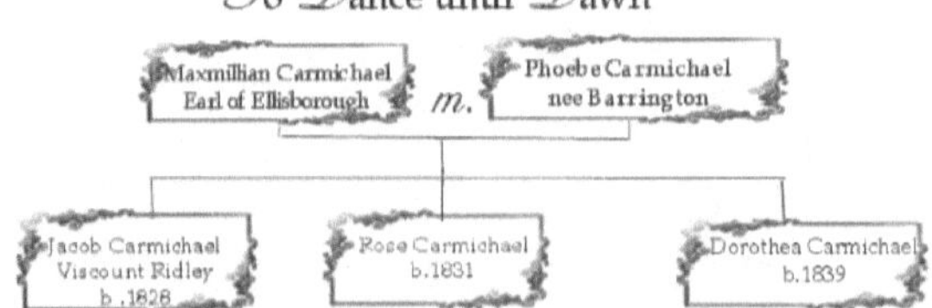
HOUSE OF ELLISBOROUGH
To Dance until Dawn
Maximillian Carmichael
Earl of Ellisborough
m.
Phoebe Carmichael
nee Barrington
Jacob Carmichael
Viscount Ridley
b.1828
Rose Carmichael
b.1831
Dorothea Carmichael
b.1839

Chapter 1

Dear Jack,

We have arrived safely in town. It's hot and dusty and smelly and I so miss the peace of the countryside and our lovely house. But I must not think of it, or I shall lose my temper all over again and what little china I have has already suffered more than I can afford. Yet I am heartsick and want to rage at Papa for what he has done to us, and at the same time I miss him so dreadfully I want to cry and not stop. Oh, what a terrible mess it all is. I cannot help but remember how frustrated I was by life just a few short months ago, and yet now with hindsight it seems my life was an idyllic existence I cannot bear the loss of.

I know I am making a terrible imposition upon you, forcing you to keep our whereabouts secret, but our stepmother cannot know where we have gone. I will not allow poor Caro to marry that vile man, not while there is breath in my body. I can only pray she will meet a good, kind man whilst she is here and marry him, and then she will be out of danger.

Our new neighbour is a Mr Larkin Weston who was so kind as to help carry the heavy packing cases inside for us, for we still have no servants. Mr Larkin's valet has been so good as to make some arrangements for us and we shall have a maid of all works, a cook, and a lady's maid arriving tomorrow. Thank heavens, for Aunt Constance is rather a trial to my nerves.

How I wish I had a female relation who could advise me. Papa was so rackety after Mama died, I never had a come out of my own and now I am feeling all at sea. I must hope I can make friends who will be good enough as to guide me how to go on.

—Excerpt of a letter from Mrs Magdelina Finchley to her friend and neighbour Mr Jack Woolgar.

17th September 1850, Berwick Street, Soho, London.

Larkin stood with a tiny brush in his hand, poised with the tiniest dab of *blanc de Krems* to add a glint of light to the eye of his latest portrait. It always astonished him how a little detail could bring such life and vibrancy to a figure that was ostensibly flat paint on canvas. Just a little touch here and—

Bang, bang, bang!

Larkin swore, snatching his hand away just in time. "Devil take the boy," he muttered, setting down the brush and hurrying to the window. It was the third time this week and Larkin was losing patience.

Bang, bang, crash, bang, bang, bang

Larkin pushed the sash up with some force before sticking his head outside.

"Master Gideon!" he shouted.

An overgrown hedge rambled along the fence below and, a moment later, a small boy appeared at a gap in the boundary. With his tumble of golden curls and big blue eyes, he appeared to be an adorable putto, but for a pair of wings and a harp. However, Larkin had concluded in the weeks since Gideon and his mama had moved in next door, this was merely a disguise. The child's namesake might have been an angel, but he had been sent by the devil to tempt Larkin back into misbehaving. Though he had never before resorted to murdering small children, drinking and carousing were all too appealing when boredom threatened, and if he couldn't work, that was an ever-present risk.

"'How you do, Mister Westie?" the boy said, cheerfully waving a wooden spoon at him.

"Mister Weston," Larkin corrected automatically before shaking his head. The child could call him what he liked if only he was quiet. "Gideon, do you remember that little chat you had with your mama about banging saucepans and saucepan lids out in the garden?"

The boy looked thoughtful for a moment and then nodded.

Good. Progress. "Excellent," Larkin said, smiling at the lad. "And do you remember what she said?"

Gideon pursed his lips, scratching his ear with the wooden spoon. "Fink so," he said, though he looked uncertain.

"Clever lad," Larkin said, encouraged. "And what was it she said, Gideon?"

Gideon stared at him for a long moment, opened his mouth, closed it again, and then ran off. The banging resumed.

Larkin groaned and closed the window.

"He's a fine, sturdy little fellow, that Gideon. Ain't he, sir?"

Larkin turned to observe his valet bearing a tray of coffee and biscuits into the studio.

"He's driving me mad is what he is," Larkin retorted, snatching a biscuit from the tray and stuffing it in his mouth.

"Well, hard for the boy, and the ladies, what with having no papa for the child," Barnes said with obvious sympathy.

Larkin sighed and rubbed a hand over his face. "I know," he said, for he felt a deal of sympathy for Mrs Finchley, whose husband, a Captain Finchley, of the Queen's troops had been killed at the Battle of Sobraon in the Punjab, barely two months after they'd married. This information had been gleaned through Barnes via the lady's maid as Larkin had seen little of her, and not a glimpse of her sister and aunt who lived with her. Mrs Finchley was a lovely young woman, though, who seemed to carry the world upon her shoulders. Larkin really did not wish to add to her troubles, but his career had suddenly taken off and he was much in demand for portraits. It was hard enough to work with Gideon crashing about but, if he had a sitter, it was also most embarrassing.

"Perhaps you could gift the boy something he could use a bit more quietly like?" Barnes said, noting his master's puckered brow.

"Paints?" Larkin suggested.

"Half of that lot could kill him," Barnes said in alarm, looking at the mess of vials of coloured powders and glass jars and bottles of turpentine and linseed oil.

"I wasn't about to get him oil paints. Just a little set of watercolours," Larkin said impatiently. "What do you think?"

"I think the lad gets enough quiet playtime with the ladies. What he needs is to let off steam. A bit of rough and tumble."

Larkin gave his valet a stony look. "I'm not becoming the child's nanny, Barnes, so don't even suggest it."

Barnes shrugged. "You want peace and quiet?"

"How about a ball?" Larkin suggested. "That's got to be quieter than crashing saucepan lids."

"Reckon so," Barnes agreed.

Larkin let out a sigh of relief. "Barnes, take what funds you deem necessary to buy such an article and have yourself a pint on the way back for your trouble."

Barnes brightened at the offer. "That's very good of you, sir. I shall, thank you."

Larkin waved this away. In his darkest moments over the past months, he had relied far too much on Barnes, who had gone above and beyond. He owed the fellow, and did not wish to risk losing him to someone else.

Watching Barnes take himself from the room, Larkin poured himself a cup of coffee and took another biscuit, regarding his painting with a critical eye. It had taken him a long time to give his work the credit it deserved. Not having spent years studying like many artists, he had worried that people only commissioned him because he was gentry, and not because he was the best there was. Yet he had worked long and hard, and he was not blind to the progress he had made. Having undertaken a personal study of the masters he admired, he now believed he was close to being worthy of placing his work beside theirs. Yes. Not bad, he thought with a surge of satisfaction. Not bad at all, though perhaps it needed a little—

Crash! Bang, bang, bang! Crash!

Larkin sighed.

17th September 1850, Berwick Street, Soho, London.

Maggie winced as she ran up to her front door, the crashing of saucepan lids quite audible from the front step. Exchanging a look of exasperation with Sally, her maid, Maggie let herself in, ran through the house, and hurried out into the back garden.

"Giddy!" she called to her son, dismayed to discover him marching about the overgrown jungle that was their garden, crashing two lids together like cymbals.

Giddy paused, the saucepan lids suspended momentarily, before giving her a dazzling smile and smashing them together once more. "How you do, Mama?" he asked cheerily.

"Giddy, what did I tell you about making such a racket in the garden? Mr Weston is an artist, and he cannot work when you make such a terrible noise."

"Not noise," Giddy objected. "Music."

"Well, we'll have to agree to differ on that score," Maggie said, hastening out, prising free one of the lids and taking the boy's hand. "Come inside. I expect Cook has a biscuit for you, not that you deserve one. You know very well I told you not to take the saucepans outside. That was a naughty thing to do."

She had also instructed Caro and Aunt Connie, *and* the cook, not to let Giddy make such uproar, but she was hardly surprised. Caro lived in a daydream, Connie in another world entirely, and Giddy could wrap Cook around his little finger.

"Mrs Moody," Maggie said, herding her son into the kitchen, where the heavenly scent of fresh baked bread and the sweet vanilla of sugar biscuits lingered in the air. "He's taken the saucepans again!"

"Ah, well, only the little one and a couple of lids," the cook—who was as far from suiting her name as night was from day—replied with an indulgent smile. "Boys will be boys."

"Yes, but this boy is driving our poor neighbour distracted," Maggie said, tugging at the black ribbons of her bonnet with one hand as she helped Giddy into a seat at the table with the other. "And I don't wish to aggravate the poor man."

Having found out a little about the man in question, the absolute last thing she wanted was to antagonise him. They had come to town intending to find Caro a husband, and it turned out Mr Larkin Weston was a most eligible *parti*. The son of a wealthy baron, his father a war hero no less, he was rumoured to be plump in the pocket and a rising star in the art world. He was also devastatingly handsome. It had all Maggie had been able to do not to gape at him upon their first meeting. After all, she had heard of him via the scandal sheets and read many stories about the wicked club he ran with his disreputable friends. She had assumed he would be old before his time and showing signs of dissipation. No, indeed. He had been tall and athletic, with an unruly shock of chestnut hair that glinted gold in the sunlight, and warm brown eyes. Not at all what she had expected, had she expected to meet him at all. It was a stroke of good fortune, though, and having had little in the way of luck since her husband was killed, Maggie was not about to let it, or him, slip through her fingers.

Admittedly, Mr Weston's reputation was concerning, but since moving in Maggie had seen no wild parties or ladies of ill repute coming and going, nor any recent mention of him in the scandal sheets, so perhaps the stories were exaggerated, or perhaps he had put such wild goings on behind him. As Mrs Moody said, boys would be boys.

"There you go, Master Gideon," Mrs Moody said, ruffling Gideon's angelic golden curls fondly as she placed a plate of biscuits and a cup of milk before him. "You tuck into those and drink your milk."

"Fanks, Moody," Giddy said, with a grin calculated to melt the hardest of hearts.

Mrs Moody, already smitten, just bent and pressed a noisy kiss to his cheek. "Oh, I could eat you up," she said with a sigh, before shaking her head and returning to her work.

"Be good," Maggie told her son, wagging a finger at him. "No saucepans, no lids. No crashing."

Giddy stuffed another biscuit into his mouth, his blue eyes dancing.

Maggie sighed and climbed the stairs to discover Caro sprawled on the floor of the parlour, cutting out pictures from old copies of La Belle Assemble and the Ladies Cabinet and adding them to her scrapbook. Having a fair hand with a pencil, Caro then filled in the scene around the figures, setting them in lavish ballrooms or elegant parlours.

"Caro, where is Giddy?" she asked, arms folded.

A pair of impossibly green eyes, framed with sooty black lashes, gazed up at Maggie.

Caroline Merrivale, Maggie's half-sister, shared their father's raven hair, which curled around her flawless face and made a sharp contrast against her fair skin. Though they saw each other every day, her beauty still made Maggie's breath catch sometimes; she had never seen a girl to rival Caro and remained utterly convinced that her sister was the most beautiful creature in the world. She was also kind-hearted, generous, and, at times, a complete ninny.

"Giddy?" Caro asked, blinking at Maggie. "Isn't he with you?"

"No," Maggie replied, striving for patience. "I went out, remember? And I asked you and Connie to ensure he did not disturb Mr Weston."

"Well, and why should he?"

"Because he was out in the back garden making enough noise to wake the dead!" Maggie exclaimed.

Caro gave a delicate shudder. "One ought not to speak of waking the dead," she reproved, before slanting an anxious glance at the ornate cuckoo clock on the wall to the left of the fireplace.

Maggie glared at her sister before throwing up her hands. She was all out of patience today. Unfortunately, at that moment, Aunt Connie floated into the room. She seemed to float everywhere, despite being built on far grander proportions than the rest of them. Her enormous bosom entered the room ahead of her, and the wide skirts in fashion did little to flatter her width, giving the impression of a fine ship in full sail. She also had Caro's lush black curls, flawless skin and flashing green eyes. According to their father the story she told of having lost her heart to an unsuitable man many years ago was pure fiction. Connie, however, was adamant. In her version of the story, her beloved had then vanished, and she had refused all others. Believing her beloved to be dead, she had retreated into her own world of romantic novels, cakes, and wistful nostalgia. Connie could certainly be alarmingly vague, but she was an absolute darling and, to Maggie's eye, was still beautiful, though she was close to fifty years of age.

"Oh, there you are," Aunt Connie said, giving Maggie a reproachful look as she wafted over to the most comfortable chair in the room and settled herself with the grace of a feather falling gently to earth. "I've been looking for you this age."

"I went out," Maggie said. She had specifically reminded Aunt Connie of this earlier but knew to her cost there was no benefit in pointing that out.

"Well, you might have told me," Connie said with a sigh, lifting a hand to her temples and rubbing gently. "Giddy has been making the most frightful racket."

"So I understand," Maggie replied, wondering if she had been terribly wicked in a past life. Perhaps that was why everything was going wrong and the people she loved most in all the world made her want to throw things, often at their heads. The trouble was, if she remonstrated it would either start a row or put everyone in a sullen mood and since their father had died, she seemed a lot less able to withstand such an atmosphere. It was simply easier to let things go and keep the peace. All the same, she could not help but ask the question. "Did you not think about telling him to stop?" *Like I asked you to do*, she did not add.

"I did," Auntie admitted. "But I was reading the bit where Darcy proposes, you know, and—" She sighed, shaking her head. "Well, you understand."

Maggie understood she was the only person in this house with the slightest grasp on reality. "I do?" she replied quizzically, though she ought to know better.

"Well, really, Maggie, darling. How could I interrupt him?" Auntie looked quite put out.

Maggie just about refrained from rolling her eyes, but it was a close thing. "Yes, yes. I quite understand. A shocking thing to interrupt a proposal in full flow. How cross they would be."

"Don't be silly, dear, they're characters in a book. They wouldn't *know,*" Auntie replied, apparently serious.

Maggie opened her mouth and closed it again. She'd only give herself a brain fever if she kept on. At that moment, the cuckoo clock—Aunt Connie's most treasured possession—chimed, apparently for no reason, as it was not yet three o'clock.

Cuckoo, cuckoo, cuckoo, cuckoo, cuckoo!

Deciding this was an opportune moment to leave her aggravating relations to their own devices, Maggie was about to go upstairs and change her gown, when there was a knock at the front door.

Pausing at the mirror in the hallway, she gave herself a cursory glance, seeing a rather harried woman with unusual blue-green eyes and thick, curling blonde hair that was escaping its pins on all sides, as usual. The sombre black dress she wore seemed to enhance her pallor and she pinched her cheeks, trying to add a little colour. People found it hard to believe she was Caro's sister, but Maggie took after her mother. Not that she had ever seen her, for Mama had died bringing her into the world, but the portrait that

Papa had moved to her bedroom when he had married Caro's mama showed a remarkable resemblance. It was one of the few items Maggie had refused to leave behind when they had run away and was still a comfort to her.

Taking a few moments to replace errant pins, Maggie smoothed her gown and went to answer the door.

"Oh, Mr Weston," she said, her heart sinking as she saw her neighbour on the doorstep. As usual, he was dressed elegantly but carelessly, his necktie shockingly askew and his hair rumpled as though he'd not long risen. His artistic temperament, she supposed, wondering how such disarray suited him when on any other man it would look dreadful. "I know why you are here, and I am so very sorry. I only went out for a short while, but Caro and Aunt Constance find Gideon rather a handful." *If they even remember he's there,* she added silently.

"Please do not trouble yourself, Mrs Finchley," he said, smiling warmly at her. "I've actually brought the little—er— *scamp* a present."

With that, he held aloft a parcel, awkwardly wrapped, but there was no disguising the shape of it.

"Oh!" Maggie gazed at him in surprise. "Goodness, but… how very kind of you."

Mr Weston grinned, and Maggie felt an odd fluttering in the vicinity of her rib cage at the engaging and surprisingly boyish expression. "In all honesty, Mrs Finchley, it's not in the least kind, but self-preservation. I thought it might be quieter and keep him away from kitchen utensils. I hope you will forgive me."

Maggie gave a sudden laugh, pleased by his ingenuity and tact. "Well, it is still kind of you. Please, do come in, and you may give it to him yourself. He'll be so pleased."

Thanking her politely, Mr Weston walked in, following her down the corridor to the front parlour. Upon opening the door, Maggie was unsurprised to discover Caro was no longer sprawled over the floor, but sitting demurely upon a chair, apparently reading a book. The black mourning gown and the copious tresses of black curls did not make her look pale but only enhanced her beauty, the soft ruby of her lips and the sooty lashes, and the impossible green of her eyes.

Mr Weston came into the room in Maggie's wake, and she was unsurprised to see his mouth fall open when his gaze landed upon Caro. She almost danced on the spot. Had that been love at first sight? How could it not be, when Caro was so heart-stoppingly beautiful?

To his credit, Mr Weston collected his wits quicker than most men did and they made their introductions. When Priddy, the maid of all work, appeared and bobbed a curtsey, Maggie ordered a tea tray be sent up and asked her to tidy Master Gideon up and bring him to the parlour.

"How are you finding the city, ladies? I'm afraid you have not seen it at its best these past weeks. It's not the place to be when it's hot, I'm afraid, but there is a good deal to see and do now the temperature is milder," Mr Weston said, his engaging manners and warm smile putting everyone at ease.

Maggie watched Caro surreptitiously, wondering what she made of Mr Weston. She had deliberately said little about him, hoping to pique her sister's interest, but Caro had not seemed curious in the least. Her manner towards him today was everything it ought to be, polite and friendly without being familiar, but the spark of interest or pretty blush Maggie had hoped for on being face–to-face with such a splendid gentleman was absent. Well, really. Was the girl blind?

"We've seen so little of it so we cannot really say," Caro said with a wistful sigh. "I had hoped to go to the theatre and—"

"A séance," Aunt Connie said, pressing her hands to her ample bosom. "So I might speak with—"

"Well, there is so much we have not seen or done," Maggie said in a rush, before Auntie could give the impression they were all as dotty as she was. Whilst Maggie was not about to swear there were no such things as ghosts or the afterlife, it was a dangerous subject to embark upon with a stranger in the house. "But it has taken us some time to make the house habitable, for it needed a little work, you understand?"

And hadn't that been an understatement? Maggie suppressed a shudder at the memory. It had been filthy and disgusting, but she was too polite to say such things, assuming the previous inhabitants might have been acquaintances or friends of Mr Weston.

"I'm surprised it didn't fall down around your ears," Mr Weston said frankly. "Old Mr Grantham was a shocking miser. I can only imagine what horrors you discovered."

"Dreadful," Auntie said, shaking her head, her lips pursed in a little moue of revulsion, though why Maggie could not fathom.

On discovering the worst of the dirt, Aunt Connie had retired to the only clean room in the house, too overcome with distaste to bear the strain. So Maggie and Priddy, bless her heart, had done it themselves. Caro had offered, though she'd not put up much of a fight when Maggie had refused. She could not have Caro ruining her lovely hands when her big chance was fast approaching. Maggie's time had come and gone, and she would not allow herself to regret that, for she had her darling Giddy to show for it, and surely that was compensation enough for the loss of her home and the life she had loved so dearly.

Cuckoo, cuckoo, cuckoo.

Drat and bother.

Maggie held her breath, hoping against hope, but no—

Cuckoo, cuckoo, cuckoo, cuckoo.

Mr Weston frowned and took out his pocket watch. "It's only twenty past three," he said, confused.

"Cecil doesn't like strangers," Auntie said, whispering behind her hand to Mr Weston, as though she did not wish the clock to hear her.

"More tea, Mr Weston?" she asked desperately, practically snatching the cup from his hand.

He jolted and looked as though he might refuse, but she was already pouring.

"Thank you," he said, before adding cautiously, "Cecil?"

"The cuckoo. Called Cecil," she said briskly. "Have a biscuit."

She thrust the biscuits at him, and he gave her an odd look but took one.

"Don't be silly, Maggie, dear," Auntie said, sounding impatient. "The cuckoo isn't called Cecil. It's just a wooden clock. Mr Weston will think you're queer in your attic if you go around saying such things."

Maggie swallowed a burst of hysterical laughter. "I beg your pardon, Auntie. Heavens, where has that boy got to, I thought he'd be here by now. I do hope he hasn't absconded with Mrs Moody's saucepans and—"

"It's my dead fiancé, you see."

Mr Weston looked from Maggie to her aunt, but Maggie could think of no way to stop the runaway train now in motion. This was it. Calamity before they had even begun. Mr Weston would tell all his friends the family were bedlamites and no one in their right mind would ever marry Caro.

"I beg your pardon," Mr Weston said, looking bewildered, as well he might. "What is?"

"Cecil," Auntie said, reaching for another biscuit and holding it between surprisingly dainty fingers. "Is my dead fiancé. He's haunting me. He lives in the cuckoo clock."

Maggie covered her face with her hand, her cheeks scalding with mortification. Any moment now, Mr Weston would excuse himself and leave and never be seen again. He'd probably move to Timbuktu if he had any sense. She wondered wistfully if he'd take her with him.

Mr Weston's eyebrows went up. "How, er—if it isn't an indelicate question—did he come to live in a cuckoo clock?"

Maggie groaned inwardly. At least she thought it had been inward, but Caro sent her a fierce glare and Mr Weston glanced in her direction, so perhaps not.

"Auntie Connie is very spiritual," Caro said, her soft voice dreamy and soothing. Lord, things must be bad for Caro to realise she must try to help. "She feels things deeply."

"How fascinating," Mr Weston said, and rather to Maggie's surprise, he did *look* interested, and not in the horrified 'wait until I tell all my friends about this' way she had expected. "But how— ?"

"Giddy!" Maggie practically shrieked as the door opened and her son came in. "Look, my darling. Mr Weston from next door has come to see you and he's brought you a lovely gift."

"Present?" Giddy said, his eyes lighting up.

"Yes, Master Gideon," Mr Weston said, smiling at the lad and reaching for the parcel beside him on the sofa. He held it out to Gideon, who glanced at his mother for approval. Maggie nodded, and the lad darted forward and took the parcel from Mr Weston.

"What do you say, Giddy?" Maggie prompted gently.

"Fank you," Giddy said, and then plopped his bottom down on the rug and began ripping the paper off. "A ball!" he exclaimed, beaming as he held the leather ball up to show his mama.

"Oh, and such a handsome ball it is, too. What colour is it, Giddy?" she asked him.

"Red and white," the boy said, touching a chubby finger to the red sections and then the white that had been sewn together to make the ball. "Play with it now, Mama?"

"You may," Maggie said, smiling at his eager expression. "But only in the garden, never in the house. Promise?"

"Not in the house," Gideon replied solemnly, and then ran from the room shouting. "Moody, Moody! Look what I's got!"

"I think he liked it," Caro said with a giggle and Maggie noted the look of admiration Mr Weston sent her and his accompanying smile.

"Perhaps it will keep him from plaguing you so with those dreadful saucepans," Maggie said, praying it would be so.

"Oh, Maggie, that boy and his saucepans. He made such a racket earlier," Auntie said, wagging a finger at Maggie. "You really ought to have told him off, the naughty boy."

Maggie swallowed the words brewing on her tongue and instead turned to Mr Weston. His eyes glinted, a look in them that suggested he knew just what she was thinking. Maggie felt colour rise to her cheeks and looked hurriedly away.

"Thank you, ladies, for a delightful visit," he said, bestowing a charming smile upon them all. "But if you will excuse me, I must return to my work."

Everyone stood, but Caro finally roused herself to ask a question of their guest.

"What kind of paintings do you do, Mr Weston?" Caro asked him before he could take his leave of them.

"Portraits, mostly," he replied, and then paused.

Maggie understood why, for the sun, which had been hidden behind thick cloud for most of the day, suddenly appeared and a shaft of golden light filtered through the lace curtains, illuminating Caro's lovely face. Mr Weston looked mesmerised, held by some unseen force as he gazed upon her.

"Has anyone ever painted you, Miss Caroline?"

"Me?" Caro said, eyes growing wide. "Good heavens, no. Why would they?"

Maggie almost laughed at Mr Weston's evident consternation, but Caro wasn't fishing for compliments. She knew she was considered lovely, but they had come from a rural place with few people and everyone, having known her from birth, had become familiar with her astonishing looks. In the city, things were different, and finding men stopping in the street to stare at her had been a shock to Caro, and one to which she was still not accustomed. That men wished to gaze at her was an idea she was struggling to appreciate. Maggie didn't blame her. It was most disconcerting.

"Because you are beautiful, Miss Caroline," Mr Weston replied candidly. "I should like very much to paint you. If you would allow it."

Caro blushed and looked to Maggie uncertainly.

"We are all proud of Caro," Maggie said with a smile, taking her sister's arm. "But this coming season is to be her first and we have no friends here, Mr Weston. I hope you understand that we must tread carefully." For more reasons than she could enumerate.

"Of course," he said at once. "I would certainly be very happy for you or your aunt to chaperone her at all times, but do you not have a sponsor, Miss Caroline?"

Caro shook her head. "Sadly not. Papa always intended for Mrs—"

"Things did not work out as we'd hoped they might," Maggie said hurriedly, sending Caro a glare of warning. They must avoid offering extra information about themselves. "So we are all at sea, I'm afraid."

Mr Weston looked thoughtful. "I wonder," he murmured. "I cannot make any promises, but I might help you there."

Maggie stared at him, heart thumping. "How so?" she asked, struggling to keep her voice calm when every instinct wanted to grab hold of his arm and plead with him, *yes, yes, please, anything!*

"If you would be so good as to leave the matter with me, I shall give it some thought. I'm certain my mother would be pleased to help, but sadly, she rarely comes to town. However, she does have a good many friends. It's possible I might at least ask one of them to make some introductions."

"Oh, Mr Weston," Maggie said, so overcome with relief at this lifeline her words trembled a little. The worry that they would be all alone and become objects of pity or derision among the *ton* had kept her awake at night. "I-I cannot tell you how grateful we would be."

Mr Weston held up a hand, shaking his head. "I have done nothing yet, and I cannot promise I will, but I shall try. Upon that, you have my word."

With that, he made his goodbyes, and his escape. Maggie only prayed he did not look back upon the visit and conclude that, temporarily dazzled by Caro's beauty, he'd gone and lost his mind.

Chapter 2

Dear diary,

I believe we are safe for now, but I wake most nights with bad dreams, terrified I will hear a fist hammering on the door and that horrid man demanding I honour my father's debt.

How can it be honourable for him to ask me to sacrifice myself and dishonourable for me to deny him? Oh, Papa, why did you do this to us? We were so happy before, why did you spoil everything?

—Excerpt of an entry from Caroline 'Caro' Merrivale to her diary.

17th September 1850, Berwick Street, Soho, London.

"Barnes!" Larkin called as he strode back into the house, setting down his hat and gloves.

"Sir?"

Barnes appeared in the hallway, immaculate as always.

"Which of my mother's cronies is in town at present?"

Barnes considered this. Larkin had long ago given up figuring out how Barnes came by his information, but the fellow seemed to be the fount of all knowledge which was a useful talent in a valet, though Barnes did far more than valet, acting as butler, secretary, and often cook too.

"I believe the Montagus have been in town this summer, which is unusual, but seeing as Dern is so close, they can come and go for a few weeks here and there. I heard tell the marquess had been working with Mr Knight on some project that required their attention. He don't go nowhere without Lady Montagu, so I reckon she's here if his lordship is."

Larkin nodded. "Send a note to Pip, tell him I'll be calling on him in the morning. Now, I've given the angelic antichrist his ball, there's half a chance I might have a few hours' peace. I am not to be disturbed, Barnes, is that clear?"

"Quite clear, sir," Barnes agreed, and then his eyebrows rose in enquiry as the door knocker sounded.

"I'll get it," Larkin said with a sigh.

Quite prepared to tell whoever it was get lost, he snatched the door open and then laughed as he saw who was standing there.

"Speak of the devil," he said, grinning at the Earl of Ashburton, who looked his cool and precise best as usual.

"Taking my name in vain, Lars?" the earl drawled, one pale eyebrow rising in an expression so familiar from his formidable sire that Larkin was struck with the sudden urge to apologise for something. He didn't know what, but Montagu had that effect on a fellow.

"I just told Barnes to write you a note, but you've saved me a journey. Come in."

Larkin held the door open and asked Barnes to bring coffee.

"Well, to what do I owe this unexpected pleasure?"

"I came to see what all the fuss is about, for I'm hearing from all sides that you're the fellow to watch so I thought I'd see for myself. I've been wanting to get a portrait done of Tilly, now there's half a chance she'll sit still for more than a minute at a time. Figured I had best get in before the rest of the world did."

"Oh," Larkin said, pleased. "Well, I'd be happy to, but you'd best come through to the studio if you want to see the latest work. For heaven's sake, *don't* touch anything," he added, eyeing Pip's exquisite tailoring with alarm. "I don't want a bill for getting paint off your sleeve."

"I think I can manage, Mama," Pip replied dryly, gesturing for Larkin to lead on.

Feeling suddenly a little anxious, Larkin went to his studio, and the newly finished portrait of Lady Cara Latimer. He turned it for Pip to look over and then stood back beside his friend. It was a stunning portrait, if he did say so himself, but then the subject matter had been exceptional too. Lady Cara's fiery red hair and lively blue eyes made her an easily recognisable figure among the *ton*. Beautiful and rather outspoken, the portrait captured her energy, a naughty sense of mischief, and her innate kindness.

Larkin glanced at Pip nervously. Ashburton was known for his exquisite taste, for being a man who accepted nothing less than perfection. Like his sire, his reputation was one of a cold, haughty man who did not suffer fools. Larkin knew much of this was simply the aura he wrapped himself in, a way of keeping the rest of the world at arm's length, but all the same….

"It's exceptional."

Larkin let out a breath and Pip turned his cool gaze towards him, his pale eyes amused. "Did you think I couldn't see it?"

"One never knows," Larkin said with a laugh. "The eye of the beholder and all that."

"I'm flattered to think my opinion matters to you," Pip said with a smile.

Larkin snorted. "You know damned well it matters."

Pip accepted this with no argument and returned his attention to the portrait. "You've captured something, not just her likeness, but the essence of Cara. I feel like she's about to leap out of the chair and go off and do something more interesting."

"She often did," Larkin said with a laugh. "I had the devil of a time getting her to keep still."

"Good practise," Pip said, smirking. "I can't wait to see how you fare with Tilly."

"Tilly and I understand one another," Larkin said loftily. "We'll be fine."

"On your head be it," Pip remarked. "When do you want to start?"

"Well, to begin, I might just come around and do some sketches. I could come tomorrow if that suits?"

Pip nodded, and the conversation halted as Barnes appeared with the coffee.

"In here, sir?" he asked, clearly disapproving of Larkin receiving such elevated guests in the chaos of his studio.

"Yes, thank you, Barnes. That will be all," he said, ignoring his valet's critical expression and reaching for the coffeepot. He poured a cup for Pip before helping himself. "There is one thing," he said, taking a tentative sip of the steaming liquid. "The reason I was coming to visit you. Is your mother in town?"

"No, but she returns tomorrow, thank the lord. My father is impossible when she's not here and he's driving me distracted. Why?"

"I've new neighbours," Larkin said. "A Mrs Finchley and her aunt and sister, and Pip, my lord, the *sister*. You've never seen such a beautiful girl in all your life, I swear. She's coming out this season, but they don't know anyone. Mrs Finchley is a widow, her husband was killed in the Punjab."

"Poor devil," Pip said, his expression darkening.

Larkin nodded. "She's got a four-year-old son, but I think their circumstances are perhaps a little straightened. I should like to help them. I believe Miss Caroline is their hope for the future and, dowry or no, she'll take, I'll swear it. With looks like that, she could catch herself a duke, I'd say. Especially when I present society with the portrait I intend to make of her."

Pip frowned, giving Larkin the benefit of one of his most penetrating stares. "Rescuing damsels in distress again, Lars? Are you quite sure that's a good idea?"

Larkin bristled. "Stow it. This is entirely different."

Pip shrugged. "Well, you're a big boy and it's your own affair, but what has my mother to do with it?"

Larkin hesitated, knowing it was a lot to ask, and that Pip might not like it. "I thought she might sponsor the girl or at least make a few introductions. I have the feeling Mrs Finchley is out of her depth and I should hate to see them flounder. You know what the *ton* is like for smelling uncertainty or the slightest sense of not belonging."

"But do they belong?" Pip asked coolly.

"Pip!" Larkin exclaimed, dismayed despite knowing he was putting his friend in a difficult position.

The earl waved away his shocked retort. "Oh, don't look so horrified. I must ask. You cannot seriously expect me to present these women to my mother, knowing nothing about them. Would you? With *my* father?"

Larkin sighed. "No. No, I accept that, but I'd swear they're respectable."

"You make sure of that first, but if they are, you may bring them. Mama always has her *at home* on a Friday when she's in town so that's the time to come. But if you foist some dreadful girl upon her, I'll murder you, Lars, and don't think I won't."

23rd September 1850, Berwick Street, Soho, London.

It was several days before Larkin could speak to Mrs Finchley again. He was making his way home from Massoul & Co, his favourite artist's supplies shop on New Bond Street, when he came upon the lady and her maid walking home along Great Marlborough Street.

Crossing the road, he smiled when she waited for him and raised his hat. Larkin gave her a polite bow. "Good morning, Mrs Finchley. How do you do?"

"Quite well, Mr Weston, I thank you, and yourself?"

"In fine fettle," he replied, admiring her well-tailored walking dress. The fit was glorious, highlighting an exceptional figure, and the rich black fabric was obviously expensive. This was the kind of garment made for a woman of means. He had noted the family all wore mourning, not just Mrs Finchley, and wondered at the extent of the tragedy that afflicted them, for Mrs Finchley no longer needed to wear mourning dress for her husband after so many years. Barnes thought it might be on account of their father, but said they were all quite tight lipped about it. "Actually, I am glad to have this opportunity to speak privately with you."

Mrs Finchley glanced up at him, her eyes alert, and he held up his hands in an expression of innocence. "My intentions are honourable, I promise, Mrs Finchley, but the truth is, the situation is a little delicate and I'm anxious I may put my foot in it. I must beg you to be lenient with me, for I have no wish to cause offence."

This, naturally, only made her look increasingly ill at ease, but there was no going back now. Larkin glanced over his shoulder at her maid, who had dropped back to a discreet distance, and lowered his voice. "The thing is, Mrs Finchley, I spoke to my friend Ashburton about Miss Caroline."

"The earl?" she asked, astonishment in her voice.

Larkin nodded. "He has agreed to allow me to bring you to meet his mother, Lady Montagu, to see if she likes Miss Caroline and would consider sponsoring her or at least give her some helpful introductions."

"Oh! Oh, good heavens." Mrs Finchley put a hand to her heart, bosom heaving dramatically. To Larkin's dismay, her eyes glittered with tears. "I-I beg your pardon," she said, fishing about in her reticule for a handkerchief.

Larkin hurriedly provided his own, and she took it gratefully, dabbing at her eyes and sniffing. "Forgive me," she said, her voice choked. "I'm not usually one to lose my wits. Only it's been such a worry."

"There is a catch," Larkin said gently, not wishing her to get ahead of herself.

He waited for the lady to compose herself, watching as her candid blue-green gaze settled upon him.

"She wishes to know if we are respectable," she guessed.

Larkin nodded.

"Quite understandable," she said with a crooked smile. "And we are, I promise you that, only… only the situation is rather a delicate one. Oh, dear. I shall have to explain, I suppose."

Worry creased her brow, and Larkin hated the need to ask such indelicate questions, but there was no help for it.

"I'm afraid you must," Larkin said apologetically. "Montagu would have me hung, drawn and quartered if I introduced scandal into his household."

"As to that," Mrs Finchley swallowed hard, the colour leaving her face. An altogether different expression settled over her fine features, the sparkle of hope he'd seen just moments ago dying a swift death. "Perhaps we should not proceed any further. I should hate to be the cause of any… any— Forgive me," she said, and picked up her pace, striding away from him.

Nonplussed by this sudden *volte-face*, Larkin frowned and hurried after her.

"Mrs Finchley?"

She shook her head. "It was foolish of me to believe anyone else could help. You are so very kind, Mr Weston, and I cannot in all conscience involve you in our troubles. I have always considered our family above reproach, but… but my father…" Her voice trembled and she shook her head.

Sensing this was a delicate topic, Larkin hesitated. "Mrs Finchley. Whilst Lord Montagu protects his family at all costs, he is not an unfeeling man. If you are deserving of help, I am certain he would bestir himself to do so, Lady Montagu certainly would. Do you think you might put your trust in me, and tell me the whole? At least that way, I might judge for myself what the best thing to do is. I promise, I shall help if I can. Even if you are correct, and Montagu is out of reach."

She stopped suddenly, staring up at him. "Do you mean that?"

There was something close to desperation behind the words and Larkin heard a little voice in his head, sounding remarkably like the Earl of Ashburton, reminding him what had happened the last time he'd helped a damsel in distress. Both he and the damsel had got burned, and he had sworn off such entanglements, preferring to concentrate on his art. This time, however, he told himself he was in no danger. Mrs Finchley was a charming woman. Attractive, too. *Very* attractive, actually, but he had no desire to be papa to little Gideon, perish the thought. And whilst Miss Caroline Merrivale was quite the most exquisite female he'd ever seen, she was only a girl and did not appeal to him in the least.

"I do," he said firmly, praying he would not come to regret his words.

"And I could confide in you and—"

"No matter what you say, I will take it to my grave," he promised her. "You have my word as a gentleman."

She stared at him for a long moment and his gaze, always alert to the beauty around him, to the fine blend of colour and light, was transfixed momentarily by the changeable nuances of her eyes. They were a pale melange of lightest green and the most heavenly sky blue, with little threads of gold flickering amid the delicate turquoise. Depending on the light, her eyes seemed sometimes bluer or greener. Her regard was unwavering, and he felt her judging what she saw, as if she could reach into his mind and discover his secrets, discover if he was worthy of her trust. He stared back, refusing to hide, though the urge to look away was nigh on irresistible. It was as if his soul were being stripped bare… not a comfortable experience. He appreciated in that moment that Mrs Finchley was perhaps more perspicacious than first impressions might have led him to believe upon meeting her and her unconventional family.

"Very well," she said, putting up her chin. "I shall put my trust in you, Mr Weston, for Caro's sake. For the truth is, since we came to town, I have realised how foolish I have been. I thought to give my sister a season, to give her the chance she deserves to shine as she ought. But I never had a season myself and we ran away in such a rush that I never stopped to consider, to realise that… that we are nobodies if there is no one of rank to sponsor us. I have been a fool, in short, and I am terrified of what will become of Caro if I fail her."

"Fail her?" Larkin said in confusion. "But what of you, Mrs Finchley? Surely Miss Caroline has parents, or guardians?"

Mrs Finchley put a hand to her head, a pained expression flickering in her eyes.

"I beg your pardon. I am a wretched fellow for interrogating you so."

"You are a deal too kind," she said, glancing up at him, something close to disbelief in her eyes. "I cannot think why you should trouble yourself."

"Call it a character flaw," he said ruefully. "I find myself compelled to help damsels in distress."

She laughed at that. "How very uncomfortable for you."

"You have no idea," Larkin murmured under his breath.

"Very well, Mr Weston. Might I prevail upon you to take tea with us tomorrow afternoon, and I shall tell you the whole story? It—It isn't a pretty story," she added, an apologetic note to her words. "But Caro, myself, and my aunt are innocent of any wrongdoing. That much I can promise you."

"I believe you," he said gently, noting the gratitude and relief that flared in her eyes.

The poor woman must be at her wits' end to trust in him so readily. For, whilst he was entirely sincere in his wish to help them, she could not know that he wasn't a trickster or some wicked blackguard intent on causing mischief for his own ends. Thank the lord she had fallen in with him and not with any of the other scoundrels who abounded in the city. The idea made a sensation like iced water slide down his spine. He shook it off. It was not for him to feel protective of women he barely knew but, as a gentleman, if he could do them a good turn, he certainly ought. Once he had them safely under the wing of Lady Montagu, or some woman of sense, at least, he might leave them to their own devices with a clear conscience.

With that thought at the forefront of his mind, he escorted Mrs Finchley the rest of the way home and bade her a good day.

Chapter 3

Dear diary,

Mr Weston is quite the kindest man I have ever encountered. Whilst I am not so foolish as to believe there is no smoke without fire, surely his reputation for hard drinking and wickedness must be fabricated? His desire to help us must be genuine, for what fool would suggest involving Lady Montagu in a scheme to help if it were not entirely respectable and had the best of intentions? Of course, his desire for Caro motivates him, I do not doubt. What man would not be smitten when faced with such exquisite beauty? Yet I worry she is rather too young for him. His involvement in a gambling club is also not what I would choose, yet the house always wins, I believe, so perhaps this proves he does not have the reckless streak poor Papa possessed. How I wish Caro did not have to marry with such urgency, for I do not believe she is entirely ready for such a step, but I must see her safe. Marriage to a man who will be kind to her and treat her with gentleness and respect is a far better fate than that which she might have faced had we not run away.

*Perhaps I have not been such a fool after all.
Only time will tell.*

**——Excerpt of an entry from Mrs
Magdelina Finchley to her diary.**

24th September 1850, Berwick Street, Soho, London.

"Do you understand, Caro?" Maggie asked, looking over her sister's head to her reflection in the dressing-table mirror as she made an adjustment to her shining black curls.

"Yes, Maggie, but really, I do not see how I am to stop Auntie from saying something to Mr Weston that will put us both to the blush. You know what she is, and besides, I cannot help but agree that there is something very odd about that cuckoo clock. I believe it is actually possessed."

"Don't be ridiculous," Maggie said impatiently. "You know Papa never believed there ever even *was* a beau, let alone that he died or that Grandpapa sent him away. And even if there was such a man, which I am not saying there couldn't be, for Papa could not know everything his sister got up to, but *why* should she think him dead? Let alone haunting the clock he supposedly gave her. And Papa always insisted the clock was a present from his great aunt Rebecca when she travelled through Switzerland. But that's by the by. Whoever the man was, perhaps he *was* sent away, or ran away, but it is easier for her to believe he died and that is why he never returned to her."

Caro sighed. "I know. Whatever the truth, it's terribly sad. Auntie ought to have married and had a family of her own."

"Yes, she ought, and so must you, my girl, which is why we must put our trust in Mr Weston and tell him the whole. I think it is our only option. It was very bad of me to bring us all to town with no clear plan of how to go on, but we have been thrown a lifeline, and I intend to make the most of it."

"Oh, Maggie, do stop taking everything on yourself." Caro turned on the stool, looking up at her sister and taking her hands. "We all agreed to come, and what other choice was there? Our home was not our own and we would have been out on the street in any case. At least here we have a chance."

Touched by this show of solidarity, Maggie bent and kissed Caro's cheek. "Thank you, dearest. What do you think of Mr Weston, by the way?" she asked, striving for nonchalance as Caro considered the question.

"Well, he seems very kind, to trouble himself with our affairs, though I expect he hopes we will move and take Giddy with us if I find a suitable husband," she added with a laugh.

Maggie smiled ruefully. "There is perhaps some truth in that, but do you not think him very handsome?"

"Handsome?" Caro, who was choosing a pair of earbobs from her jewellery box, looked up in surprise, as though the question had not occurred to her. "Oh. Well, yes, he is very handsome, I suppose."

"And his manners are exactly as they ought to be," Maggie added encouragingly.

"Hmmm? Do you think the pearls are best?"

"Yes, perfect," Maggie said, a little exasperated. "I think he was rather taken with you, Caro."

"Who was?"

"Mr Weston," Maggie replied, holding onto her patience. "He was taken. With you."

"Mr Weston?" Caro repeated, frowning. "Isn't he rather old?"

"Indeed, he is not. He can only be in his early thirties. In his prime, one would say."

Caro looked doubtful. "He seems rather old to me."

Maggie sighed. "Yes, I suppose he must, dear. Oh, lawks. That's the door. He's here. Hurry, Caro, we cannot leave him alone with Auntie. Now, do remember, try to help me keep her from scaring him off."

"I'll try," Caro said doubtfully. "But I make no promises."

24th September 1850, Berwick Street, Soho, London.

A neat maid in a pristine white apron showed Larkin into the parlour where Miss Constance Merrivale, the ladies' aunt, was already ensconced. She glanced up from the book in her hand, a dreamy look in her eyes which faded gradually as she focused upon him.

"Mr Weston," she said, extending a hand to him with all the grandeur of an empress. She had the look of such an impressive creature, dressed as she was in a voluminous gown of plum satin so dark it was almost black and that seemed to explode out of the chair she sat in on all sides. "How good of you to call upon us again. My niece tells me how terribly kind you have been. It's a rare thing, in these troubled times, to find such kindness. Especially in the city. Such a heartless, brutal place it is, when you have no friends or companions to comfort one. I miss the countryside," she said with a heavy sigh. "Do you like the countryside, Mr Weston?"

"I do, very much," Larkin said, a little uncomfortable to still be standing and staring down at her, but as the lady had not yet deigned to invite him to sit, he had little option but to remain on his feet.

"Then why are you still here?" she asked. "If, like me, you feel the countryside in your soul, the rivers that flow like your own life's blood, why do you remain in the turmoil and hurly-burly of this vast, brutal landscape?"

Larkin blinked, a little taken aback. "Er… my work," he said cautiously. "I am an artist, Miss Merrivale, but to further my career, it is better for me to spend time in town. At least for the moment. I hope once my reputation is fully established, I might return to the countryside, especially in the summer months, for London is a trial to the senses in hot weather."

"And to the soul, Mr Weston," the lady exclaimed, putting a hand upon her expansive bosom. "And to the soul."

The door opened and Larkin admitted himself relieved to see Mrs Finchley and Miss Caroline Merrivale enter the room. Once again, his gaze travelled to Miss Caroline automatically, still finding it hard to believe such a beautiful creature was really flesh and blood. The only woman he had ever seen to rival her was Lady Kilbane. Cat was generally acknowledged to be the most beautiful woman in the country, but she was a stunning ice blonde. Miss Caroline, with her raven hair and green eyes, was quite a different prospect.

"Mr Weston. Thank you for coming. I am afraid we are trespassing upon your time quite shamelessly," Mrs Finchley said with a smile. "And please, do take a seat," she added, shooting a disbelieving look at her aunt, who seemed oblivious to her error.

"Not at all, and I beg you will remember my promise and not feel in the least uncomfortable. I will help you as best I can. You have my word."

Once everyone settled, all eyes turned to Mrs Finchley and in that moment, Larkin realised what a burden rested upon her shoulders. For all she was a widow, she looked to be no more than two and twenty. Yet she was mother to a small boy, and responsible for her unmarried sister, and a maiden aunt who was certainly a little eccentric. His heart went out to her, and he understood why she had become tearful upon hearing his offer of help. Looking closer at her now, he saw the shadows under her lovely eyes, the signs of strain upon a face made for smiling. The poor girl was exhausted with worry.

"Well, there is no easy way of saying it, so I shall be frank, Mr Weston. Our father was a wonderful man, kind and generous to a fault, but he had a fatal flaw. Gambling, in short. When he remarried two years ago, the marriage… was not a success." She spoke carefully, but with a candid air that he appreciated. It was clear she was mortified, her cheeks blazing with colour, but she held his gaze, her chin up. "In his unhappiness, my father lost large sums of money, but it only seemed to spur him on to greater recklessness. One night this summer, he gambled and lost our family estate in Norfolk, and everything we possessed, to a man—I will not say gentleman—who now seems to believe we, too, are his property."

Larkin stared at her, appalled and sensing there was worse to come. She had said their father *was*—past tense. "I am so sorry."

Mrs Finchley inclined her head a little but seemed determined to get the worst over with. "Our father is dead, Mr Weston." The words hung in the air, the shock of what followed bringing an oppressive silence in its wake. "He could not live with the shame of what he'd done and took his own life."

Larkin's breath caught. *Hell. Bloody, bloody hell.*

"I see," he said, once he could bring himself to respond.

"We will understand if you feel unable to help us any further," Mrs Finchley said, her hands clenching and unclenching nervously in the skirts of her dress.

Larkin looked at her, at the dignity of her bearing, at a woman who would do whatever it took to keep her family safe, no matter the cost to herself, he suspected.

"Of course I shall help you," he said quietly, a dart of pain piercing his heart at the relief that shone in Mrs Finchley's eyes. "But I must ask you some personal questions, if you can bear it?"

Mrs Finchley nodded, and Miss Caroline, who had been sitting beside her on the sofa, reached over and took her hand.

"Your father's name?"

"He was John Merrivale, youngest son of Viscount Fothersham."

"The viscount?" Larkin suggested, only to be met with a fierce shake of her head. "My father fell out with the family many years ago. Our stepmother has already approached the new viscount, my father's brother, though I warned her it was a mistake. I am afraid they made it very clear they wanted no part of such a scandal. In short, they have disowned us."

Larkin started at that. Though he knew I happened often enough, he could not help but wonder at the callousness of a family that could wash its hands of the downfall of their own flesh and blood. Larkin remembered hearing of the scandal at the time. Mr Merrivale, or 'Merry Merrivale' as he was known, had been a respected fellow and well liked, though he did not move among the higher circles of the ton.

"You are still in mourning," he observed. "When did your father die?" For it would not be possible for Miss Caroline to make her come out before a year was passed.

"In May. Mr Jenkins appeared three weeks later, and he gave us a month to make up our minds. We ran away in June but were forced to stay in temporary lodgings for a time before we found this house to let. And yes, I know if Caro comes out in February we will only have mourned for ten months, but our father has destroyed our lives by his actions. I will not allow him to ruin my sister's chance for happiness by missing a season, for our finances are not such that we can afford a second. My husband left me a small sum that would do well enough if it were just myself and Gideon, and Aunt Constance has helped as much as she can, but none of us are independently wealthy, and I have Gideon's future to think of too. Have I shocked you?" she asked, looking anxious and somewhat defensive.

"I think you have managed a dreadful situation as well as you possibly could, and I agree it would be pointless to keep such a lovely girl hidden away for another year." He smiled at Miss Caroline, who blushed and looked away. "And what of the man your father lost to?"

"A Mr Jenkins," she said, the distaste she felt for the man writ large on her face. "In his desperation, it appears my father resorted to the less refined gambling establishments, as his own club would no longer extend him credit."

Larkin nodded. It was an all too familiar story. He wondered if the lady knew of his involvement in the Sons of Hades, and if she did not, if she would think ill of him.

"Mr Jenkins is not the kind of man a lady would wish to depend upon, Mr Weston," Mrs Finchley said, and Larkin sensed her growing agitation. "He—He turned up at our house and… and had the temerity to imply that Caro—that she *belonged* to him, that he had won her, along with the house, and if we did not wish to be thrown into the street, we would do well to agree to her marrying him."

Larkin swallowed a litany of bad language that would likely have had Miss Caroline and Miss Merrivale swooning, though he suspected Mrs Finchley was made of sterner stuff. As it was, he shot to his feet, raking a hand through his hair in his agitation. He took a moment to calm himself before sitting once more.

"I cannot tell you how very sorry I am that you were forced to endure such… such vile behaviour," he said, finding it hard to keep a lid on his temper. He reminded himself that these women were strangers to him, not his kin, not his problem, and yet he knew he would do all in his power to see them safe. If he ever came across Mr Jenkins, he'd have a few things to say to him, too, preferably with his hands wrapped about the bastard's throat.

"Thank you, Mr Weston. I am afraid, however, that our stepmother was of the opinion that Caro ought to sacrifice herself.

She is not a kind woman, and I am ashamed to say we have been at odds since the moment Papa brought her home as his wife. I am willing to admit this may have been my fault in part, for I have been mistress of our family estate since Caro's mama died."

· "Oh, no," Miss Caroline said fiercely. "That is quite untrue. Maggie did everything she could to make the horrid creature welcome, but nothing pleased her. She's intolerable, and it's her fault Papa is d-dead. If not for her, he would not have stayed away so long and got himself into such trouble. He was always a little reckless, but never—never—"

With a sob, Miss Caroline got to her feet and ran from the room.

"Oh dear," Mrs Finchley said, but before she could follow her sister, their aunt had risen and moved to the door.

"I'll go, Maggie dear. I know how best to soothe her when she's like this."

Miss Merrivale went out of the room in pursuit of their niece, closing the door behind her. Larkin glanced at it, about to get to his feet and object but then he noticed the misery on Mrs Finchley's face. The poor young woman. To have lost her husband and then her father and her home in such a short period, and to have her son, her sister, and her aunt relying upon her to put it right… it must be a heavy burden to bear.

"I did say it was not a pretty story," she said with a wan smile. "I imagine you rue the day we moved in next door to you, what with Giddy destroying your peace and now—"

"Not at all," Larkin said, though she was not entirely wrong. Still, if he could get her under the protective wing of Lady Montagu, all would be well. It might also be an idea to discover more about this bastard Jenkins. Perhaps there was more practical help he could offer them. "I believe, from what you've told me, that Lady Montagu would be pleased to help you, but I cannot answer for her. If you are willing, I will escort you to Montagu

House to pay her a call on Friday. I will arrange for us to go rather earlier than is usually acceptable, and then we may be private with the lady for a while before the world and his wife descends upon her."

"You are very good, Mr Weston," she said, gazing at him in wonder. "Like a benevolent angel, come to our rescue."

He laughed at that, quite unable to do otherwise. "You don't read the scandal sheets, do you, Mrs Finchley?"

"Actually, I do, or at least, I have in the past," she admitted, a tinge of colour cresting her cheeks.

"Then I wonder you can say such things with a straight face," he remarked, trying to cheer her spirits a little.

To his relief, she rallied, a mischievous light dancing in her eyes.

"I confess, when you introduced yourself, I was torn between chagrin and delight. I feared loud parties and many dreadful goings on would entertain us at all hours of the day and night, but I have concluded the scandal sheets got it all wrong. You are a paragon, Mr Weston. It's very bad of you to pretend such wickedness to impressionable females and not to live up to it."

He grinned, rather delighted that she dared speak to him so. "Forgive me for disappointing you, Mrs Finchley. The truth is that I have turned over a new leaf and put such… wickedness behind me."

"Ah, well, a country mouse like myself ought to be content to see this great city at all. I never thought I would, so I must console myself with that."

"Did you never have a season?" Larkin asked, too curious not to delve a little.

"No. When Caro's mama died, Papa and the household went to pieces. She was such a dear creature, and so very lovely, and poor Caro was only four. I was eleven, though, and rather precocious, and so I took over the running of the house as best I could and continued to do so thereafter. Poor Papa was an absolute dear, but rather a henwit. Everyone called him *Merry* Merrivale, and it suited him wonderfully. The sun always shone when Papa was home, but it never even occurred to me that I would come out and Papa never suggested it. By then our finances were feast or famine, depending on his success, and I was used to our way of life."

"And then you met your husband?"

A wistful smile touched her lips, and she nodded. "I met him at a local assembly. William swept me off my feet, for he was so very handsome in his regimentals. Papa liked him too, and so when he asked me to marry him, I said yes. We'd only known each other two months, and we were married for two weeks before he had to return to India. And that was the extent of my married life."

Larkin stared at her, aghast. "That's— My word, Mrs Finchley. I am so very sorry."

"So am I," she said softly. "And for a while, I believed my life was over, but then I discovered I had been blessed with a child and everything changed. In truth, after my mourning period was done, I found I was content enough at home with Giddy and Auntie and Caro. Until Papa married again. He needed an heir, he said, before it was too late, but how that dreadful woman got her claws into him—" She coloured, pressing her fingers to her lips, her expression one of shock. "I beg your pardon, Mr Weston. I forgot myself, only it is so nice to speak to someone and—and you are such an excellent listener, I'm afraid you tempt me into speaking a deal too frankly."

He laughed at that, shaking his head. "Please, Mrs Finchley, I pray you will count me as a friend and speak without reservation. I much prefer to hear the unvarnished truth. Indeed, the truth has become something I prize rather highly."

She gave him a piercing look and Larkin realised he had spoken rather too forcefully. He cleared his throat. Mrs Finchley was also far too easy to talk to, and he was in danger of letting his guard down.

"Well, I had better be going. I ought not to have remained once your aunt had left you without a chaperone."

She laughed at that, looking genuinely amused. "Good heavens do not concern yourself with such trifles. I am a mature lady, a widow, no less, and a mama. I think such days are long behind me."

Larkin gave her an amused glance, wondering if she had any idea how lovely she was. Besides her stunning sister, she might fade into the background, but she was a beauty in her own right, and she looked to be not very much older than the lovely Miss Caroline. "You speak as if you are in your dotage," he teased.

"Well, perhaps not that, but past the age of worrying about my reputation," she told him, smiling as she got to her feet and escorted him to the door.

"You don't wish to remarry?" he asked, shocked to think this lovely creature would never consider finding love again.

"Oh, no. That's all done. I have my darling Gideon, and so long as I can see Caro happy, that is enough. Auntie and I shall rub along together quite well, I promise you."

Larkin thought this most unlikely, having met the aunt, but forbore to say so.

"Well, I shall call for you on Friday and escort you to Montagu House, but do not hesitate to contact me if there is anything you need," Larkin said, accepting his hat and gloves as she handed them back to him.

"I pray we do nothing to make you regret your kindness to us," she said, the anxious pucker of frown lines pulling her fine eyebrows closer together.

"I am certain you will not," Larkin said, and bade her a good day.

Chapter 4

Lady Montagu,

I expect Pip has already given you notice of my intention to call upon you with my new neighbours on Friday. I beg you will forgive me for the imposition and understand I would not do so if I did not believe them worthy of your time.

I would like to explain a little about their circumstances, so you might judge for yourself before they arrive.

—Excerpt of a letter from the Hon'ble Larkin Weston to The Most Hon'ble Lady Matilda Barrington, The Marchioness of Montagu.

25th September 1850, Berwick Street, Soho, London.

The next afternoon, Larkin returned from a visit to sketch Tilly and sat in his studio, reviewing what he'd done and considering the portrait he wished to produce. Tilly was a saucy little minx who knew she was adorable, and Larkin did not envy Pip the trouble that would ensue when she finally came out. He'd have his hands full, that was for good and certain. Lady Montagu had been out visiting friends when he'd been there, so he'd been unable to speak to her about Mrs Finchley, but he'd left a brief note outlining their situation. He knew Lady Montagu to be altruistic and discerning, not the kind to dispense charity solely at a distance, and he hoped that the ladies' plight would be something she would wish to help with.

A thud against the window he sat beside had him jumping in shock and he looked up to see a muddy circle on the glass before him. Larkin sighed.

Getting up, he undid the window fastener and then pushed up the sash, glancing down at the ground beneath. There lay a small leather ball.

"Westie! *Westie!*"

Larkin looked over the fence to where Gideon was waving at him.

"Day to you, Mister Westie. Can I have my ball… *please,*" he added after a tense moment of concentration as he remembered his manners. The plea was followed by an angelic smile.

"Very well, you little menace," Larkin said, though he smiled back at the lad. After all, it had been an impressive throw, or kick, to lob the ball so far. He wondered if the lad had done it on purpose. "Wait there."

Larkin went out of his studio and down the stairs to the back door. Opening it, he walked along to where the ball lay and picked it up. He straightened, expecting to throw it over the fence, when a voice spoke from directly behind him.

"Fanks."

Larkin started and spun around to see Gideon holding out his hand.

"Where did you spring from?" he demanded.

"Spring?" the boy said in confusion.

"How did you get into my garden?" Larkin clarified.

"An 'ole in the fence," Gideon said, pointing to the far end of the garden, which was long and narrow.

Larkin had a gardener come now and then to tend the grass and keep the place in some semblance of order, but otherwise he had done nothing with the place, which was little more than a barely contained wilderness. Next door was even worse, having been neglected for so long.

Larkin looked down at Gideon. The boy's golden curls were mussed, his shirt had clearly snagged on a bramble, tearing a small hole, and his knees were muddy, his ankles scratched.

"What have you been up to then?" he asked, feeling a sudden shaft of pity for the lad. It wasn't much fun playing ball all by yourself, and now he came to think of it, he doubted there was much open space in the garden to kick the ball around.

The boy shrugged, kicking the toe of his shoe against the brick edge of the path.

Larkin held the ball up, and Gideon's eyes followed it. Larkin threw it gently down to the boy, who fumbled and missed it.

"Try again," Larkin said, reaching down and picking the ball up. "Move away a bit."

Gideon's eyes glinted with delight, and he hurried back, waiting. Larkin threw the ball again, and again the ball hit the ground unimpeded.

"Never mind," Larkin said. "You need a bit of practise is all. Look. Hold your hands like this, and you'll be ready to catch it when it comes."

The boy mirrored Larkin's stance, holding his hands out in front of him, palms up. Larkin threw the ball again. This time, Gideon got his hands on it but dropped it.

"Good work!" Larkin told him with a grin. "You almost got it that time."

The afternoon sunlight shone through the leaves overhead, their russet autumn shades turning gold. The lingering warmth felt good on Larkin's back and brought back memories of playing with his father and sister in the rambling gardens at Mitcham Priory, the ancient home that had been in their family for generations. His father had always been willing to spend time with them, though his injured leg made some games challenging for him. He had always been patient, though, kind even when Larkin had suspected he was in pain. His sister and he had always said they were bored with the game at that point, not wanting their father to be the one who had to call a halt. He was a proud man, and rightly so in Larkin's view, for he was a hero in every sense of the word, wounded in battle and yet fighting on, ensuring his men were safe and that they triumphed against the French despite being vastly outnumbered.

How fortunate he'd been, how blessed, to have his father beside him as he grew up, to have his kindness and his guidance, even his anger when Larkin pushed his luck too far.

He looked at Gideon as the boy patiently tried and tried again to catch the ball, and something in his heart twisted. Finally, the lad made a solid catch, his little hands clasping the ball and holding on to it tightly.

Gideon gave a little yip and Larkin shouted too, finding a sudden burst of joy in the way the lad's face lit up.

"I catched it! I catched it!" Gideon said, his face flushed with pleasure.

"You certainly did, a magnificent catch. Well done, sir," Larkin said, giving the boy a gentle slap on the back in an echo of how he might with one of his friends.

"You saw how I catched it?" Gideon gazed up at him, round blue eyes shining with happiness.

"I did," Larkin said, crouching down to observe the boy. "It was very well done."

The boy hugged the ball to his chest and seemed to swell visibly with pride at Larkin's words. How little it took to make the child's day.

"Well, after all that exertion, I think you must be famished. How about a glass of milk and some cake?"

"Cake?" If Gideon had looked pleased before, this invitation seemed to have given Larkin heroic status. "I like cake," he said solemnly.

"So do I," Larkin confided. "Come along, then, but I had best send Barnes round to tell your mama where you are, or she'll worry when she discovers you've escaped."

Larkin led the boy into the kitchen and sat him at the table there. He had a cook who came four days a week, and the woman prepared meals for the other days, to which Barnes saw. Barnes was a tolerable cook himself, and Larkin wasn't a fussy fellow who wanted a dozen different dishes on his table every night. A good stew followed by a pudding that stuck to his ribs was exactly the type of fare he preferred, rather than fancy sauces and complicated dishes that were more for show than for tasting. He did like cake, however, and there was always something in the pantry if he found himself peckish.

As if summoned, Barnes appeared.

"Sir?"

"Ah, Barnes. Tea, a glass of milk, and some cake, if you'd be so good. Master Gideon is starving after his sporting endeavours. Would you also be so good as to pop next door and explain that he has paid an afternoon call upon me and will return whence he came in half an hour?"

Barnes looked a little surprised by this but nodded.

"Come and wash your hands first, if you'd be so good, Master Gideon," Barnes said, ushering the lad to the scullery first, where he liberally applied soap and water.

Gideon didn't protest overmuch, no doubt used to such attentions in a household composed only of women. Larkin meekly followed suit, not wishing to give a poor impression. They returned to the kitchen and Barnes filled the kettle and swung it into place, fetched the cake, two plates, and the cake slice. Then he gave Gideon a glass of milk and hurried next door.

"Splendid fellow, is Barnes," Larkin said, lifting the glass dome covering the large fruit cake that Gideon was considering with an avaricious glint in his eyes. "He keeps me in order," he explained as he cut two generous slices and handed one to Gideon.

"Big as my head!" Gideon exclaimed in delight, staring at the large slice in awe.

"Is it too big?" Larkin asked. He hadn't wanted to give the lad a smaller slice than he had, and he really was famished. Perhaps it was too much for a small boy, however, judging the size of it against the size of Gideon.

"*No!* Oh, no," Gideon said in alarm, clearly anxious it would be taken away again. He stuffed a large piece into his mouth before such a dire thing could come to pass and chewed frantically. "S'good," he mumbled, cake crumbs flying in all directions.

Larkin laughed and reached out, ruffling the boy's hair. "It is, though don't choke yourself on it, for heaven's sake. Your mama will not be pleased with me. It's all yours and it's not a race."

With this assurance, Gideon relaxed, and Barnes returned a moment later, just as the kettle began to boil. "I spoke to Miss Smith, sir, and she will pass the message on to Mrs Finchley," he told Larkin, pouring a little boiling water into the teapot and swirling it about to warm the pot before emptying it into a basin.

"Miss Smith?" Larkin queried, frowning.

Barnes nodded, spooning tea leaves into the warmed pot as the kettle sang once more. "Miss Sally Smith. She's their lady's maid, sir. A lovely young woman she is, too," he added with a slightly wistful sigh that was most unlike Barnes.

"Sally's pretty," Gideon said, chasing crumbs about his plate, as Larkin noticed with some astonishment that the cake had disappeared. "Mama is pretty, too. Not as pretty as Caro, but pretty."

"I don't think anyone is as pretty as Caro," Larkin said with a laugh.

"Auntie is big and squishy," Gideon added, clearly not wanting to leave anyone out. "She gives good cuddles, but s'hard to breave," he said confidingly.

Larkin and Barnes exchanged amused glances.

"Can I have some more?" Gideon asked, gazing at Larkin with a worshipful expression.

Well, he'd done it now. He'd not only played ball with the lad but fed him cake. If he'd not wanted to be the boy's best friend in the world, he might have thought a bit more about that. Too late now.

Larkin looked at Barnes, uneasy. "He'll burst," he said, wondering if Mrs Finchley would be cross with him for stuffing the boy with cake.

"In my experience, boys have hollow legs," Barnes said with a shrug.

"What experience is that?" Larkin asked, wondering if there was something about Barnes he didn't know.

"I was one," his valet said in amusement, placing a tray with the teapot, a cup and saucer, and the milk jug on the table.

Larkin laughed. "So you were and, thinking about it, I could have eaten that entire cake single handed as a lad. Actually, I did once, and our housekeeper, Mrs Norrell, chased me around the garden with a broom!"

"A formidable lady, Mrs Norrell," Barnes said, having met the lady on several occasions whilst visiting the priory. Though she had long since retired, Larkin's father had given her a cottage on the estate, and she kept a close eye on all the goings on.

"Join us," Larkin said, gesturing for Barnes to sit down as he cut Gideon another slice of cake. This one was not quite as large as the first, just in case.

Barnes poured them both a cup of tea and they considered Gideon as he worked his way happily through his second slice. Larkin smiled as he noticed the boy picking out the cherries and putting them to one side to eat last, just as he himself had done as a boy. The cherries had always been the best bit of the fruitcake.

"How did he get into the garden?" Barnes asked quietly.

"A hole in the fence, so he tells me."

Barnes nodded, regarding Larkin thoughtfully. "You going to get it fixed, then?"

Larkin frowned, glancing at Gideon and shifting in his seat. He'd been wondering the same thing. "Probably, but… well, there's no rush, is there?"

"None at all," Barnes said, though his lips quivered a little. "I reckon you'll be getting more visits, then."

Larkin sighed. "I reckon you're right."

Once tea was done, Larkin asked Gideon to show him the hole in the fence. To his surprise, Gideon took his hand, leading him down to the end of the garden where the fence was in far worse repair than Larkin had realised. An entire section had collapsed, lying flat on the ground. There had been high winds and heavy rainstorms back in August, which must have done damage to the already rotten wood.

"Ah," he said, as Gideon marched straight over the wood. "Now I understand."

At the far end of the garden on Mrs Finchley's side there was a large apple tree, windfalls littering the grass. As they approached, Gideon looked up at the tree with an excited light in his eyes and gripped his precious ball against his chest. "Climb up?" he said hopefully.

Larkin looked at the huge old tree, gnarled and with twisting branches that curved off in all directions. It was catnip to any small boy, practically demanding it be scaled.

"No," he said firmly. "No climbing trees unless someone is here, and certainly not now. Your mama will be worried about you."

Gideon sighed and led him past the tree, back down Mrs Finchley's garden. Larkin noticed the grass was knee deep and the trees and shrubs badly overgrown, brambles encroaching on all sides and scrambling up into the branches overhead. Of course, Mrs Finchley would not have the funds available to see such work done and with winter approaching, it was hardly a priority. Yet a garden for a small boy was a necessity, in Larkin's view.

As they approached the house, the back door opened, and the lady herself hurried out. She started in shock upon seeing him, a blush climbing up her throat and pinking her cheeks. Larkin thought this a little odd, but assumed she was only embarrassed about him bringing her errant son home. He watched as she composed herself and addressed herself to her son.

"Gideon!" she said, her voice calm, though she was clearly exasperated. "What have I told you about disturbing Mr Weston? And now you trespass into his garden too!"

"Wasn't 'sturbing him," Gideon objected, glowering a little. "We played ball and ate cake. Lots of cake," he said with a touch of defiance.

Mrs Finchley groaned and put her fingers to her temples. "Oh dear." She looked at Larkin, her expression pleading, and putting him so forcibly in mind of her cherubic son, he almost laughed. "I'm so terribly sorry, Mr Weston. What must you think of us?"

Larkin shook his head, smiling at her. "No harm done. Indeed, I've had a most entertaining time, and it's a shame to waste such a lovely afternoon stuck indoors."

"You are very kind, but I'm afraid he's been a bother to you," Mrs Finchley said, lowering her voice so Gideon couldn't hear her words.

"I thought he was going to be," Larkin admitted. "But I meant it. I enjoyed his company. I may even invite him again," he added, before he had too much time to think his words through.

Mrs Finchley gazed at him in wonder and Larkin realised he'd best watch his step. He'd already made a cake of himself over Elmira, inserting himself into her life when she'd never explicitly invited him to be there. He had played knight in shining armour, expecting them to live happily ever after, without ever asking Elmira what it was she wanted. With hindsight, he suspected she'd needed him to be a friend and a confidant, and he'd read more into the relationship than there was. He had assumed he'd had all of her trust, all of her love, and finding that had not been true had been more painful than he'd imagined. He would not make such mistakes again. Mrs Finchley was a woman in need of his friendship and support, and he must be careful she did not believe he was offering more than that or allow himself to want to give more. He needed to concentrate on his career for the next few years. Perhaps then he would be ready to again consider finding a wife. *Perhaps.*

"Well, now Gideon has been returned to you, I shall bid you a good afternoon," he said, going to raise his hat before he realised he wasn't wearing one. Belatedly, he realised he wasn't wearing a coat either, just his waistcoat. He was in his shirtsleeves. Not only that, they were rolled up to his elbows. Suddenly, he felt oddly naked, and wondered that Barnes hadn't stopped him. No wonder Mrs Finchley had stared at him so oddly. Going about with no coat on was tantamount to wearing no trousers in society's opinion. Added to that, he was in her back garden, and she had no chaperone. Mrs Finchley might believe she was past the age of needing one, but no one else would agree. Belatedly realising what a difficult position he'd put her in, Larkin executed a somewhat awkward bow and retreated with all haste.

"Thank you, Mr Weston!"

"Fanks, Westie!"

Her and her son's voices followed him down the garden as he negotiated the overgrown lawn and the invading brambles. One caught his hand as he passed and he muttered an oath, putting the bloody scratch to his mouth. No wonder Gideon's shirt had been torn, his ankles scratched. The lad was lucky the scratches hadn't been worse. Larkin must ask Rogers, his gardener, to come over and sort it out. Then Gideon might be less inclined to trespass next door. It would be for the best.

Chapter 5

Dear Jack,

I hope all is well with you. I have the most exciting news. Our neighbour, Mr Weston, has been an absolute godsend. Tomorrow, he is escorting us to meet Lady Montagu. He is close friends with her son, Lord Ashburton, and assures me she will know how best to assist me in launching Caro into society. To have such a respected woman, from the highest echelons of society, take an interest in our affairs is more than I could ever have dreamed of. I do not know how I shall ever repay him for his kindness, not only to myself and Caro and Auntie, but to Gideon, too. He played with darling Giddy yesterday and even had him stay to tea. Can you imagine? Giddy can speak of nothing else but when he can see his friend 'Westie' again.

Of course, I don't doubt he's trying to win Caro's affections, but it shows me what a good-hearted man he is. Caro would be safe if she were to marry such a kind and caring fellow, though his past and notoriety for gambling and drinking are a worry, I do not wish her to find herself with a man like Papa, but he says such days are behind him. If I remember correctly from the gossip around him, there was a woman involved, a broken heart, perhaps. If so, I must hope that he is mended now and the love of a beautiful girl like Caro is enough to make him forget all others. If only I can bring her to encourage his suite.

I hardly dare ask, but how are things at home? Has that dreadful man moved in yet, and how are poor Wallace and Mrs Goodall? Please give them all our fondest love and good wishes, for you may rely upon them not to give us away. Is our stepmother still in residence? Have they any idea of our whereabouts?

—*Excerpt of a letter from Mrs Magdelina Finchley to her friend and neighbour Mr Jack Woolgar.*

27th September 1850, Berwick Street, Soho, London.

"Perhaps I ought to have worn the green?" Maggie fretted as Sally put the final touches to her coiffure.

"Oh, Maggie, do stop worrying so. You look beautiful. The blue is stunning against your lovely eyes. Such an unusual colour they are," Caro said, looking up from her position at the window, poised as lookout for Mr Weston.

Sadly, Maggie had assigned her the position as Caro still seemed oblivious to Mr Weston's charms. A pity she had not been in the garden when he had brought Gideon home, for that had been a sight to stir any woman's heart. It had certainly stirred Maggie's.

Nonsense, she told herself briskly. She was a widowed lady with a son; such romantic nonsense was behind her. Yet the vision of Mr Weston's powerful physique, clad in his shirt and waistcoat, and with his sleeves rolled to the elbows, holding Gideon's small fingers gently in his far larger hand, was one she was having a good deal of trouble banishing.

She returned her attention to the looking glass, giving herself a critical once over. What would Lady Montagu see? Was the woman in the looking glass the picture of a respectable widow, the kind of lady who would do nothing to cause the woman any anxiety when deciding whether to take Caro under her wing? Did she look mature and decent? *Mature?* Really? Mature was *old.* Was she old now? Were those crow's feet about her eyes? Surely not. Maggie peered closer, squinting at the tiny little lines.

"Mrs?" Sally said, her frank gaze upon her mistress. "Is aught amiss?"

"Are those wrinkles?" Maggie said, her heart thudding. She told herself she was becoming hysterical, but that didn't seem to help.

"Where, missus?" Sally asked, putting her face very close to Maggie's. "I can't see nowt."

"There!" Maggie said, certain she was being ridiculous now.

What did it matter if she had the first signs of wrinkles? It didn't matter if she was covered in them, head to toe. No one cared what she looked like, her time was done. She must stop forgetting that. Caro was all that mattered. Nothing else. She would go on very well with Auntie once Caro was married. They would have Giddy to dote upon and to fill their days. Well, until he was old enough to go to school, and… and then university, and then to marry and go away and have a life of his own.

Maggie swallowed, the coming years yawning before her like a great gaping maw, ready to swallow her up.

"Maggie!" Caro said, and Maggie jolted from her nightmarish thoughts at the unusual level of exasperation in her sister's voice. "He's here."

"Oh!" Maggie leapt to her feet with such haste she knocked over a silver-backed hairbrush, a bottle of scent and a ceramic container of pearl powder. The expensive articles crashed to the floor but mercifully didn't break.

"It's all right, Mrs Finchley, I'll deal with it. You run along now," Sally said, shooing her mistress out of the door before she could wreak any further havoc in her anxiety.

"Come along, Maggie, dear," Caro said, taking her arm and steering her towards the stairs. Maggie frowned at her little sister, unused to being the one needing guidance and careful handling.

"I'm quite all right," she said with a touch of indignation as she made her way down the stairs.

To her relief, she discovered Priddy had greeted Mr Weston and shown him into the parlour, which was blessedly free of Aunt Connie, who'd not yet come down.

"Mama! Mama! Westie is here—" Gideon cried, barrelling past her as she reached the bottom of the stairs and darting out of her reach before she could grab him.

"Giddy, he's not here to play with you," she told him, hurrying in his wake as he burst into the parlour.

"Aha! Master Gideon, how do you do?" Mr Weston said, crouching down and holding out his hand.

This at least had the effect of halting Gideon in his tracks as he remembered grown-up people shook hands first. Maggie winced as her son wiped his nose on his sleeve before taking Mr Weston's hand and shaking it vigorously.

"You come for tea?" Giddy asked. "To play ball?"

"Not today, my fine fellow, but I did bring you something." Giddy watched as Mr Weston produced a small parcel wrapped in muslin. "I saved you some cake for your tea. It's a good big slice, but you may only have it if you are a good boy whilst I take your mama and your aunties out for a little while."

Gideon gazed at the cake, apparently mentally weighing the merit of a large slice of cake against several hours of good behaviour. Finally, the cake won out.

"I'll be good," he said solemnly.

Maggie gave Mr Weston a grateful smile, one of her anxieties somewhat relieved. Mrs Moody was a good sort, and she trusted her to keep an eye on Gideon up to a point, that point being where he used his cherubic smile and persuaded her he was allowed to do something that would be obviously diabolical in any other child. Unfortunately, her kindness constantly undermined Maggie's efforts to keep her lively son in line.

"Caro, take Gideon back to Mrs Moody and give her the cake, which he is only to have if he is good," she added sternly, before crouching down and giving him a hug. He pressed a kiss to her cheek, burying his nose in her hair.

"Smells good," he said, nuzzling closer.

Maggie laughed. "As good as cake?"

"Nah!" Giddy said, pushing out of her arms and running back down the corridor.

"Dreadful boy," she said fondly, getting to her feet and watching her son as he thundered across the parquet floor, giving the impression he weighed several stone more than he did. A small elephant would likely make less of a commotion. "Thank you for the cake. That was a marvellous idea, and very thoughtful of you."

"I cannot take the credit," Mr Weston replied, smiling at her, his brown eyes twinkling. "Barnes suggested it, but I thought it might be an excellent incentive not to get into mischief in your absence."

"We can only hope," Maggie replied, not entirely sanguine about leaving the house. She had given Mrs Moody strict instructions that Gideon was not to be allowed into the garden unless someone was with him, but the child was adept at slipping out when the grownups were busy with other things.

Caro returned, giving Mr Weston the benefit of one of her dazzling smiles. It was even more lovely for being entirely unselfconscious. Caro was simply a lovely girl with the kindest heart and that was plain to see.

Maggie glanced back at Mr Weston, unsurprised to see him looking somewhat dazed. It was not an unusual state for gentlemen when in Caro's presence.

"Well, are we ready then, ladies?" Mr Weston enquired. "We ought to be going if we are to arrive ahead of everyone else."

Maggie looked at Caro. "Have you seen Auntie? You did tell her what time we were leaving?"

"Of course I did, but when did that ever make a jot of difference?" Caro replied frankly. "I'll go and chivvy her up," she said with a sigh, making her way back up the stairs.

Maggie fidgeted, trying desperately to think of a topic of a conversation to entertain Mr Weston while they waited. The trouble was, whenever she looked at him, she remembered how he had looked in his shirt sleeves, remembered the powerful, muscled forearms and the dark gold hair that covered them from wrist to elbow. She wondered if that intriguing hair continued beneath the shirt and was so shocked by her own thoughts that she felt her cheeks burning. Hurriedly she turned away, moving down the hallway to the hat stand where she reached for her bonnet, standing before the mirror on the wall to tie the black ribbon under her chin.

"I'm afraid Auntie has only the vaguest notion of what time it is," Maggie said, avoiding Mr Weston's gaze as she fiddled with the bow under her chin for longer than was necessary.

At that moment, the wretched cuckoo clock decided to stick its oar in.

Cuckoo, cuckoo, cuckoo.

"I'm not surprised. It's only one o' clock," he said, regarding his pocket watch.

"Ah, but if it chimed once, it would be five thirty," came a dreamy voice from the stairs.

Maggie winced again. She had grown used to her aunt's eccentricities over the years and it was only now, viewing her through the eyes of a stranger, that she realised how odd the dear creature really was. Still, if anyone were ever to remark upon it in her hearing, she'd have a few things to say. Auntie might be a little peculiar, but she was also the kindest creature in the world, and often strangely perceptive despite her sometimes inexplicable conversation. Still, Maggie wondered what on earth Mr Weston must think of them. She looked up to see Aunt Connie making her way down, resplendent in a deep navy-blue pelisse-robe with a matching pardessus. This last made her appear even grander than usual, adorned as it was with extravagant black zigzag trimmings and a faux hood trimmed with black silk tassels. Papa had been more than generous with their allowances before he'd died, bless his soul, even to his unmarried sister. Whilst Connie only had to wear mourning for six months for her brother, she always favoured deep, dark colours that highlighted her beautiful skin and luxuriant black hair.

"Are we all ready?" Auntie said, holding out a languid hand to Mr Weston. "How good of you to accompany us, Mr Weston, but we had best be going. We do not want to keep Lady Montagu waiting."

With that, she swept down the hallway to the front door, blithely unaware that she was the one they'd been waiting for.

Maggie sent Mr Weston an apologetic glance and thought perhaps his lips twitched, but she could not be certain.

Larkin watched Mrs Finchley as the carriage Lady Montagu had been so good as to send took them the short distance to St James's. The closer they got, the paler she became, her hands clasped tightly in her lap and knew how much she must be relying on this introduction to give them an entrée into society. If Lady Montagu took a shine to Miss Caroline, their acceptance would be guaranteed.

Her sister and aunt were looking out of the window, both exclaiming with interest over the shops and fashionably dressed people as they made slow progress down Regent Street.

"There is no need to be nervous, Mrs Finchley," Larkin said, smiling at her as she looked up. "Whilst I cannot speak for Lady Montagu or to the extent, she might be willing to help you, she is a lovely woman, and not at all the kind to put one to the blush. Do not be thinking you are facing a tyrant and are about to be subjected to an interrogation, for I promise you it will be nothing of the sort."

"But Lord Montagu has such an intimidating reputation," she said in an undertone. "Will… Will he be there?"

Larkin shrugged. "He usually avoids morning callers. Montagu is not a terribly sociable fellow, but he's not half so terrifying as you might think. Actually, no, that's a lie," he amended with a laugh. "He *is* terrifying, but actually he's very kind at heart and not half so fierce as one might think."

Mrs Finchley let out a shaky breath but looked a little less daunted.

"Just be honest with her," Larkin suggested. "She's very perceptive, in any case, and not the kind to be shocked easily, or to judge."

"You are very patient, Mr Weston. I cannot think what possessed you to trouble yourself with us, but we are all indebted to you. We shall never be able to repay such kindness," she said, her expression so grave and so earnestly sincere Larkin almost blushed.

Good lord, it had been a long time since anyone had provoked a reaction like that from him.

"Indeed, you are not," he said, belatedly realising he'd spoken with too much force, for Mrs Finchley started, looking somewhat taken aback. Larkin cleared his throat, wishing he'd not snapped at her, but he did not wish them to feel beholden to him. "I am doing what anyone with a grain of decency would do, and that is all," he said, careful to moderate his tone this time.

Mrs Finchley seemed a little uncertain but nodded and offered him a hesitant smile. Larkin looked up, relieved to discover they had arrived at St James's.

"Here we are," he said, as the carriage drew up outside Montagu House.

Larkin climbed out, waving away the footman that hurried down to greet them, and gave the ladies his hand to help them out.

"Heavens," Miss Caroline said faintly, gazing up at the imposing edifice of Montagu House and suddenly looking as daunted as her sister had moments earlier. "Maggie, look. It's so very grand."

"A splendid house," Miss Merrivale said, her green eyes sparkling with delight as she gazed up at the grand building. "And I am so looking forward to meeting Lord Montagu."

If Mrs Finchley had been pale before, this pronouncement turned her the colour of alabaster.

"Oh, n-no, Auntie, we are not to see Lord Montagu. Only Lady Montagu, my dear, and we are to remember that if we make a good impression, she might help our darling Caro find her place in society. So we must *all* remember to mind our manners and not to talk too much," she said with a touch of desperation.

Her aunt waved this away, the tassels on the magnificent pardessus she wore trembling and swaying with the movement. "I always make a good impression, Maggie. Do stop fretting needlessly. Come along then, my dears," she added, sweeping up the steps beneath the elegant portico and toward the front door.

"Oh, dear," Mrs Finchley said faintly. "Perhaps this was a bad idea."

"Nonsense," Larkin said, his tone brisk as he offered her his arm. "Everything will be fine," he assured her, though even he quailed at the idea of a meeting between Montagu and Aunt Constance.

Still, there was no going back now, so he escorted the ladies inside.

Maggie's heart was thundering as a very grand butler guided them through the house. Their father's estate in Norfolk had been a modest one by these standards, but Maggie had loved it dearly. An ancient, rambling manor house, parts of it dated back to the sixteenth century. Age had softened all the sharp edges, and the mellow brickwork and neat weatherboarding combined with riotous climbing roses made it the most beautiful place in the world as far as Maggie was concerned. Melancholy pierced her heart as she realised she would never see her beloved home again. No doubt that horrid man was already there, making changes, destroying all that they had loved so dearly.

With an effort, Maggie shook the wretchedness away. This was Caro's future at stake, and she would let nothing, and no one interfere with that.

Finally, the butler escorted them into a large, formal drawing room. Maggie heard Caro's swift intake of breath and could not blame her for it. The space was bright, lit by five huge, full height windows. Tastefully decorated in soft shades of blue, every wall was a feast for the eyes, decorated with beautiful paintings, both portraits and landscapes. Their footsteps fell softly upon a complex Aubusson carpet, its warm tones giving the room a surprisingly cosy aspect despite its size. An imposing white marble fireplace dominated the lovely scene, a fire crackling in the hearth. The comfortable, elegantly fashionable furniture invited visitors to sit and relax in an atmosphere of graceful and effortless style.

Maggie felt certain that such exquisite taste was very far from effortless and someone with a fine eye for detail and colour had carefully chosen every stick of furniture and artwork. She did not need to look long for that person, for seated upon a gorgeous silk covered divan was Lady Montagu.

The lady looked up from the book she was reading as the butler announced them. "My Lady, Mr Larkin Weston, Mrs Finchley, and the Misses Merrivale."

"Thank you, Carlton. We will take tea, if you please."

The butler withdrew and, as he moved away, Maggie got her first proper glimpse of the noble lady. Her breath caught, for here was a woman of wealth, power, and great beauty, and to be in her presence truly was an honour. As they drew closer, Maggie was struck not only by her lovely face, still smooth and relatively unlined for a woman of her years, but by the kindness shining in her vivid blue eyes.

"Larkin, my dear, how lovely to see you," Lady Montagu said as Mr Weston took her proffered hand, but leaned down and pressed a kiss to her cheek.

"Matilda, the pleasure is all mine, and how ravishing you look. Have you persuaded Lord Montagu to allow me to paint you again? I swear you look younger than the last time I made the attempt, but I believe my skills have improved. Perhaps this time I shall come somewhere close to doing you justice."

She laughed, waving him away. "Dreadful boy. Don't think pouring the butter boat over me will get you your own way. Besides, Lucian has already agreed, though I believe Tilly is your next commission?"

"Yes, but I also have ambitions to paint the most beautiful girl in London, which is why we are here. My Lady Montagu, may I make known to you, Mrs Magdelina Finchley, Miss Constance Merrivale, and Miss Caroline Merrivale?"

"Oh, my," Lady Montagu said, her hand going to her heart as she looked upon Caro for the first time. "Goodness gracious, but you speak only the truth as ever, Larkin. What a gorgeous creature you are, but then three lovelier women are seldom seen all at once," she added, looking between them with interest glittering in her eyes. "Please, be seated."

Maggie sat down, finding herself poised on the very edge of the sofa opposite Lady Montagu, as if ready for flight. Caro sat close beside her, but Aunt Connie drifted over to a lavish gold framed chair upholstered in a pale yellow chinoiserie silk that Maggie ought to have realised would catch her aunt's eye. Settling herself down with her usual grace, Aunt Constance spoke before anyone else could gather their wits.

Chapter 6

P.S Whilst I have not the slightest doubt you will treat the ladies with the utmost kindness, I must make you aware that the eldest Miss Merrivale, their Aunt Constance, appears to be more than a little eccentric.

——Excerpt of a letter from the Hon'ble Larkin Weston to The Most Hon'ble Lady Matilda Barrington, The Marchioness of Montagu.

27th September 1850, Montagu House, St James's, London.

"Do you have a cuckoo clock?"

Maggie had to give Lady Montagu credit, for she did not so much as bat an eyelid.

"I'm afraid we do not," she said, with apparent regret. "My eldest daughter, Phoebe, brought one home after a holiday in Switzerland and I thought it the most charming thing, but Lord Montagu disagreed. He said it gave him a headache and refused to get me one. He was quite adamant, which is rare, for he is a most generous husband as a rule. Do you possess such a thing?"

"I do," Aunt Connie said with a contented smile. "Though mine is rather unusual. It's—"

"It's such a great pleasure to make your acquaintance, Lady Montagu, and so good of you to spare the time to meet with us,"

Maggie said in a rush, praying the lady would not think her horribly ill-mannered for so rudely interrupting her aunt.

"Not at all," Lady Montagu replied, turning her attention to Maggie. "Indeed, if you will forgive me for my frankness, Larkin has given me a brief outline of your situation and I have been impatient to meet you all. My dears, I am so terribly sorry for all you have suffered. I cannot imagine what a trial you have endured these past months, and to come to London, to face society all alone, well, you are very brave indeed, and such courage ought to be rewarded."

"I'm not certain it was courage so much as foolishness," Maggie admitted, hardly daring to believe the lady had already decided to help them. "But I did not know what else to do. I could not have Caro marry such a wicked man as Mr Jenkins appeared to be."

"I should think not," Lady Montagu said, anger flashing in her blue eyes. "Men such as those believe women are property, things to be possessed. But we will not speak of him for the moment. Of course, you are in mourning for your father at present, which would normally present certain difficulties, but Larkin tells me you are prepared to defy convention to a degree?"

Maggie nodded. "I know it is rather outrageous to launch Caro before the year is up, but we do not have the funds for a second season. Indeed, if she does not marry, we will need to quit London and find somewhere cheaper to live. There is no point in denying the fact or allowing people to believe otherwise. Caro has no dowry, but she has great beauty and is very accomplished, as well as being the dearest creature that ever lived. But I cannot pretend that I am not afraid of the less than respectable offers such a situation might attract."

"Miss Caroline, how old are you, my dear?" Lady Montagu asked her gently.

"I am eighteen, my lady."

"Oh, so young," the lady said with a sigh, sorrow in her eyes.

Maggie felt her throat tighten. "I would not, for the world, force my sister to wed. I wish I could give her the time to enjoy life, to meet a young man whom she could esteem and fall in love with, but I fear what will become of her if she does not marry." To her dismay, Maggie's voice trembled as she spoke, her eyes prickling with tears.

"My dear Mrs Finchley, please do not feel the need to justify your decision. The world is not kind to women, especially not to unmarried women with no fortune, and who have no male relations to protect them. I understand your choices and your decisions far better than you may believe. However, if it is not an indelicate question, do you not consider this an opportunity for yourself as well? Do you not wish to remarry?"

"Oh! Oh, no," Maggie said at once. "No, this is all for Caro. Once she is safely settled, I shall be at ease. I have my little boy, Gideon, to think of, and Auntie and I plan to buy a little cottage in the country somewhere. We will be quite content, I assure you."

"But, my dear, you cannot be over three and twenty. That is a little young to turn your back on the world, is it not, and perhaps Miss Merrivale too might find herself a beau?" Lady Montagu suggested, smiling warmly at the eldest Miss Merrivale.

Aunt Connie gave an almost girlish giggle but shook her head. "You are a dear to say so, my lady, but sadly I lost my beloved years ago and I cannot ever love again, for he was my soul mate. That is why he hau—"

Maggie cut in before her aunt put them all to the blush. "I am five and twenty, my lady, and as you see, my aunt is determined to live the rest of her days as a spinster. I promise you, the state does not terrify me." *Much*, she added silently as her stomach twisted into a knot.

But her future did not matter. She did not wish for Lady Montagu to feel burdened by the idea of finding them all husbands when the only one who needed one was Caro. There was no way she could impose upon the woman's generosity further than that, but if it got Caro into society and gave her opportunities Maggie could not provide her with, then she would certainly take advantage of her kindness on her sister's behalf.

"Well, we shall see," Lady Montagu said with a smile. "To put your mind at ease, I should be delighted to sponsor Miss Caroline for her come out."

"Oh! Oh, my lady, thank you!" Caroline said in astonishment, her hands flying to her cheeks and Maggie was so overcome for a full minute she could not form a coherent word.

She simply gazed at Lady Montagu, her hand covering her mouth as she fought to keep from breaking down and sobbing with relief and gratitude.

Thankfully, the butler returned at this moment and for the next few minutes, Lady Montagu was occupied with preparing tea to everyone's preferred taste.

Once Maggie had regained some semblance of calm, she spoke, finding the words trembled and quavered as she fought to keep her emotions in check. "I have no words to thank you, my lady, for your kindness and generosity. You may be certain that we shall never forget what we owe you and will ensure to do all we can to act in a manner that will not make you regret your decision."

Lady Montagu laughed, shaking her head. "Oh, pish. As to that, I cannot abide a milk and water miss. I admire a little spirit, I assure you, but perhaps if you could steer clear of any great scandal, it would be best for all concerned."

"Oh, my lady, we would never—" Maggie began, only to be hushed by Aunt Connie.

"Hush, Maggie, you little goosecap. Her ladyship is funning, that's all," Connie said serenely, quite as if she took tea in such elevated circles every day of the week.

"I am," the lady said, somewhat apologetically, smiling over the rim of her pretty porcelain teacup. "And I did not mean to fluster you, so do forgive me. In sponsoring Miss Caroline, I hope you understand I mean to include you and Miss Merrivale in all the events that we will attend. I am certain Miss Caroline will feel more at ease knowing you are close at hand. In the meantime, there is not a great deal I can do for you, seeing as you are in mourning and society at this time of year is rather limited. However, we must consider Miss Caroline's gown for her presentation at court, which I, as her sponsor, will provide, naturally. Also, I would be pleased to further our acquaintance in the meantime. As silly as it is, simply being counted among my intimate circle will do you much good in the eyes of the *ton*. I believe you have a little boy. Gideon, is it?"

The news that she and her aunt were also under the lady's patronage, and that Caro's court dress was no longer a cost she must bear, left Maggie speechless. It was an enormous expense, and she had steeled herself to sell her mother's pearls, the only jewellery she had of her own mama's save for a few trumpery trinkets with little value. But the pearls were very fine, and it would have hurt her to part with them, but for Caro's sake, she would have done so. To discover now that she need not… she had to be dreaming. This was all too good to be true.

"Maggie, answer the lady," Connie said, shaking her head before turning back to Lady Montagu. "Poor dear Maggie has been under a tremendous strain of late, so I beg you will forgive her if she appears a little… vague. She has taken us all on, a significant burden, as a perceptive woman like yourself will understand. Magdelina, my dear. Tell the marchioness about Gideon."

Maggie blinked, startled to realise she was the one making them all look foolish, and not Aunt Connie. "Gideon," she managed, and then cleared her throat. "He—He's four years old, my lady, and the joy of my life."

"Ah," Lady Montagu sighed and turned her head, gesturing to a portrait on the wall. "I miss those days, I admit. It all seems so long ago and yet like yesterday all at once. Time passes so quickly, but when one is young and busy, one does not notice. But then suddenly you look around and your children are grown, and the house is quiet," she said, her voice wistful. "Until they all come home for a visit, at least," she added with a merry twinkle in her eyes.

Maggie regarded the portrait, which showed a solemn boy on the cusp of manhood, tall and slender and utterly beautiful. His ice blonde hair and cool blue-grey eyes looked out of the portrait, surveying the viewer with a detached air. His younger brother appeared full of mischief, his hair a darker gold, his eyes a deeper blue. Between them, the boys each held the hand of a china doll of a girl. Maggie wondered if even Caro could have matched the beautiful child with her tumbling fair curls and the magnetic quality of her eyes, which appeared more silver than grey.

"They are beautiful children, my lady."

"They are, though they are grown now. Ashburton has yet to settle down, I am sad to say. We have been blessed with a granddaughter though, his natural child, you understand. She has brought such laughter and merriment back to the family. There is nothing like children in the house, is there, Mrs Finchley?" She gave Maggie a direct look, a contemplative gleam in her eyes. "Have I shocked you?"

Maggie let out a breath of laughter. "Yes, a little, but only with delight. I know not all noble families set aside those born outside of the rules of convention, but it warms my heart to discover it is true."

Lady Montagu nodded her approval of Maggie's words. "Then perhaps you would care to bring Gideon to meet our darling Tilly. She is rather older than he is, but she adores small children and is very patient with them. Indeed, it is the only time the wicked girl *is* patient," she added with a laugh. "But now we must part, I fear, for I hear voices. I believe today's callers are upon us."

"Yes, indeed, for we have already imposed upon your time far longer than our allotted span, I fear," Maggie said apologetically.

"Not at all. Come back next Thursday afternoon if it pleases you and bring your son. We shall be delighted to see you all again. Larkin, my dear, thank you for bringing me such a treat. I've had a delightful visit and shall look forward to the coming season with interest and anticipation."

Mr Weston, who had sat quietly, discreetly allowing the women to talk, took the lady's hand and kissed her fingers. "Thank you, Matilda. I knew I could depend upon you."

The lady nodded and smiled and bid them all a good day and Mr Weston escorted them out as a chattering gaggle of women entered, eyeing them speculatively as they passed.

"Good day, Mr Weston," they chorused, the younger ones casting him flirtatious looks from under their lashes.

Maggie bristled a little at their coquetry before scolding herself. Who was she to feel annoyed at their behaviour? But she had no energy to consider any other feelings than those of elation. They had done it. Or at least, Mr Weston had done it. Without him, they would never have been given such a wonderful opportunity. Maggie was almost bubbling over with excitement as the butler showed them out to the carriage.

She could barely contain herself and the moment the door closed upon them, she turned to Mr Weston and grasped his hands.

"Oh, sir, I do not know how to thank you for this day. I never… never expected, never dreamed… but now Caro is to have the chance she deserves. I—I—" Maggie snapped her mouth shut and pulled her hands away as she realised what she'd been about to say.

I could kiss you!

It was no more than the truth, but not at all the thing a lady said in any circumstances, and especially not when the lady harboured hopes that the gentleman would marry her sister.

Mr Weston shook his head. "But I did nothing at all," he protested, laughing. "I only presented your delightful selves to the lady who could see as easily as I could that there were never three more deserving or enchanting ladies in need of a little help. I assure you, Lady Matilda will take a great deal of enjoyment in outfitting Miss Caroline for her court appearance and in guiding you all through the melee of the *ton*."

"Still, Maggie is quite right, Mr Weston. It was a wonderfully generous thing for you to do and… and I am quite overcome by the prospect," Caro said.

Though she had said little during the visit, she had acted just as a young girl ought. Now, however, she simply glowed, her cheeks pink with excitement, her lovely green eyes alight with happiness.

Maggie glanced at Mr Weston to see him gazing at the enchanting vision before him and experienced a little shaft of pain. Lucky Caro, to have gained the admiration of such a man, and so easily. Belatedly, she realised she was guilty of feeling rather jealous which was an appalling and uncomfortable truth. Suddenly wretched, she spent the rest of the journey home giving herself a stern talking to.

Once home, Maggie changed into her oldest and most comfortable gown and went down to the kitchens in search of Gideon. She found him kneeling on a chair, a large tea towel fastened around him, playing with pastry scraps that Mrs Moody had given him.

"Mama!" he exclaimed, standing up on the chair and holding out his floury hands to her.

Congratulating herself on having the forethought to have changed before she came in search of him, Maggie hurried forward and hugged him tightly. "Oh, Giddy. I have missed you," she said, planting him a kiss on the cheek.

"Missed you, Mama, but look. I made a graff!"

Maggie looked down at the creature that had four short, stubby legs and an oddly distorted neck. "That is certainly the finest giraffe I have ever seen, Giddy, well done, love."

"Fanks," Giddy said, before settling himself back on the chair and squishing the giraffe in his chubby little fist. "Make a helephant now," he announced with a grin.

"Well, missus? Did it all go a'right?" Mrs Moody asked as she set the kettle on the range to heat.

"It went perfectly," Maggie said, too elated to bother that she was discussing personal family business with the staff.

At home, the staff had been more family than employees, having been at the estate since before Maggie was born. It was a hard habit to break, and Mrs Moody did not strike Maggie as the sort to tattle about her family's doings.

"Then Miss Caro will get her come out?" Mrs Moody asked, looking as pleased at the news as if she had been her own flesh and blood. But then everyone loved Caro.

"She will," Maggie said, settling herself down at the kitchen table. "I still cannot believe it."

"Caro go to the ball, like a princess?" Gideon asked seriously.

"Yes, just like a princess, for Lady Montagu will provide her court dress for her." With that, Maggie's voice trembled and the tears that had been threatening all day finally overcame her. She put her head in her hands, sobbing at the table like the greatest ninny in Christendom.

"Mama!" Gideon said in alarm, scrambling off the chair and running around the table to clutch at her arm. "Mama!"

"Oh, darling, it's all right," Maggie said, laughing and crying at once now. "Mama is just very happy and so… so very relieved."

Without saying a word, Mrs Moody went off and returned with a bottle under her arm, a glass in one hand, and a clean handkerchief in the other. She handed Maggie the handkerchief. "Have a tot of my peapod wine. It's good for what ails you, pet." So saying, she uncorked the bottle and poured Maggie a generous glass.

"Get that down you and it will set all to rights," she promised with a wink.

Maggie wiped her face and blew her nose. She eyed the pale liquid dubiously but hadn't the heart to refuse. "Thank you," she said, and took a tentative sip. The wine hit the back of her throat and turned into liquid fire. "Heavens above!" she exclaimed, coughing and spluttering.

Mrs Moody grinned at her. "Not bad, eh?"

"Mama cough?" Gideon said, pounding her on the back as Maggie's eyes watered.

"Fine…" she croaked, gazing at the glass with dawning respect. "I'm fine, Giddy."

"Go on, try again. I dare you," Mrs Moody said with a chuckle.

Maggie did, more cautiously this time. Though the fiery liquid still took her breath, a warm glow began in the pit of her stomach and the muscles in her shoulders eased a fraction.

"Oh," she said, letting out a breath which she was certain must be flammable.

"Good, isn't it?" Mrs Moody said with a knowing smile.

Good wasn't exactly the word Maggie would have chosen, but as she sipped, she found she grew used to the rather astringent flavour and the way it had of stealing her breath. It was worth it for the lovely glow that surrounded her and made her feel more relaxed than she had since before Papa had died.

"Good?" Gideon said, sniffing the glass and wrinkling his nose. *"Pooh!* Bad. Very, very bad," he exclaimed, and hurried back around the chair to continue mangling his pastry scraps.

Maggie laughed, deciding this reaction was for the best and finished her glass, believing she might sleep soundly for the first time in months, and it was all thanks to Mr Weston. She closed her eyes, sighing, and allowing herself the wickedness of remembering how handsome he had looked out in the wilderness of their back garden. Once more, Maggie could not help but consider those powerful arms and wondered idly what it might feel like to be held in such a strong embrace.

Guilt hit her square in the chest. Not only was she daydreaming about a man she hoped would marry her sister, but she was betraying the memory of poor, dear William. Yet those scant weeks they had shared seemed like a dream to her now, faded and grown misty with time. The harder she tried to recall William's face, the more difficult it became, for she had no portrait of him, no drawing or likeness to gaze at and help bring him to mind. He had been a gentle soul, quiet and bookish and ill-suited for army life. He'd confided to her once that he found it hard to believe he had dared to court her so assiduously, but that he had fallen in love with her at first sight and it had given him courage. Maggie had never been a romantic soul, having been occupied with the running of the house since a young age, but William had spoken to some long-neglected part of herself that still believed in dreams. During those strangely idyllic days she had forgotten her self-imposed responsibilities and become someone else, a carefree girl with foolish hopes. For a time, she had been content to sit and listen to him read love poetry to her—both his own and others he admired—or to gaze up at the stars for hours in silence.

In recent months, she had looked back upon their all too brief marriage and wondered how they would have fared if he had come home to her. They had been so young. Maggie had just turned twenty when they married, and William was only two and twenty. Having lost his own parents when he was young, he loved Maggie's irreverent father and aunt and thought her sister a delight. She thought perhaps he had married her because of them, as much as for her own sake, but perhaps they would have grown up together and found their way to a happy future. She liked to think so. But such a short life it had been for her poor, sweet boy, gone before he'd even had time to understand he would be a father.

Maggie's eyes grew misty as she looked across the table at Gideon. He looked more like her than William, she realised, and felt her throat tighten with regret that even this echo of his father was lost to her. She swallowed hard and lifted the glass to her lips, a little shocked to discover it was empty.

Mrs Moody came over and topped it up again, giving Maggie a gentle pat on the shoulder. "Drink up, missus. It's all right to feel things now and again, it does a soul good to let go and to feel sorry for oneself. So long as it's only now and then, the world won't end, I promise."

"You're very kind, Mrs Moody," Maggie said, thinking the woman was wiser than she had given her credit for, and sipping at her drink as she watched her son, so strong and healthy and happy, and counted her blessings.

Chapter 7

Dear Mrs Finchley,

I write this in haste, hoping it will arrive before your visitors. Your step-mama left two days ago, gone to live with her sister and her family in Bath, by all accounts. She barred the door to Mr Jenkins for several weeks, but he forced his way in. Still, she refused to leave, making things as difficult for the fellow as she could. It has been a wretched place since you ladies left and no mistake. The thing is, Wallace and Mrs Goodall stuck it out as long as they could, hoping you'd be back. With the ways things were, I'm afraid I let slip that you were settled and not likely to return. Well, then they badgered and badgered me, and I'm afraid I gave them your address. They left this morning, determined to work for you or no one. I hope you can forgive me, but they were in such a pother, I didn't know what to do for the best.

—Excerpt of a letter from Mr Jack Woolgar to

Mrs Magdelina Finchley.

28th September 1850, Berwick Street, Soho, London.

Larkin sat before the window in his studio. He'd been up early for once and had spent the morning mixing paints and readying his supplies before his return to Montagu House that afternoon. He had decided it would be best for Tilly to paint her in familiar surroundings, where she would feel more at home. Also, if she got too bored, she could go off and play for a bit and come back again. It would be their first sitting today, and he wanted to be certain he'd remembered everything he would need. He stared down at the list he'd prepared earlier in the week, and ticked off the last item, racking his brain for anything he'd forgotten. Suddenly, a prickling sensation travelled down the back of his neck, and he had the strangest feeling he was being watched. Looking up, he discovered he was correct.

"Argh!" Larkin jumped back in shock, a hand pressed to his heart. On the other side of the window he'd been sitting in front of, Gideon, whose face had been mashed against the glass, dissolved into laughter. Larkin let out an unsteady breath as his heart returned to normal. "Little devil," he muttered, though he could not help but snort with amusement as Gideon was practically doubled up in hysterics at Larkin's reaction.

Undoing the catch, Larkin pushed the sash open. "Funny," he deadpanned, shaking his head. "Most amusing."

"I m-made you j-jump!" the boy chortled, holding his stomach. "You jumped good!"

"Yes, you did, you dreadful boy. What are you even doing here? Does your mama know you're here?"

"No," Gideon said, wiping his eyes and then his nose on his sleeve. "She got a sore head. Moody knows, though."

"Hmmm," Larkin said, sighing inwardly. He hoped the cook would not treat him as an unofficial babysitter when she'd had enough of the boy. "Well, you'd best come in, I suppose. Have you had breakfast?"

"Er," Gideon said, clearly torn between the truth and the prospect of more cake. "Yes, but I'm still hungry."

"You astonish me," Larkin replied, shaking his head. "Go to the door and I'll let you in."

A few minutes later, Larkin escorted Gideon into the kitchen where the enticing scent of frying bacon made him realise he'd not yet eaten, even if Gideon had.

"We've got a visitor," Larkin said, guiding the boy to a chair at the table and sitting him on it.

"You don't say," Barnes said, his expression amused as he regarded their uninvited guest. "How do, Master Gideon. Hungry, are you?"

"Yes. Is there cake?" he asked hopefully.

"No cake," Barnes replied, his voice firm. "You can have bacon and eggs, though."

"I like cake."

"I know you do, but there's bacon and egg. Take it or leave it."

Gideon considered this for a moment. "Bacon and egg, please."

"A sound decision," Barnes replied with a nod.

With the deftness of many years' practise, Barnes filled a plate with two fried eggs, some fried mushrooms, and some crispy fried bacon. He set it in front of Gideon before addressing Larkin.

"Sorry, sir. I'll cook some more."

Larkin's stomach growled, but he could hardly snatch his breakfast back.

"Need help with that?" he asked Gideon, who nodded.

"Well, this is a turnup, not only are you eating my breakfast, but I must help you do it," Larkin said ruefully, leaning over to cut the bacon up for the boy before handing him the fork. "Do your worst, brat."

Gideon grinned at him, stabbed a piece of bacon with his fork, and stuffed it in his mouth. "S'good," he said, chewing happily.

Larkin sighed.

2nd October 1850, Berwick Street, Soho, London.

On returning the boy to his mother, Mrs Finchley had been mortified that Gideon had once again invited himself around, but Larkin assured her it was no trouble. Still, the little rascal must have had a telling off, for the next few days were quiet and Larkin got a deal of work done, including two good sittings with Tilly, and finishing a commission he'd begun some months earlier. He'd worked late the previous night, into the early hours of the morning, in fact, eager to clear his commitments so he could concentrate on Tilly and then Miss Caroline's portraits and he'd no intention of getting up before Barnes had brought him up his breakfast. He'd left a note asking Barnes to wake him at eleven and no earlier.

Now, he drowsed in bed, uncertain what the time was and not caring. A sliver of sunlight shafting through a gap in the curtains had woken him, but he couldn't be bothered to get up and close them properly. Instead, he turned his head, determined to go back to sleep again.

He drifted, pleasantly sleepy, as he slipped into a dream. It was an odd sort of dream, not like his usual. A tropical jungle surrounded him, great towering trees and exotic shrubs on all sides, vines with wicked thorns reached out, snatching at his clothes, tearing them until he cast aside his ruined coat and waistcoat. Soon his shirt was tattered too, and he cast that down as well, pushing on through the increasingly difficult terrain. A voice reached him though, and he realised he was searching for someone. She was lost, somewhere in this vast jungle. How ever would he find her? Yet suddenly, in the way of dreams, she was right before him.

Mrs Finchley—for it was she—had got herself caught up in the same vines that had slashed his clothes. They wrapped about her wrists and slender waist, holding her off the ground. Her long golden hair hung free, cascading like a silken curtain down her back and over her shoulders. At once he was put in mind of Andromeda, chained to the rocks, waiting for a sea monster to come and devour her. There did not appear to be anything monstrous in this jungle save for the vines, but a fellow could hope. As he drew nearer, he saw she wore only a thin chemise and the bright sunlight beat down upon her, turning it all but transparent. A splendid landscape of lush curves revealed itself to his hungry gaze, and as she turned to him, her sea blue, sea-green eyes beckoned him on.

Well, now, *this* was getting interesting.

He fought harder, trying to get to her but the thorns kept growing faster and faster and—

"Mornin', Westie!"

Larkin cracked one eye open and—there was a face, inches from his own.

"Argh!" He scrambled up in the bed, suddenly wide awake. Blinking in disbelief, he regarded the smiling angelic countenance of Gideon, golden curls tumbling about his face.

"You a slug-a-bed," the boy said, snorting with amusement.

"Barnes!" Larkin shouted, feeling quite unequal to dealing with Gideon, especially when he wasn't wearing anything under the covers, and he'd been having the most astonishing erotic dream about the boy's mother.

"Sir?"

Barnes hurried in and stopped in his tracks as he regarded Gideon.

"Well, I'm blowed. How the devil—"

"Precisely what I should like to know, Barnes," Larkin said, a little tersely. He felt guilty and bothered and quite out of sorts. What the devil had that dream been about? Mrs Finchley, of all people! A respectable widow. Good God. What was wrong with him? "Do we not have a functioning lock on the back door any longer?" he demanded.

"Why, yes, sir, but I stepped out into the garden for a breath of fresh air, lovely morning it is, too, but the little rascal must have slipped past me."

Larkin groaned, rubbing his face with his hand. "What time is it?"

"Half past seven, sir."

"In the *morning?*" Larkin protested. "Dam— *drat* the little fellow," he said, struggling to modify his language.

"Get up, Westie. Time for breakfast," Gideon piped up, his cheerful tone far too shrill and merry for Larkin's tattered nerves to endure at such an ungodly hour.

"Barnes," Larkin pleaded.

"S'all right, sir. I'll deal with it. Come along, Master Gideon, you little tyke, you'd best come with me."

"For breakfast?"

"I suppose so, but this is the last time," Barnes warned him sternly.

Undeterred, Gideon smiled in anticipation. "Got cake, Barnsy?" he enquired sweetly.

Larkin listened to the two as they went out into the hallway and down the stairs.

"No cake. Eggs."

"But I like cake."

"I know it. But we got eggs."

"Got no cake?"

"Not for breakfast."

"But I like cake."

"Not for breakfast."

"Why?"

"Because."

"Why?"

"Cause I said so."

"Why?"

"Because we got eggs, no cake!" exclaimed an increasingly agitated Barnes as their voices faded and the sound of the kitchen door left Larkin in merciful peace.

"Heaven preserve me from diabolical infants," he muttered, settling himself back against the pillows. But his bed, which had been so wonderfully cosy and comfortable just moments earlier, was now all wrong. He pounded the pillows into submission, rearranged the covers, and tried again to go back to sleep. It was no good. Besides, if he went back to sleep, he might have another peculiar dream about his neighbour. Whilst that was oddly tempting, it was a bad, bad idea. *Very* bad. Anyway, he was bloody well awake now, so he might as well get up.

Muttering all the while about other people's children, he got up, slung on his dressing gown, shoved his feet into a pair of leather slippers, and headed downstairs.

He pushed the kitchen door open, unsurprised to find Gideon at the table, tucking into a fried egg sandwich. Larkin sent his valet a baleful glare.

"Coffee," he said, or possibly grunted. He really wasn't at his best.

The dream bothered him still, tugging at the edges of his consciousness. It felt like he'd done something wrong, like spying on her in the bath. Of course, it wasn't the least bit like that, and he didn't feel he could be held to account for what his troublemaking brain got up to when he wasn't looking. Still, the uneasy sense of guilt lingered, and he didn't like it.

Barnes set a cup of coffee in front of him and Larkin took it gratefully, adding several lumps of sugar before taking a sip. He watched Gideon, smacking his lips with pleasure as golden yolk oozed out from between two thick slices of bread. Larkin's stomach growled.

"Barnes."

"Yes, sir?"

"I'll have the same as Master Gideon," he said, gesturing to the messy sandwich. Gideon had dripped it down his shirt, despite the tea towel Barnes had tied about his middle but looked to be enjoying himself.

"Is it good?" Larkin asked, amused despite his rude awakening.

"Mmm. Good," Gideon mumbled, pausing to lick his fingers.

"As good as cake?" Larkin asked innocently.

"Oh, sir!" Barnes protested, giving him a reproachful glare.

Larkin snorted as Gideon set down the remains of the mangled sandwich.

"Not as good as cake, but good," he said gravely. "Any cake, Barnsy?"

"No!" Barnes said and stalked out of the kitchen, muttering.

"No cake," Gideon said, holding his hands up in a 'what can you do' expression that made Larkin snort with laughter.

"No. No cake, you wicked child. I tell you now, if Barnes quits on me, I shall know who to blame."

"Me?" he asked, looking pleased with himself.

"Yes, you. Now eat that up, brat."

"Yes, Westie," Gideon said obligingly, and picked up the remains of his sandwich and tucked in once more.

Larkin sighed and had just taken a sip of his coffee when there was a sharp knock at the back door. It flew open, and Mrs Finchley hurried inside.

"Gideon!" she exclaimed, clearly torn between shock and relief.

Larkin stood, as one must when a lady entered, but felt entirely unprepared for the encounter. His sinful dream about the lady was far from forgotten, and… and he was in his dressing gown and nothing else, drat the woman! It wasn't a modest article by any stretch of the imagination. Being an artist, he took a good deal of pleasure in colour and in rich fabrics, and he'd had the dressing gown specially made. It was a bright orange in a heavy silken fabric and ornately embroidered with a chinoiserie design in yellow and green. His friend Ash had coveted it so badly, he'd had one similar made for himself, also in orange, but with black embroidery. However, Larkin was quite unprepared to face Mrs Finchley while wearing it, especially as it was all he was wearing.

It seemed she was also unprepared, as she froze upon seeing him, her mouth falling open, and a hectic flush of colour rising up her throat to blaze at her cheeks.

"Oh, good heavens!" she exclaimed, and promptly turned her back. "I am so—*so* very sorry, Mr Weston. I—I was so anxious about Gideon I did not stop to think and… and… oh, how you must regret us moving in next door when you never get a moment's peace!"

Despite everything, Larkin was not beyond seeing the funny side of the situation.

"Mrs Finchley, please do not upset yourself. I'll admit, I had something of a rude awakening this morning, but there is no harm done. I am not in the least upset." Not about anything Gideon had done anyway, he amended silently.

"Oh, Lord. Don't tell me he woke you up?" Mrs Finchley said, sounding so utterly mortified, Larkin felt wretched on her behalf.

"It's just as well, for I have a deal to do today," he replied amiably. Now the coffee was kicking in, he felt a little less like eating small children for breakfast and could even look at the little devil with something approaching fondness. "I'm afraid he's made rather a mess of his shirt, however."

"That is hardly news," she said with a sigh. "He cannot stay clean for above five minutes. I swear he could be sitting still, looking at picture books and when I turn back, something is torn or dirty or hanging off."

"You sound like my mother," Larkin said ruefully as his gaze roamed over the back view of Mrs Finchley. She really did have a splendid figure. Such a neat little waist, and whilst one could only imagine what lay beneath all those layers of petticoats and yards and yards of fabric, he could certainly envisage—*no!* No, he could not imagine or envisage. He *must* not.

Suddenly feeling rather out of sorts again, the impropriety of the situation struck him with some force. Here he was, barely dressed, and there she was, alone with him, with only her small son as chaperone.

"Gideon, have you finished your sandwich?" Larkin asked the lad.

"Nah," he said, the word muffled, spoken as it was with a mouthful of eggy bread.

"Gideon, please hurry," Mrs Finchley said, sounding exasperated now. "We cannot impose upon Mr Weston any longer. It is very bad of you. I'm afraid I shall have to keep you confined to the house if you cannot be trusted not to come next door. I will get the fence mended at once, Mr Weston, so you need not fear any further interruptions."

It was difficult to carry out a conversation with the back of her head, but Larkin did his best. "Actually, Mrs Finchley, that fence is mine and my responsibility. So all the while it is down, you are not in the least at fault."

"Oh," she said, and he heard the relief if her voice. He knew their finances were somewhat stretched and the extra expense would not be welcomed. "Oh, well, all the same. I ought to be able to keep one small boy in check."

"From what I've seen of Master Gideon so far, I think it would take an armed guard to keep him in one place for any length of time. Still, he's a nice lad, even if he does eat like a starving horse."

He watched some of the tension drain from her as her shoulders sagged a little with relief. "I feel I am always apologising to you, Mr Weston," she said with a sigh.

Larkin remembered the dream and had the wildest urge to apologise for that, which he knew was ridiculous, but his gaze kept returning to the neat coil of plaited hair at her nape and remembering how it had cascaded over her barely covered body. His heart gave a disconcerting thud, and he held his tongue before he could do or say anything stupid.

"Finished!" Gideon said, wiping his hands on the tea towel. "Want to play ball, Westie?"

There was an indignant gasp from Mrs Finchley. "Indeed, Mr Weston does not wish to play ball, you naughty boy. Now, apologise for waking him up so rudely."

Gideon's bottom lip protruded, and he folded his arms. Larkin caught his mutinous gaze and lifted an eyebrow at the lad. Gideon sighed and capitulated. "Sorry, Mr Westie. Sorry I waked you up."

"That's all right, Gideon. I don't mind you coming for a visit now and then, but perhaps next time, wait for an invitation."

"You invite me?" he said at once, which Larkin ought to have expected.

"Giddy! You are the outside of enough."

Apparently having reached the end of her tether, Mrs Finchley turned and grasped her son's hand, studiously avoiding looking at Larkin. She towed him towards the door. "Thank you for your patience, Mr Weston. If I could suggest you get the fence fixed with all haste, it might be best for all concerned."

With that, she left, the kitchen door banging shut behind her.

Chapter 8

Information desperately requested concerning the whereabouts of Mrs Magdelina Finchley, Miss Constance Merrivale, and Miss Caroline Merrivale.

Please contact their heart-broken uncle at the following address.

—Excerpt of an announcement in the London Evening Star

2nd October 1850, Berwick Street, Soho, London.

"I was never more embarrassed in all my days!" Maggie confided to her aunt as she sat down at the breakfast table, pressing her palms against her cheeks. Though an hour had passed since she'd fetched Gideon home, she was still in a flurry of confusion. "And there was Gideon, bold as brass, eating an egg sandwich!"

"And you say Mr Weston wore only a silk banyan?" Aunt Connie asked, her eyes agog with delighted interest.

"Yes! Bright orange it was, and embroidered all over," she said, and then covered her face with her hands and let out a groan. "Oh, kill me now. I wanted the ground to open up and swallow me."

"Whatever for?" Aunt Connie protested. "Then you'd never have got to see such a splendid sight, and it seems as though he was not vexed with you."

"Oh, but he was. He must have been! How could he not?" Maggie protested. "He has the most engaging manners and is so very kind and polite, but how can he not be at his wits' end? He'll move, you mark my words."

"Oh, Maggie, settle your feathers," Aunt Connie said with a sigh. She reached across the breakfast table and lifted the teapot, pouring them both a cup. "You are getting yourself in a lather about nothing. If you ask me, it was the sight of Mr Weston in such a state of undress that has addled your mind."

"Auntie!" Maggie exclaimed, mortified by the accusation, not least because it was nothing but the truth. It was the only thing she could think of. For now, not only did she know that Mr Weston had strong, muscular arms, dusted with dark golden hair, but she knew too that his chest was similarly covered, and was powerful and broad and– *oh, good heavens!*

"I cannot blame you," Aunt Connie carried on, adding an extra lump of sugar to Maggie's cup before handing it to her. "Mr Weston is a splendid figure of a man, so athletic, and so very handsome," she added with a sigh, lifting her cup to her lips.

Cuckoo! Cuckoo, cuckoo, cuckoo!

"Oh!" She almost dropped her cup and turned to glare at the clock. "Cecil! That was not funny and quite unnecessary. You know you are my true love!"

Cuckoo!

Connie rolled her eyes. "He must always have the last word," she muttered, reaching for a slice of toast. "Now, drink your tea and have some breakfast. Mrs Moody has sent up some of that bramble jam she made and it's quite delicious."

Maggie sighed and did as she was told. They ate in comfortable silence for a little while. Caro was not yet down, having volunteered to tidy Gideon up as Priddy was busy cleaning.

"Was there any post today? I thought we might have had a reply from Jack by now," Maggie said, reaching for a second slice of toast. The jam really was delicious.

"Oh! Yes, I forgot. I thought I recognised the handwriting. It's on the mantelpiece."

Maggie spied the letter behind the clock and got to her feet, just as a knock sounded at the door. She turned to look at her aunt in alarm. "Whoever could that be?"

As no one knew they were here, they hoped, and they knew no one other than Mr Weston and Lady Montagu, any visitors were viewed with deep suspicion.

Connie frowned and gave a delicate shrug. "I see no way that horrid man could have tracked us down. I'm sure it's nothing. A salesman, I'll warrant."

"At this hour?" Maggie said sceptically but went out to the hallway to listen as Priddy bustled up the stairs and hurried to the door.

"Might the lady of the house be at home? You may send in my card."

The deeply resonant and well-modulated voice reached Maggie's ears, and she gasped in surprise.

"Wallace!" she exclaimed and rushed past a startled Priddy to see the lugubrious face of their family's butler. "Oh, Wallace!" she said, and was so overcome with shock and affection for the older man that she clasped his hands and held on tight, tears pricking at her eyes.

"There, you see! I told you she'd be needin' us. Didn't I tell you?" The smug words were spoken from behind the man and Maggie gasped in astonishment as she saw the familiar face of their housekeeper, Mrs Goodall.

"Oh!" was all Maggie could say, too overcome for words as she flew from the front door and hugged the woman tightly.

"There, there, my dear. It's all right. We're here now."

Maggie stood, gazing down at the diminutive but plump woman who, alongside Wallace, had been the mainstay of their family for all their lives.

"Where are my manners?" Maggie said, shaking her head. "Here we are, making a spectacle of ourselves for all to see. Come in, come in. Goodness, won't Connie be surprised?"

She ushered them into the front parlour, where Connie leapt up with a shriek of mingled delight and shock, which set the blasted cuckoo clock off again. A moment later, Caro and Gideon appeared, both laughing and dancing about with delight at seeing such welcome visitors. Chaos reigned.

Yet, despite her joy in seeing them, Maggie felt deeply uneasy. For they were both carrying suitcases and if they expected her to employ them, what on earth was she to do? They already had Mrs Moody, who had been a godsend and was so very kind. Maggie could hardly give the woman notice and reduce Mrs Goodall to the position of mere cook. And what on earth did she need with a butler? And where would they stay? There was room enough for Mrs Goodall, just about, but Wallace? What was she to do with him? Her head spun with the dilemma.

Finally, the hubbub dimmed a little, but Maggie had a job on her hands to persuade the two to sit down and take breakfast with them.

"But it ain't proper," Mrs Goodall said, shocked by the prospect.

"Oh, bother proper," Maggie retorted, guiding the woman to a seat. "We need to hear what has been happening, and you clearly need a strong cup of tea, for you look worn to a thread."

"Well, that I am, and I don't mind admitting it," Mrs Goodall said, sinking gratefully onto the chair. "Up at dawn yesterday, we was, and travelling all day, and then we stayed the night in a very poor place. Them beds weren't aired, leastways mine wasn't, and so I told the landlady, an uppity bit of work she was an' all. A shocking disgrace it was, and that dinner last night," she tsked, pulling a disgusted face. "Runny mash and a rabbit that died of starvation, you ask me. Well, I wouldn't eat breakfast there if you'd paid me, so we left at first light and here we are."

Maggie gaped at this information. That her very proper butler and their housekeeper had not only run away together but spent the night in the same establishment… well! She hardly knew what to think except that they must have been desperate to do such a thing.

Aunt Connie was clearly agog also, staring from Wallace to Mrs Goodall and back again as she poured them both tea. Maggie sent a curious Priddy down to ask Mrs Moody to send up scones and bread rolls and more butter and jam, and anything else she thought appropriate for their guests.

"Whilst we both lamented the need to leave the manor, I would like to assure you that we did as we thought best for the family, as we always have done," Wallace said, his tone grave. "And whilst our journey together was not what we would have liked, propriety was observed at all times," he added, looking mortified to have to say such a thing.

"Oh, Wallace," Maggie said, touched by his need to put this right. "We would never have thought otherwise. But what are you doing here?"

"Well, and where else ought we to be?" Mrs Goodall asked with some acerbity. "We've been looking after your family since before you was born, Mrs Maggie. You're dear to us, you are, and it was bad enough after the master w-went and did for himself and th-that awful woman but stay in that house a moment longer with that—that—*pig!*"

To everyone's astonishment, the redoubtable Mrs Goodall burst into tears.

"Martha!" Wallace exclaimed, hurrying around the table to press a handkerchief into the woman's hands.

Auntie Connie got up and went to the sideboard, searching in the depths and coming back with a bottle of cognac Maggie had not been aware they'd owned. Connie tipped a generous measure into the lady's tea. "Drink that up, Goody. You'll feel much more the thing."

Mrs Goodall did as she was told, and the sobs subsided enough that Wallace felt able to sit down again.

"We could not stay," he said gravely, his narrow face tense with worry. "It was intolerable. The man is, as Mrs Goodall so rightly said, an animal with no manners and no respect. I sent the maids away within hours of his arrival, for it was clear they would not be safe."

"And our stepmother?" Maggie asked.

"She stuck it out, I'll give her that," Mrs Goodall said with a grimace. "Though only because she's as greedy as he is and didn't want to lose her nice comfy house. Oh, and to hear the two of them go at each other. I never heard such language! And her supposed to be respectable. She ain't never been, you ask me. Born in a bawdy house, I reckon, with a mouth like that on her."

"Martha!" Wallace exclaimed, shocked.

"Well," Mrs Goodall said, looking somewhat embarrassed to have spoken so in polite company. "I beg your pardon, ladies, but I speak as I find."

Wallace looked at Maggie and then around at the house, which was a fraction of the size of the manor, and obviously did not need a butler.

"We ought not to have come," he said, his naturally morose face set in an expression of dejection.

"Oh. No! Don't say so," Maggie said, her fondness for the pair making her determined to do right by them. "You would never desert us, and I am touched that you've sought us out. We will not desert you either, but… but I am afraid things might be a little tight financially."

Wallace held up his hand before she could say any more. "Bed and board is all we ask for now. We want to help you. You've come here to keep Miss Caro safe, we know that, and we approve, for I would kill the fellow myself before he got within a mile of her," he said stoutly, despite being dreadfully lanky, certainly a good many years older and a few stone lighter than Mr Jenkins.

"Oh, Wallace!" Caroline, deeply touched by this, got up and ran around the table to hug him. Startled, Wallace turned a deep shade of red. "You dear, dear man. How we have missed you. Both of you. And as if we would turn you out! Would we, Maggie?" she turned a beseeching look upon Maggie, who smiled.

"Of course not," she said, for what else could she say? "But it is going to be a little awkward. You see, we have a cook, and she's been so very kind to us and—"

"Say no more." Mrs Goodall raised her hand this time. "I said, didn't I, Fredrick, that if they was overburdened with staff, I wouldn't be the one to rock the boat."

"Oh, no! Goody, you won't go anywhere!" Maggie cried, appalled. "I-I-I think my neighbour might need a cook, though it's a dreadful come down for you I fear?"

"Like I care about that," Mrs Goodall said with a snort.

Nodding, Maggie did not waste a moment. "I shall ask him at once," she said, pushing to her feet and hurrying to the backdoor.

The moment the words were out of her mouth, she regretted them, but Mr Weston was the only one who could possibly help… providing they had not vexed him too far and pushed his good manners to breaking. He might be packing at this very moment. She could hardly blame him.

Whilst she knew it was deeply inappropriate for her to go around to the backdoor of his home, it had to be better than setting the neighbours' tongues wagging if they saw her go in the front door. At least her overgrown garden had the benefit of shielding it from view. Besides, she was no innocent miss, but a widow, and far past worrying about such things as propriety. So long as she did nothing that would reflect badly upon Caro, there was no need to get in a fret about things. Mr Weston would not give her away, she knew.

Still, she was careful to knock loudly at the door this time, and to wait until it opened instead of bursting into the poor man's house unannounced.

"Mrs Finchley," Barnes said, smiling warmly at her. "Do come in."

"Thank you, Barnes," she said, grateful for his politeness, and that he didn't bat an eyelid at her odd behaviour. "I didn't want to get curtains twitching up and down the road by coming to the front door, but I must speak with Mr Weston if he could spare me a moment."

"Of course. If you would be so good as to take a seat, I'll see if he is at home."

Maggie nodded and sat at one of the kitchen chairs, wondering if Mr Weston was cursing his rotten luck. Yet barely two minutes later she heard footsteps coming downstairs and then there he was, striding into the kitchen and making the previously cosy space feel suddenly rather stifling. How was it he seemed to use up all the air in the room whenever he appeared? He was dressed elegantly as always but with a slightly careless attitude that spoke of his artistic temperament and yet suited him admirably. She wondered if his valet despaired of his informal manner of tying his neckcloth or if the artful disorder was actually his own work, for she suspected it was harder to achieve such perfect imperfection than to be entirely tidy.

As he moved closer, Maggie's heart gave an excited little leap in her chest, which she told herself sternly was simply nerves.

Really, she was pushing her luck and, if he threw her out with a flea in her ear, it would be no more than she deserved. Yet he smiled as he saw her, and such a smile it was. Surely this man must have females throwing themselves at him on all sides, for it was such a warm expression, designed by some beneficent god with the sole intention of turning women into fools whenever they saw it.

"Mrs Finchley, we meet again," he said, and she prayed that really was amusement in his voice and not well covered exasperation.

"I am afraid so," she said, so nervous now that her clasped hands tightened, the knuckles turning white. "I beg your pardon for intruding once again."

Mr Weston noticed her stiff posture at once, and his smile faded. Moving to the table, he drew out a chair and sat down. "Not at all. But something has happened. What is it? Is there a problem?"

"Yes," she said, and then sighed. "No. Not exactly. At least, it is a problem but not one I ought to complain about, only I'm in such a fix and I do not know what to do and—and I'm not making the least bit of sense, am I?" she said, shaking her head as she noticed his rather bewildered expression.

He laughed and reached out, patting her clenched hands, which rested on the tabletop. The touch was brief, yet Maggie had come out in such a rush she wore no gloves and the brush of his bare skin against hers made her tingle all over in the most peculiar way. Good Lord, but she was a wicked creature. What was wrong with her? Wasn't this the man she hoped would marry Caro? Yet here she was getting herself in a dither like the veriest schoolgirl because he was kind and handsome and – well, maybe it wasn't such a surprise, after all, but it must stop at once. How uncomfortable it would be to feel such a forceful attraction to her sister's husband. No, indeed, that would not do.

"Why not start at the beginning?" Mr Weston suggested. "I'm in no rush. Tell me all and if I can help, I shall."

Maggie groaned and put her head in her hands. "You really ought not to say such reckless things to me."

He laughed at that, shaking his head. "I mean it."

Maggie frowned down at her clasped hands, aware she had not only overstepped the mark by coming here but gone far beyond it. "But I am coming to depend upon you and that—that is not at all appropriate, nor fair. We are not in any way your responsibility. If we were living at home, I should know far better how to go on, but here, so far from everything that is familiar, I feel all at sea and—"

"Hush now," Mr Weston cut in, his tone firm but not unkind. "I hope we are friends, are we not? And what is a friend for if not to help in times of difficulty?"

Maggie looked up, touched by his words. "But you hardly know me," she said in wonder and then reminded herself sternly that it was for Caro's sake he was so kind.

Mr Weston hesitated for a moment, his brown eyes studying her. "Perhaps. But I know a good deal, and I admire what I see very much."

Of Caro—he admires what he sees of Caro, Maggie told herself, yet her ill-behaved heart gave a joyous little leap in her chest all the same.

"Now then," he carried on. "This problem of yours, tell me all."

Taking a deep breath, she explained about the unexpected arrival of their devoted servants, and her dilemma of what to do with them.

"I simply cannot turn them out," she said desperately. "They are like family to us. Wallace has been more of a father to us than Papa ever was, if I'm honest, and dear Mrs Goodall has been cook and housekeeper and so much more. She nursed us when we were poorly and has been a shoulder to cry on so often for all of us. They have been with us all our lives and are dear to us, and all they ask is bed and board and the opportunity to be of use to us, but Mrs Moody too has been a godsend, and I cannot be so shabby as to turn her off after all her kindness."

Mr Weston was silent for a moment, his expression thoughtful.

"I have a cook who comes four days a week, she also prepares food for the other days which Barnes deals with. However, it is purely a business arrangement, and I should have no qualms in ending it, for the lady is doing very well, as I understand. The only reason she is not full time is that I was used to being out so often, but now I am more settled, there is no reason I cannot employ someone on a regular basis. So, I could certainly take on one of your ladies, though I do not believe she will wish to live in a bachelor establishment. As to the question of Wallace, however, there is a spare room in the attic. I should not mind if he made use of it, whilst working for you during the day. I shall have to speak to Barnes but he's a very amiable fellow and I do not think he would mind. We could give it a trial period for a few weeks and see how it goes? Does that work, do you think, at least to be going on with?"

Maggie stared at him. It was more than she could have hoped for, but ought she to accept? She was so much in this man's debt already, to ask this of him too seemed outrageous, yet how could she refuse when it was an answer to her prayers?

To her mortification, Maggie felt her eyes fill. She fumbled for a handkerchief but found none and gave an exasperated sob as Mr Weston proffered a pristine one of his own.

"This is the second time I've soaked one of your handkerchiefs. I swear I'm not usually like this," she said, taking it from him and pressing it to her eyes. "Before I married, I was always said to be a resourceful girl, no-nonsense and… and a deal t-too managing," she said shakily.

"You've had a great deal to endure," Mr Weston said, his voice soft and sympathetic. "You've lost a husband and a father and your home and become a mother too in such a short space of time. That's enough to give anyone fit of the dismals, and I know what it's like to have your emotions all turned upside down and everything you thought you knew about yourself called into question. I-I know you've read the scandal sheets about my, er… drunken escapades. I hope you will believe me when I tell you it was only because I was deeply unhappy. Not that I didn't do such things when I was a younger man, but that was different. An excess of animal spirits, as my parents' old housekeeper used to say. But people deal with emotional turmoil in different ways, you see. I'm afraid such behaviour is not a solution for you, however, as you really would cause a scandal," he said, his eyes twinkling with humour, though they grew serious again as he continued. "In truth, I cannot recommend it, for it only masks one's feelings for a while. It solves nothing. Time is the only thing that really heals, as trite as it may sound. That and the realisation that no one is perfect, and that we all ought to be a deal kinder and more understanding."

Maggie wiped her eyes again, watching him with a growing sense of admiration as his words rang true. She had been so used to dealing with things in the past and never once felt overwhelmed, whereas since their father died, she seemed to be forever on the brink of drowning under the weight of responsibility. That he saw her with such clarity was at once startling and comforting, and how easily he spoke of such things. She had never known a man ever speak openly of his feelings, or to show such empathy, either. Her father had been of the type who never spoke of his troubles, and she did not doubt this was in part the reason he had ended as he had. As for William, they'd had so little time to get to know each other there had been little chance for such serious discussions. He had spoken of his feelings for her in the most romantic terms, but the opportunity to weather the vicissitudes of life had been denied them.

"You are the kindest person I've ever met," she said, speaking from the heart and without thinking first. She ought not to say such things to him, especially when they were alone, with no chaperone. Yet she did not wish the words unsaid, for they were true.

He smiled and shrugged. "I had wonderful parents who taught me kindness, for boys are often not taught such things, you know. We are taught to be brave and not to look as if we care about anything or anyone. But my father taught me it is possible to be brave and strong and still to be kind, and he's the best man that ever lived."

Maggie smiled at the certainty of his words. "A war hero, I believe?"

He nodded. "The kind one reads about in books," he replied, his eyes lit with such pride she could see the depth of regard he held for his sire.

As he spoke, Maggie found herself leaning closer to him, drawn to him by some invisible pull. The room around her faded until she forgot where she was or why she had come, only wanting to hear him speak, to tell her more about himself. She hung upon his every word as he carried on speaking.

"I wanted to be a soldier too, when I was a young man. I was hell bent on his buying me a commission, and when he wouldn't, I said I'd enlist as a common soldier. We had the worst row we'd ever had then, for he forbade me. I was wild with the injustice of it until he sat me down and told me things I had never known, the truth about his time in the army, about what it really is to be a soldier, and his words showed me he was a greater hero than I had ever imagined, for all he endured."

"But you did not become a soldier," she said with a smile.

He shook his head, his smile rueful and a little wistful. "No, and my father was right to stop me. I'm his only heir, for one thing, and it would have destroyed him and my mother if I'd been killed. I could not do that to them."

Maggie studied his face, wondering if he regretted not forcing the issue, or if he was truly content now. "Your father saw the truth, though, that you had an uncommon talent, one that you might not pursue if you went to war."

He nodded. "Yes, he did. He was wiser than I ever gave him credit for. I see that now. But I see a good deal more about him and about myself these days. To be honest, I think that's why I took so long to apply myself and to take my work seriously. Even though I understood my father's reasoning, I think I resented his interference for many years. I wanted to be a hero, like him, and I think I have unconsciously let that ambition colour my life, instead of concentrating on the things I ought to have taken more seriously."

"But now you see your way more clearly?" she asked, wishing she might have such an epiphany.

"I do," he said, nodding. "My work is my passion now and, whilst it might not be heroic, it is not so frivolous as I once believed."

"Frivolous!" Maggie exclaimed, startled. "But how could you think it?"

He laughed at that. "Well, it is only paint upon canvas, after all."

"Oh, indeed it is not!" she said, with far more passion than she had intended, but she could not leave the words unsaid. "You are painting Lord Ashburton's daughter, are you not? And in one hundred years, in two hundred years, more even, her ancestors will look at that portrait and see the truth of the woman who came before them. A great artist not only captures a likeness, but the essence of that person, the spark that fires them. And think too, of how much it means to a person or a family who loses someone they love. How comforting to look again upon the face of one so beloved. I have no such portrait of my husband, and I fear I am forgetting what he looked like… and poor Giddy, he will n-never know the face of his father."

Maggie swallowed hard, determined not to weep again, but Mr Weston was staring at her, his expression filled with warmth and compassion. He reached out and took her hand this time, holding it tightly. "Thank you. That is certainly what I aspire to achieve, and that you see that so easily means a great deal to me. I am sorry, however, that you have not such a portrait of your husband. That must be a great sorrow to you."

Maggie blinked, wishing he would not say such things that threatened to unravel the tightly woven threads of her life. For it always had been a great sorrow, but she had believed herself content enough. She had believed she would continue to find comfort in her son and that she could be satisfied to live a smaller life than the one she had imagined as a girl. But now here was Mr Weston, making her feel things she had believed were no longer possible for her, or even allowed.

Now she felt Mr Weston's hand cradling her own, and it was strong and warm, and he was so very alive and… and she had no business thinking about such things. Besides all else, he fancied Caro, not her, and the entire reason they'd come to town was to get her sister safely married. Who could be better for Caro than this wonderfully kind and compassionate man?

Mr Weston looked around then, and a moment later Maggie heard what he had: footsteps on the stairs. He withdrew his hand just as Barnes entered the room.

"I beg your pardon, sir, but I thought I ought to remind you of your appointment this morning."

"Oh, good heavens!" Maggie jumped to her feet, horrified she had done what she always seemed to do whenever Mr Weston was around, weeping all over him, making a nuisance of herself and taking up his valuable time. "I am so sorry, I—"

"Stop!" he told her, quite firmly too, his expression serious. "You've done nothing wrong, and I am glad to help. Either Mrs Moody or Mrs Goodall may start whenever they choose. Barnes will be pleased not to have to cook for me any longer, I know. Eh, Barnes?"

"No cooking?" Barnes expression lit up so comically Maggie had to laugh. This much was no more than the truth, at least.

"There, you see?" Mr Weston said, grinning at her. "And I'm certain we can accommodate Wallace, but he must work for you, for I cannot have anyone stepping on Barnes' toes."

"Oh, no indeed, but truly, I do not know how to thank you—" Maggie began, only for him to hold up his hand to silence her.

"It's my pleasure."

"Mine too, if I don't have to cook no more," Barnes said with a grin before he left the room again.

Mr Weston laughed and turned back to her.

"Barnes is eternally grateful."

Maggie let out a breath and nodded and turned back to the door but hesitated. She knew she ought not to say it, but she had already said a deal too much, and he deserved to hear the words after all he'd done. "You *are* a hero, Mr Weston, for me and my family, that is exactly what you are, and we shall never forget that."

Chapter 9

My Lord,

Would you be so good as to spare me a moment of your time? I am escorting Mrs Finchley and her son, and the Misses Merrivale for a visit to Lady Montagu and Miss Barrington on Thursday if this is

convenient.

—Excerpt of letter to The Most Hon'ble Lucian Barrington, The Marquess of Montagu from The Hon'ble Larkin Weston.

2nd October 1850, Berwick Street, Soho, London.

Larkin watched the door close as Mrs Finchley left the room, feeling oddly elated and yet bereft.

You are a hero, Mr Weston, for me and my family, that is exactly what you are, and we shall never forget that

It was sweet of her to say such a thing, but he knew she was refining too much upon his actions. It pleased him to help her and her family, and he truly believed anyone with a grain of decency would do likewise. His parents certainly would, his sister too, and his friends he was sure, but all the same the words settled inside him and glowed like the first sip of a fine brandy, warming him.

Though he did not have as much difficulty as some of his friends in speaking of his feelings, he was still a little startled by their conversation. Larkin hadn't intended to give her so much personal information when he'd been hurt before by giving too much of himself, regardless of whether that confidence was wanted. He must be careful not to overstep the mark and invite too deep an intimacy between them.

Though he wanted to be Mrs Finchley's friend, such friendships between men and women were fraught with problems with the outside world too ready to assume the worst. Moreover, she was vulnerable, and he ought not to give her the impression he was looking for more than friendship when he wasn't. But she was so easy to confide in, and so quick to understand, too. He felt a strange tug of kinship to her of the kind he had never known before. Uneasily, he turned his attention to his feelings for Elmira, something he'd not done for some time. Whilst the memory of her no longer gave him pain, he had learned to avoid thinking of her, not wishing to stir up the past. Had there been this same sense of familiarity, of ease? He knew the answer without having to consider it.

Elmira had been his heroine, his muse, the first one to make him take his art seriously as he tried to capture whatever it was about her that fascinated him. He knew now that it was the combination of fragility and strength she exuded, and that the reason he could never capture her truly was because she had held herself back. She had not wished for him to see everything about her, to know her entirely, and so he had become increasingly fascinated and frustrated. When he discovered she had lied about her son, about who she was and where she had come from, about everything, it had been devastating. He had trusted her with so much of himself and she had never reciprocated. If she had understood who he really was, why had she not trusted him to protect her and the child she had taken on as her own?

The entire episode had shaken his confidence in himself, and he had felt a fool. He did not wish to feel that way again, and so he must tread the path of friendship with Mrs Finchley with great care.

3rd October 1850, Berwick Street, Soho, London.

"Westie!"

Gideon came barrelling through the front door and launched himself at Larkin. Thankfully, Larkin had been prepared for the assault and swept the boy up before he could do him an injury.

"Master Gideon. Well, you are looking fine as fivepence today," Larkin observed, as Gideon looked adorable and remarkably tidy in his sailor suit.

"Got to keep it clean," Gideon said, pulling a comically tragic face.

"Oh, dear," Larkin said with a deal of sympathy, remembering many, many scoldings from his nanny and mother when he had ruined some new outfit in a matter of minutes just before visitors arrived or they were due to leave for some event. "That is a trial."

"'Tis." Gideon nodded sadly. "And I can't bring my ball!" he exclaimed, his expression turning from merely incomprehension to one of outright indignation.

Larkin met Mrs Finchley's eye as she followed her sister out of the house. "Indeed, I should think not. Can you imagine him throwing it and knocking over some priceless piece of porcelain?" she said, closing her eyes in horror and shuddering. "I should have to run away and live abroad."

Larkin laughed. "I do not think such drastic measure would be required. In my experience, the Montagus are somewhat intimidating unless you are under the age of twelve, in which case you can get away with murder."

"Well, let us pray he does not need to get away with murder," she said under her breath as Larkin handed her up into the carriage.

As they were a little tight on space, Gideon had to choose a lap to sit on and Larkin was given this honour.

"Are you sure you don't mind?" Mrs Finchley fretted.

"I already told you twice. Gideon and I are quite all right," Larkin said, rather touched by the way the boy leaned against him, so trusting and confident he was safe.

"Gideon, mind your boots on Mr Weston's trousers, love."

"Stop worrying!" Larkin remonstrated, shaking his head at her.

"Yes, Mama, stop worrying," Gideon repeated, wagging his finger at his mother and gaining himself a reproving look from Larkin.

"Don't cheek your mama, you little devil," he said, though not unkindly. "And mind your shoes on my trousers."

Gideon snorted. "All right, Westie."

"I am so looking forward to meeting Lady Montagu again," Aunt Connie said, smiling in her serene way. "I felt we made a connection. I believe we are kindred spirits. Though I do wish you had let me explain about Cecil, Maggie. You were very rude last time, keeping interrupting me as you did. I know you were nervous, but really…! She is just like the rest of us, you know, even if she is a marchioness."

Larkin watched, amused, as Mrs Finchley coloured a little. "I beg your pardon, Auntie, I shall endeavour to do so, but—but do you think you ought to mention Cecil? You know how funny people can be about ghosts and… and things of that nature."

"Oh, *people*, certainly, but not Lady Montagu. She is a woman of sensibility, like myself and I feel she is certainly in touch with the spirit world as I am," Connie said with utter conviction.

Larkin watched as Mrs Finchley bit her lip in consternation, obviously wracking her brain for a different tack to take.

"Yes, but, isn't the er… your relationship with Cecil a rather private story?"

Mrs Finchley cast him a worried glance, and he wondered what the story was. Had Aunt Connie been a naughty girl? Not that he cared if she had. Propriety and the rules of society were ridiculous, in his opinion, certainly where females were concerned. Their standards would have labelled both his mother and his sister as outcasts and fallen women. Not that he was about to volunteer this information, but he certainly would not judge Miss Merrivale, or any woman, for such indiscretions.

"Well, of course it is private, but Lady Montagu is not the kind to tattle. You read that novel that was written about her and Montagu, The Eagle and the Lamb, just as I did. Such a romantic story," Connie said with a wistful sigh, one hand pressed to her enormous bosom. "And it shows the kind of woman Lady Montagu is, passionate and determined, no matter the circumstances. She would do anything for the man she loved, as I would have done if I'd had the chance."

She trailed off, tears shimmering in her eyes.

"Oh, Auntie." Miss Caroline took her hand and squeezed it tightly. "We know that, and I'm sure Cecil did, too."

Her aunt summoned a smile and nodded, covering her niece's hand with her own. "I know, dearest Caro, and you and Maggie and darling Gideon are such a comfort to me. I am very blessed and ought not to repine, but sometimes I miss him so dreadfully. I know we will be reunited one day, though. Once I pass through the veil between this world and the next."

"There, there," Gideon said, reaching over and giving his aunt a gentle pat on the shoulder. "All better?" he said, looking a little anxious.

"Yes, all better, you sweet creature," Aunt Connie said with a chuckle, apparently restored to her usual humour.

Larkin regarded their aunt with renewed interest. He must paint her, he decided, once he'd finished Caro. Whilst, like all artists, he had to take commissions to increase his status in the art world by being seen to paint the great and the good, Larkin was independently wealthy thanks to his interest in the gaming club he ran with his friends. He had long since told his father he no longer needed his financial support, a matter of no little pride to him. This also meant he could pick and choose his subjects, however. Whilst he might paint some subjects because they would get him noticed, others he chose because they interested him. Caro, with her stunning beauty, was one, Aunt Connie was another. Whilst he knew most men would not consider her a beauty, for she was too old and too large for such conventional judgements, to Larkin's eye, she was truly lovely. All the Merrivale family seemed to have been blessed with skin that glowed with some inner light, and then there were their eyes. Startling green for the two Misses Merrivale, and Mrs Finchley's were even more intriguing to him, for they changed with the light, sometimes an unusual aquamarine, other times green or blue. He wished to paint her too, he realised, but that was not a good idea.

Unbidden, the images from his dream rose in his mind and he shoved them away, down into some mental cupboard where they ought not to bother him. Yet they did, because he knew they were there.

"Are we there yet?"

Gideon wriggled on Larkin's lap, twisting to look up at him. Relieved to be taken from his own troubling thoughts, Larkin glanced out of the window.

"We are indeed, Master Gideon," he said, as the carriage slowed and came to a halt.

"Now, Gideon, remember what I told you," his mother fretted as they all climbed out of the carriage and went up the stairs to the grand front door. "Say please and thank you and do try not to get into mischief."

"Yes, Mama," Gideon said with a sigh.

Larkin gave the boy a sympathetic smile and Gideon took his hand, looking suddenly a little intimidated as they were taken into a grand entrance hall.

The butler greeted them as before and footmen took their coats and hats, but before he could lead them through the magnificent house, light footsteps sounded on the polished marble floor and Tilly appeared, fair ringlets bouncing.

"Good morning, Mr Weston. Good morning, ladies. I'm Miss Ottilie Barrington. I've come to meet Master Gideon."

Gideon sidled closer to Larkin, his eyes very wide as he stared in awe at the beautiful girl before him. Larkin smiled, understanding the boy's sudden shyness. Tilly had inherited her looks from her grandfather, with her white-blonde hair and strange silver eyes. One day she would cause as much of a sensation among the *ton* as her Aunt Catherine had, that much he was certain of.

"Master Finchley, this is Miss Barrington, say how do you do to her like a gentleman," Larkin prompted him.

Gideon glanced at his mother, who returned an encouraging smile and a nod. "Go on, dear."

"How you do?" Gideon said, looking a little flustered.

"I'm very well, thank you," Tilly said. "Would you like to have tea with me and my governess? Mrs Harris is very nice, and we have cake."

"Cake?" Gideon repeated eagerly, perking up.

"Oh, yes. Three kinds," Tilly said, grinning at him. "A fruitcake, a strawberry jam sponge, and a whole plate of little queen cakes. They're my favourite," she added confidingly.

"Three kinds of cake!" Gideon looked as though he might burst at the very idea of such abundance. "Mama! Three kinds of cake!"

Mrs Finchley pressed her fingers to her lips to stifle a laugh. "Well, you had best run along with Miss Barrington then, but mind you are a good boy."

Tilly held out her hand to Gideon, who took it with a look of dazed happiness, allowing her to lead him away in search of cake.

"How adorable they look together," Aunt Connie said with a sigh. "Like a couple of little angels."

"Do not let my daughter's looks deceive you," remarked a deep voice from behind them. "She's the naughtiest creature and I am afraid I let her get away with murder."

The ladies turned and Larkin heard Miss Caroline's breath catch as she came face-to-face with Lord Ashburton.

"Good morning, Pip," Larkin said, shaking his friend's hand. He made the introductions, intrigued by the varying reactions of the ladies.

Caro blushed, gazing up at Ashburton with stunned admiration, like Apollo had appeared before her. Her Aunt Connie, also openly admiring, but not the least hindered by inhibition, performed a deep and surprisingly balletic curtsey, as if she were being presented to a king instead of a mere earl. Pip looked a little startled but took it in his stride as he did most things. Mrs Finchley greeted him politely, with the perfect mix of warmth and restraint, and Larkin refused to admit himself relieved that she did not gaze upon his friend with such obvious admiration.

"Are you taking tea with us?" Larkin asked his friend with a smile, knowing Pip would avoid such an encounter, if at all possible.

"Sadly, no. I have business to attend to. I believe my father is expecting you, however," he said to Larkin, before bidding the ladies a good day.

"Oh, my," Caro said, letting out a breath once Pip was out of earshot and they were following the butler through to see Lady Montagu. She took her sister's arm, whispering in her ear, but Larkin still caught the words. "I never saw such a handsome man in all my days!"

Mrs Finchley glanced at her with a little frown. "Did you think so? His is a rather cold beauty, in my opinion."

"Maggie! How can you say so?"

Her sister shrugged and Larkin tried very hard not to feel pleased by her words.

Once again, Lady Montagu was everything that was elegance and charm, and Larkin left the ladies to their visit, taking himself off to visit Lord Montagu.

"Come," replied a commanding voice from behind the heavy oak door as Larkin knocked.

"Ah, Larkin, how are you, my boy?" Lord Montagu rose, and once again, Larkin was struck by the resemblance between him and his eldest son.

Mrs Finchley was quite correct too, it was a cold beauty, austere, and utterly compelling. High cheekbones and a chiselled jaw gave them both a rather unearthly aspect, but Montagu's eyes were a strange glinting silver and oddly penetrating.

"I am well, sir. Thank you for seeing me today. I know how busy you are."

Montagu waved this away. "Sit down. What can I do for you?"

"Well, it's a little delicate," Larkin said, frowning. "And has to do with the ladies I brought today. Has Lady Montagu told you of their circumstances?"

"Indeed, a sorry business and I hardly wonder at her wishing to help them. I never met Mr Merrivale, but I remember the scandal. Fothersham ought to have stepped in, of course, but he's an unfeeling brute, and quite remarkably stupid, I'm afraid."

Larkin smiled at this brisk assessment and nodded, hoping this implied Montagu would help him as he hoped. The marquess had a vast network of contacts throughout the country and always seemed to know everything and everyone. Larkin knew he also worked closely with Gabriel Knight, and the whispers about things the two of them may or may not have done to those that crossed them, or their families, were many. Would he help the ladies, though?

"The viscount has abandoned them sadly and this vile creature, Mr Jenkins, has taken possession of their family home. I know it is a source of great sorrow to them all, and… and I wondered if you might help me to discover something about the man."

"Larkin," Montagu said, a warning note to his voice. "I sense a plot in the making. Can you not leave things alone? My lady wife seems to have things in hand. Surely you have saved enough young ladies through the refuge at Gillmont?"

Larkin stiffened but knew better than to rebuke the marquess. "This is different."

"How is it different?" Montagu asked mildly, and sat back in his chair, his long fingers steepled together as he regarded Larkin. Finally, he gave a heavy sigh. "Let me guess. You wish to tempt Mr Jenkins into a card game at that wicked club you run and see if you can't win back what they lost."

Larkin felt his colour rise, for that was precisely what he'd been considering. "It could work," he said defensively, feeling like a small boy caught doing something foolish. "I'm the best card player at the club and I'd like to see anyone try to cheat me. I know all the tricks there are."

"It's still a risky strategy. You must stake something of equal value, remember, and all this for women you hardly know. People will talk," Montagu warned him.

"I do know how cards are played," Larkin retorted and then cleared his throat as his lordship raised one elegant eyebrow. "I beg your pardon. But I very much doubt a creature like this Mr Jenkins has the skills to outplay me and, as for the talk, if things are done discreetly, no one need know it was me."

Montagu sighed and shook his head. "I will make enquiries about the repugnant Mr Jenkins and see what I can discover. But you will do *nothing* in the meantime. Is that understood?"

"Of course."

Montagu nodded, regarding Larkin with the unnerving gaze that he was known for throughout the *ton*. "Why do you wish to do this?"

"Because it is an injustice," Larkin said with a shrug. "Mrs Finchley lost her husband in the war, and then her fool of a father kills himself. She and her sister and aunt lost their home, as did her son. Gideon will never know his father, or his grandfather, and he won't even have the security of growing up in the place his family have loved and built up over generations. I cannot help but think how I would feel if someone I despised turned me out of Mitcham Priory and took my place. It's unbearable. The place that means so much to them all is in the hands of a man unfit to cross its threshold. It's wrong."

Montagu's expression softened, but his words were implacable. "There are many injustices in the world, Larkin. You cannot undo them all."

Larkin scoffed. "And how many injustices have you resolved in your own inimitable manner? How many times have you interfered when society would have had you turn your back?"

"I know not to what you refer," Montagu replied coolly, though his eyes sparkled with amusement.

"That's what I thought," Larkin replied, shaking his head.

"Just don't go doing anything foolish. I'll help you if the plan is sound, but I won't help you to ruin yourself for no good reason."

"I have no intention of doing anything of the sort," Larkin replied sharply. "I'm not entirely a fool."

"You are in no way a fool, but you are a romantic soul and are always too quick to go riding in on your white charger, wishing to rescue the damsel in distress. I only ask you to consider your own happiness before you put it at risk. *Again,"* he added, putting such emphasis on the word that Larkin had to fight a blush.

That was the trouble with going to pieces: people always fretted you'd repeat the error.

"I will," Larkin said stiffly, too embarrassed to reply with equanimity.

"Very well," Montagu said. "You may leave it with me."

"Thank you," Larkin replied gratefully, but did not rise.

"Was that all?"

"Actually, no, sir. I wondered if you might do one other thing for me. It's regarding Mrs Finchley's husband—"

Chapter 10

Georgette stared at her reflection in the looking glass. Her hair, once glossy and a rich chestnut, now appeared a dingy mud colour, her eyes obscured by spectacles. Surely, in this guise, she would be safe, and no one would recognise her.

Excitement rose in her breast, the future before her suddenly full of possibilities. She had thwarted her grandfather's scheme to marry her off and now she was free. The vile Lord Hanover could find another poor little heiress to marry, for it would never be her.

—Excerpt from 'His Grace and Disfavour', by an anonymous author.

3rd October 1850, Montagu House, St James's, London.

"—and then I discovered he was haunting the cuckoo clock he gave me," Aunt Connie said with a tragic sigh.

Maggie groaned inwardly and closed her eyes. Well, this was it. If Lady Montagu decided they were too peculiar for her to wish to be associated with, they would know shortly. Gingerly opening her eyes, she discovered Lady Montagu did not look the least bit dismayed by this unusual confidence, however, but intrigued.

"How fascinating. I wish I could introduce you to our old housekeeper, but she is very elderly now and prefers to stay at home. But she is—well, I suppose one would say a wise woman," Lady Montagu said with a smile. "And the things I have seen her do would open your eyes to a great many possibilities about life and about feminine power and... oh, a host of things. I certainly do not dismiss the possibility of ghosts, and why not the cuckoo clock, if it was his only connection to the woman he loved? It's terribly romantic, though such a sad tale. I am so sorry for your loss," she said, reaching over to pat Connie's hand.

"Thank you, my lady. I felt sure you would understand. I said to Maggie just this morning that I sensed you were a woman who is in touch with the *other side."* Connie mouthed these last words as if they were too powerful to speak aloud.

"Well, I cannot say as to that," Lady Montagu replied thoughtfully. "I have never had such interactions personally. Truthfully, I believe I am rather afraid of the possibility. For it is one thing to allow that such things exist, but quite another to invite them into your life."

"Would you not like to attend a séance, then?" Connie persisted.

"That would be a little difficult, I fear, even if I did, which I am not at all certain of. But so many of those who purport to have such talents are charlatans; it is terribly hard to discover someone who truly has the gift. My husband is rather protective of me, I'm afraid, and he would not like me mixing with anyone if he did not trust their motives were genuine."

"A pity," Connie said with a frown, but before she could persuade Lady Montagu into accompanying her to some dodgy séance, the door opened, and Miss Barrington appeared with Gideon in tow.

He was still gazing at his companion with a look that bordered upon worshipful, but he looked relatively clean, and though

Maggie discerned a jam stain on his previously pristine sailor suit, she sighed with relief. The two children were obviously still friends, and nothing had been torn or ruined beyond saving.

"Ah! Tilly, darling, come and give me a kiss," Lady Montagu said eagerly, holding her arms open for Tilly to run into. "And who is this handsome fellow?"

"This is Master Gideon," Miss Barrington replied, kissing her grandmother on the cheek. "But he prefers to be called Giddy," she added with a giggle.

"Mama!" Giddy said, running to hug her. "We had cake!"

"And so did we," Maggie said, laughing and tweaking his nose. "Aren't we all lucky?"

"What cake you had, Mama?"

"I'll tell you later," she whispered. "Make your bow to Lady Montagu now, just like we practised."

Maggie gave her son a gentle push, and he stepped forward. "Good day, lady," he said solemnly and gave a very low bow.

"Nicely done, Master Gideon," Lady Montagu said, smiling warmly at him. "What a fine gentleman you are."

"Fanks," Gideon replied, and ran back to bury his face in his mother's skirts.

"He's adorable," Lady Montagu said, laughing, before turning back to her granddaughter. "Did you have a nice time?"

"Yes. He's very funny, and he certainly loves cake," Miss Barrington said, grinning.

Everyone, certainly Gideon, deemed the visit a splendid success, and when Mr Weston returned, they said their goodbyes. Once settled in the carriage, everyone had something to say.

"So much cake!"

"—and did I not say we had a connection? She is certainly as spiritual as I believed."

"—and Lady Montagu is sending her own modiste to *our* home, to measure me and begin work on my gown for my presentation at court!"

Maggie laughed and nodded and tried to speak to everyone at once, relieved and delighted that they were all in such high spirits. She looked up, a little disconcerted to discover Mr Weston watching her. He was the only one who had not spoken, and she felt the strangest sensation as his eyes met hers. Warmth surged beneath her skin, and an odd, ticklish sensation fluttered inside her. She smiled at him uncertainly.

"Did you have a pleasant visit with Lord Montagu?" she asked him.

"Thank you, yes. He sent his apologies for not coming to meet you, by the way. He's rather busy this morning, and I was lucky he made time for me."

"He's an important man, and one who takes his responsibilities seriously, from what people say."

"Certainly that," Mr Weston replied with a smile, but he seemed distracted and not in the mood for conversation, so Maggie let the subject drop.

Instead, she listened to Connie, Caro, and Gideon chattering about the splendid time they'd had, and turned her gaze to the view passing them by. How different London was from home, and how she missed the manor. By now, the leaves would be changing colour in the woodland that bordered the estate, a riot of gold and yellow, red and orange, and there would be the scent of wood smoke from the many chimneys. Their parlour was the cosiest room imaginable, filled with old, well-loved furniture, covered in cushions, and woollen rugs to snuggle into on the coldest nights. They would sometimes roast chestnuts on the fire of an evening, and the kitchen always smelled of fresh bread. The sound of her father's laughter and the scent of his cigars were never far away, and her mare, Starlight, would nicker a greeting when Maggie came to see her. That she would never hear her father laugh again, and that her beloved horse was in the hands of a man who might not be kind to her made sudden tears spring to her eyes.

Maggie blinked hard, nostalgia and longing filling her heart. She knew it was normal to feel such sadness, but it seemed ungrateful when she had so much to be thankful for. She'd had a splendid morning, visiting a marchioness of all people. Caro was to have the come out she'd always dreamed of, and even Auntie Connie seemed content. Surely, she had no business feeling homesick and so very sorry for herself. Taking a deep breath, she pushed the feeling away, reminding herself that Wallace and Mrs Goodall were with them now and she had many reasons to be cheerful in the light of such good fortune. Yet when she looked up again, she found Mr Weston's gaze upon her once more, such sympathy in his expression that her throat tightened all over again.

"How is Mrs Goodall settling in? Did you have a splendid breakfast this morning?" Caro asked Mr Weston, which relieved Maggie as it took his attention from her.

"So splendid I fear I will need a new wardrobe in a matter of weeks. I think she believes I need feeding up in the manner of a Christmas goose," he replied ruefully.

"Mrs Goodall does like to see people eat well," Aunt Connie replied with a smile. "Oh, you must get her to make you her plum duff. It's the most heavenly thing you'll ever eat."

"I shall, indeed, and to answer your question, she seems very pleased."

"Does she? Truly?" Maggie asked anxiously. "I feared it might be something of a comedown for her to be a mere cook when she's been our housekeeper for so long."

"I think she is so relieved to be near you all, she'd take a position as a kitchen maid if it were necessary."

"Dearest Goody," Caro said with a sigh. "And Wallace too. I have missed them so much. They really are like family to us, aren't they, Maggie?"

Maggie nodded but said nothing, fearing her emotions were too close to the surface and she might embarrass herself. Gentlemen did not like weeping women, that much she knew, and she did not wish to make Mr Weston ill at ease.

Still, she felt him watching her but dared not look up again for fear she was correct. What might her foolish heart make of this circumstance if she was, and what if she was wrong and it was lovely Caro he gazed upon with rapt admiration? What then?

So she avoided his eye until they had turned onto Berwick street and was startled when he addressed her directly.

"Mrs Finchley, am I to take it that you and the Misses Merrivale have as yet seen nothing of the sights of this fair city?"

Maggie hesitated but could only answer honestly. "No, sir. We have not."

"Might I be so bold as to invite you ladies to take a little outing with me? Tomorrow if the weather remains fair. We could do a little shopping on Regent Street, and perhaps then go to the Parthenon Bazaar?"

"Oh!" Caro exclaimed. "Oh, Maggie, may we go? Please?"

"Why, that does sound rather marvellous," Aunt Connie said, her eyes alight with anticipation for such a treat. "What say you, Maggie?"

Maggie stared back at them, unwilling to be the one to spoil their fun, and yet she turned back to Mr Weston with concern. "Are you quite certain you wish to? That you can spare the time? I fear we have been a dreadful trial to you already."

"Not a bit of it," he said, sounding so genuine she had no reason to doubt him. "It will be a pleasure to see the places I know so well through your eyes, and I shall look forward to it."

"Well then. If you are quite certain, we should be glad to accept."

Caro squealed with excitement. "Oh, thank you, Mr Weston! I have heard so much about the bazaar and longed to go."

"You are most welcome, Miss Caroline. Indeed, it is worth it just to see your beautiful smile."

Maggie's heart sank at his words, and she scolded herself for a fool. This was why he bore with them, with her, so that he could further his interests with Caro. Of course it was. Why would he look at her, a widow with a son already, when her younger, far more beautiful sister was at hand. This was a wonderful development, she reminded herself and told herself she ought to be glad of it for Caro's sake.

She only hoped that, if he was serious about her sister, he would hurry the courtship along, so she was not forced to watch it unfold before her eyes for months and months to come. Whilst she could not resent Caro for her good fortune, she was not so generous that she wished to watch the two of them fall in love. For it was plain to her now, despite all her best intentions, that she harboured some foolish feelings for Mr Weston: inappropriate, inconvenient, and very ill-timed feelings. But there it was. Admitting it to herself was hard, as it was far easier to bury her head in the sand and pretend otherwise, but she had never been one to run away from the truth. He was thoroughly splendid, handsome and kind and funny and talented and, whenever she saw him, it was as though the world became brighter and more colourful than it ever had before.

But even if Caro had not been the one, she knew better than to think he would choose *her*. It was simply his innate kindness that drove him to help them all and his desire to spend more time with Caro, and she would do well to remember that.

♡♣◇♠

Maggie was sitting at her dressing table applying her night cream when Caro cracked open her bedroom door.

"Can I get into your bed? It's freezing!" she exclaimed, running across the bare wood floor on tiptoes and leaping onto the mattress.

Maggie watched, amused, as Caro burrowed under the covers and pulled them up to her neck. She looked so very young, her hair all tied up in rags to make it curl, her lovely features gilded by the candlelight.

"Wasn't it a marvellous day?" Caro said with a sigh.

"Marvellous," Maggie agreed, smoothing the cream into her neck.

"Lady Montagu was very kind, wasn't she? And so sweet to Auntie. I admit I was holding my breath when she explained about Cecil. People have been so cruel to her in the past, I was simply quaking in case the lady took exception to her eccentricities, but she was simply wonderful."

"She was indeed, and she looked genuinely interested too, not just politely going along with her," Maggie said, putting the lid back on her cream pot before slipping under the covers beside her sister.

"Do you think her son is as kind as she is?" Caro asked tentatively.

"Caro," Maggie said, smiling at her. "Love, don't go getting ideas about Lord Ashburton. I know he is very handsome and that he has piqued your interest, but he's heir to a vast and powerful inheritance. I'm afraid even a girl as lovely as you is unlikely to capture him. People of that station rarely marry for love, though I grant you his parents did. Still, he'll be looking for a powerful alliance, I don't doubt."

Caro rolled her eyes. "Oh, Maggie. I wish you would not take everything so seriously. I'm not planning on throwing my cap at him. He's just so beautiful and—" She sighed, shaking her head. "Never mind."

"But what of Mr Weston?" Maggie asked, smoothing the bedsheets with her hands and not looking directly at her sister.

"What of him?"

"You thought he was handsome too, did you not?"

"No, you did," Caro said, looking sulky now. "I mean, yes, he is handsome, but he's not someone I'd like to marry."

"B-But whyever not?" Maggie said, genuinely outraged, for she could think of no finer man than Mr Weston, who was the kindest and most caring man, not to mention gloriously handsome and athletic and funny, and intelligent too. "Has he not shown you how worthy he is of your admiration? He has done everything he can to help us, to make the way easy for us and—"

"Oh, drat Mr Weston," Caro said crossly. "I do esteem him and like him very much, and he has been most kind to us all, but I shan't marry him. He's too old, for one thing."

"But I'm certain Lord Ashburton is the same age as he is, and you said—"

"Oh, Maggie!" Caro exclaimed, throwing back the bedcovers and getting out. "I just came for a bit of a gossip with my sister, to laugh and exchange silly nonsense about a handsome fellow I saw today. I know I must marry, for you've explained over and over that there is no other choice if I want to have a life of my own and be safe, but can you not understand that I *don't want to*! I don't want to marry anyone yet! Not Mr Weston and not Lord Ashburton. I want to go home to the manor and go back to our lives, that's what I want, but I cannot and whether or not I know it to be true, it's still not fair!"

With that, Caro went out, slamming the door behind her.

Maggie stared at the door for a moment and then put her head in her hands, her throat tight and her eyes burning. She breathed steadily, trying to calm herself. Caro was right, it wasn't fair, but what else could they do, any of them? They could not impose upon Lady Montagu for a second season, and even if they could, by then they would all need new wardrobes, something Maggie could not possibly pay for. The London house was the best they could afford in a genteel neighbourhood that would not make them look too shabby, but it was shockingly expensive. Papa had outfitted them all splendidly for the year, as he always had, though after his death she'd discovered he had not been able to afford it, as the bailiffs had quickly come knocking. But next year, their gowns would be out of fashion and the little nest egg Maggie had put aside all gone. Only hers and her aunt's income would support them all, and they would not be able to remain in this house beyond the summer, as small as it was compared to the manor.

A soft knock at the door heralded Aunt Connie, who took one look at her and bustled in.

"Oh, my dear," she said, the voluminous fabric of her nightgown fluttering with dozens of pink ribbons and lace frills as she hurried around the bed. "There, there, Maggie, darling. As soon as I heard that door slam and Caro's raised voice, I knew you were getting yourself into a tizzy, fretting yourself to death over every little thing. You cannot control our fates, love, but I'm certain Cecil is looking after us. All will be well, I promise you."

"Oh, but how can you promise?" Maggie said, more startled by her aunt's perspicacity than her certainty that Cecil was keeping them safe, which was nothing new. Still, it was nice to be cossetted, and Maggie could not help but give into the tears that seemed always too close to the surface of late. "I knew it from the start, but I fear Caro is simply too young to marry. If she cannot see that Mr Weston is the best chance she has for happiness, then I despair of her."

Her aunt gave her an enigmatic smile and stroked her hair. "I know just how you feel, darling," she said with a touch of amusement. "But Cecil is certain it will all come right, and I believe him. You'll see."

"But what are we to do? All this is to launch Caro into society so that she can find a husband. She has this one chance, auntie, only one! Whether or not it is fair does not come into it. We simply cannot afford to keep her clothed as well as she ought to be, not to mention feeding us all, on top of the cost of rent and all the staff, and Giddy is growing like a weed and wearing through clothes at such a rate—"

"I know, love, but it is only October. The season does not begin until February, and that is a lifetime when one is only eighteen. Let us see what the coming months bring. We have Christmas to look forward to, remember, and you know how much you enjoy that now that Gideon is old enough to get excited about it."

"Yes," Maggie said, wiping her eyes. "But we all ought to be at the manor for Christmas. All our little traditions are impossible here. We can't go gathering holly and ivy on Regent Street, can we!"

"Now, now, pet. You're becoming overwrought," Connie said sternly.

Maggie sniffed and nodded. "I am. I know it. I'm an ungrateful wretch who has not the good sense to realise how lucky she is. Forgive me, Auntie. I beg your pardon for being such a trial."

"Goodness, Maggie, you are not a trial. We are the trial, as we all know. We all look to you, expecting you to put things right, to know just what to do and how and when, and you have always done so, but it is a strain on your nerves, anyone can see that. My brother was a dear man, and we all miss him despite the trouble he has brought down upon us, but I think his death has been hardest on you, so soon after losing William, and with a lively son to care for too. Now, stop being so hard upon yourself and do stop fretting. We have a lovely outing promised tomorrow, so let us just look forward to that and let the future take care of itself for now. I promise you it will."

"Yes, Auntie," Maggie said too weary to object, laying back against the pillows.

"There's a good girl," Connie said soothingly, pulling the covers up and smoothing them out. "Night, night, dearest. I'll see you in the morning."

Chapter 11

Larkin,

Yes, of course I'd be willing to help you. Do you want me to call a meeting of the Sons? I could manage it next week sometime if that suits?

—Excerpt from a letter from Mr Leo Hunt (Son of Mr Nathanial and Mrs Alice Hunt) to The Hon'ble Larkin Weston.

4th October 1850, Berwick Street, Soho, London.

The next morning, the household was a flurry of activity as the ladies prepared to show themselves in society. Dresses and bonnets were chosen and discarded and Sally and Priddy darted back and forth with this pair of gloves and that ribbon, trying to make sense among the general hubbub.

"Oh, Caro, you do look splendid," Maggie said, stifling the smallest twinge of envy as she regarded her little sister. She had never been jealous of Caro's glorious, good looks before, and told herself she was not now, except she wished she might capture Mr Weston's admiration as Caro had.

"Thank you. It is pretty, isn't it? I've been just dying to wear it, but what with being in mourning—" She stopped, suddenly ill at ease. "You do not think we shall look too much like country bumpkins among the fashionable town set, do you?"

"Don't be a silly goose," Aunt Connie replied soothingly. "Your papa was many things, but he knew what was up to snuff and what wasn't. Mrs Ledbetter might not have been a London modiste, but she got all her patterns direct from Paris, and much of her fabric too. She'll not let us down."

Maggie had to agree, for Caro looked divine in her promenade dress *en redingote* in a striking lavender taffeta. It was not black, however, which they well knew they ought to be wearing, and was probably even a little too dashing for half-mourning. But Mr Weston would not judge them, Maggie felt sure, and no one else knew who they were, so why not enjoy the day without the suffocating pall of heavy mourning fabrics, which made everyone look at them with pity? If they were to laugh or to appear to enjoy themselves too much, those looks would become censorious too, and Maggie thought they had suffered enough from her well-meaning but rackety father's behaviour and its consequences.

She turned back to the looking glass to review her own toilette with a critical gaze, aware she had dressed with far too much care this morning. It was foolish of her to choose her gown in hopes of drawing Mr Weston's eye. Wicked, too, when she purported to support his suit towards her sister, but she seemed unable to help herself. Besides, it was too late now to don her widow's weeds again. Instead, she had chosen a gown of deep green satin, with a fitted jacket embellished with black silk frogging. It hugged her waist and emphasised her bust and, whilst Maggie had never been vain—who could be with Caro to compare oneself to? —she did think she looked rather pretty.

"What do you think?"

Maggie turned as Aunt Connie came in, resplendent in a dashing ensemble of puce silk with three large, fringed flounces on her skirts that swished when she moved. The bodice was intricately ruched and tucked and seemed to make her impressive bosom even more notable.

"Auntie!" Maggie said, as her aunt twirled before her, looking as pleased as Caro did with her outfit. "You look quite magnificent and shall cast us both in the shade."

"Oh, you silly creature, as if I could," Connie said, but she blushed with pleasure all the same. "I declare, I am so excited! I know we came to town for Caro's sake, but to have a shopping trip all of our own and to see something of London… well, I am quite beside myself with delight."

"Indeed, it is a rare treat, and well deserved," Maggie said, pulling on her gloves. "We shall enjoy ourselves excessively, but if I may be the voice of doom for just a moment—"

"Oh, Maggie, no!" Caro said, sitting on Maggie's bed with an aggravated flounce and folding her arms.

"Yes, dear," Maggie said firmly, determined to make her point. "We are on a budget, and you are not to spend more than the amounts we discussed, and only on the items we decided are necessary to us. Is that clear?"

"Yes, Maggie," Caro replied, stony-faced.

"Of course, my dear," Aunt Connie said, patting her arm.

Maggie gave her aunt a stern look, aware Connie was the most likely of the two to get carried away, but Connie floated off, murmuring about having forgotten to apply her scent.

Maggie sighed, wishing she was not the one who had to remind them of such things and spoil their pleasure. Picking up her bonnet, she made her way downstairs, reaching the bottom just as a knock sounded. As Wallace was in the kitchen, she opened it and had to fight not to catch her breath as Mr Weston's tall, powerful frame filled the opening.

"Good morning, Mr Weston," she managed, wishing she did not sound quite so breathless, but the morning was bright, and sunshine gleamed upon his hair, making it shine gold and bronze, and highlighting the warm glints in his brown eyes.

For a moment she thought he hesitated too at the sight of her, his eyes widening a little, his mouth opening as if to speak but closing again. Maggie instantly fretted that she had something stuck in her teeth, though she had cleaned them very carefully, or that her skirts were caught up somehow, but a quick survey reassured her all was as it ought to be with her dress.

"Good morning, Mrs Finchley. That is a most charming outfit, if I may say so."

Maggie returned a quick smile, careful not to show her teeth before hurrying to the looking glass to put on her bonnet. Assuring herself that Mr Weston was not looking, she checked her teeth, reassured to discover nothing appalling lurking there.

"Good morning, Mr Weston. Forgive me for not opening the door to you," Wallace said, giving Maggie a reproving look for having done so herself.

She returned an apologetic smile before looking back at Mr Weston. "We are almost ready," she assured him, glancing up the stairs and hoping Connie would not keep them waiting too long.

"Mama!"

"Master Gideon!" Priddy exclaimed, hurrying after Gideon, who had clearly escaped from her clutches. "Beg pardon, Mrs Finchley, he got away from me."

"That's quite all right, Priddy," Maggie said, bending down to kiss her son's cheek. "He just wants to say goodbye, don't you, darling?"

"Yes, Mama. You going with Westie?"

"We are," she agreed, pushing his golden curls from his forehead. "And if you are a very good boy, I shall bring you a present."

"Cake?" he asked, his eyes lighting up. "Westie bring cake too?"

"Not cake," Maggie said, laughing. "Something good, though, but only if you behave," she added, wagging a finger at him.

"I be good," he replied, looking grave indeed.

"Wallace."

Maggie looked up as Mr Weston spoke, seeing Wallace turn towards him. "Yes, sir?"

"That matter I spoke to you about last night. He'll start today."

Maggie looked between them, a little perplexed.

"Nothing to trouble yourself about, Mrs Finchley. A private matter between Mr Weston and myself," Wallace assured her soothingly.

"Oh, of course," Maggie said, wondering what matter that could be when they barely knew each other. Still, it was none of her affair. Wallace was entitled to his private life as much as she was.

Finally, Caro and Aunt Connie arrived, and the party set off in high spirits, all looking forward to the day ahead.

The carriage Mr Weston had hired dropped them after they had survived the madness that was Piccadilly Circus, though the noise, the weight of traffic, and the chaos almost sent Aunt Connie into a swoon. She recovered with alacrity, however, once she was travelling again under her own power and surrounded by the delights that the fashionable shopping street had to offer.

Before they chanced to look in a shop window, however, the magnificent sight of the Horse Guards caught their eye, riding up Regent Street on their way to St James's. Caro gazed upon them open-mouthed, and even Maggie, who had been once so beguiled by a red coat, admired the impressive picture they presented on their gleaming mounts. Their helmets were adorned with flowing black plumes, the standard they bore flapping eagerly in a brisk autumn wind that also tugged at the ladies' bonnets and skirts as they trotted smartly past.

Once the imposing display had passed, they stopped at the very first window they came to, Caro and Connie drawn by the colourful display of stuffed birds. Brightly arrayed parrots and hummingbirds were arranged in lifelike poses, settled upon branches or suspended from cleverly hidden wires. Birds-of-paradise, with their exquisite plumage, gazed glassily back at them and made Maggie shudder with pity.

"I don't disagree," Larkin murmured with sympathy. "I find them rather unnerving myself. They would have been so free and beautiful in life; this seems rather undignified."

Maggie smiled at him, pleased he understood her disquiet without her having to explain.

Hurrying past a funeral monuments shop in silent accord, they ignored the obelisks and draped urns in the window, pulled onwards by the promise of more agreeable sights. An Italian statuary shop drew Aunt Connie, who lingered for longer than was appropriate over a scale model of Michelangelo's David until Maggie tugged her away. Next was a filter shop, at once somewhat revolting yet fascinating, with its display of clever machines for turning foul water, thick with mud, into something sparkling and clear.

Next, they came across a magnificent emporium, which they dared to enter to peruse the goods on offer. Wines from France and Italy, sweetmeats and preserves, liqueurs and condiments, Bayonne ham and honey from Narbonne all tempted them to spend their carefully counted allowance for the day. Mr Weston found he could not resist the lure of Bologna sausage, which he confided to Maggie was his valet's favourite thing in all the world. He bought a quantity, and had it sent to his home, laughing with amusement at how pleased Barnes would be when it arrived out of the blue. That he would think of and buy such a treat for his servant only elevated him higher still in Maggie's estimation and she found she hardly dared look at him for fear of gazing at him like a complete ninny.

Aunt Connie could not quite contain herself either and succumbed to a pot of clotted cream and a jar of *pâté de fois gras*. This, Mr Weston was kind enough to add to his own order so the items might be delivered together.

They gazed next into the windows of fancy watchmakers and stationers, before the ladies dragged poor Mr Weston into a haberdasher's shop in which Maggie feared he might be forced to spend the rest of the day. Here, Caro ran amok, despite being reminded they still had a great deal to see. An hour later she was finally dragged out, looking dazed but delighted by her haul of ribbons, lace, and silk flowers.

Once more, Maggie looked upon Mr Weston with admiration, for he had not by look nor deed shown even a little impatience with them when she had felt sure he must be bored witless. After another hour or more of meandering and window shopping, Mr Weston suggested they stop for tea in a charming tea shop, for he was certain everyone was famished. No one contradicted him.

The proprietress, who greeted them warmly, seated them in a table near the window so they could watch the world outside while they ate, and promised them a delightful lunch would be provided at once. Aunt Connie was very taken with the place and admired the pretty china and the lovely chintz wallpaper. They all exclaimed when the lady returned with two serving girls who carried an extraordinary selection of dainty sandwiches, scones, cakes, and biscuits.

"Good heavens!" Maggie exclaimed, looking at Mr Weston in astonishment. "However, shall we eat it all?"

"I think we can manage it. I'm starving myself, so I promise to do my part," he added, winking at her and helping himself to a selection of sandwiches.

"Oh, Maggie, can you imagine what Gideon would say if he saw all this?" Caro said, laughing.

"You must not tell him, Miss Caroline," Mr Weston said, wagging a finger at her. "The poor boy will be bereft. However, I shall make it up to him and bring him another day. What do you think, Mrs Finchley?"

Maggie gazed at him, colour rising to her cheeks. "I-I think he would be the happiest boy that ever lived," she managed, hardly able to believe he meant such a thing. Would he really bring Gideon here? Why should he trouble himself with her little boy? Did it mean anything, or was she over-interpreting a kind gesture? Never having had a come out, she was uncertain how a gentleman might act towards a female friend in town and whether this would be considered quite unexceptional or not. In the countryside a neighbour might well invite your child in for tea, or give them a game of cricket, but to take them out to a tea shop in town? Was that usual?

Overwhelmed and disarmed, she busied herself pouring the tea and preparing it to everyone's taste before she ate and was a little surprised when Mr Weston handed her a plate filled with a little of everything that looked nicest.

"I thought I had best lay claim to some for you before we eat it all. I told you we would," he said with a grin.

"Thank you," she said, reaching for the plate.

As she took it, their fingers touched. The oddest sensation raced over her skin and her foolish heart skipped.

Maggie glanced up at him, wondering if he'd felt it too, and discovered his warm brown eyes upon her. He held her gaze far longer than he ought before he replied, "You're welcome," in a low voice that made her breath catch and warmth bloom inside her.

Maggie looked away, flustered, wondering if she was imagining things. Was he flirting with her, or was she being an idiot? She tried to remember how she had felt when William had courted her. Though it seemed a lifetime ago, as if it had happened to another version of her when she had been innocent and relatively carefree, she recalled the excitement she had felt, but had it been so tangible then? Had the brush of William's hand sent her pulse racing, had she felt the lingering touch like she had been branded somehow, the warmth persisting long after it had ended?

Though they all exclaimed that they did not know how it was possible, Mr Weston was proven correct, and little remained of their lunch but crumbs. Once Mr Weston had paid, they thanked him excessively for the rare treat until he laughed and held up his hands, imploring them to stop.

"I told you it was my treat, and I promise you I enjoyed it as much as you did! If you wish to repay me, then I shall come to tea again and you may stuff me with cake to your heart's content."

"Indeed, we shall do so," Aunt Connie said firmly. "Shan't we, Maggie?"

"Certainly, if you would like to come, we will be pleased to see you. I believe you must know by now that you are always most welcome," Maggie replied, finding her words were rather more earnest than perhaps they ought to be.

Mr Weston's gaze met hers and he smiled, a smile that tugged at her heart and made her dream impossible dreams. "I shall hold you to that," he said, and then turned to speak with Caro, making her laugh as he drew her attention to a shop window, leaving Maggie in a stew of happiness and confusion. Could she have been wrong all this time? Could it be that Mr Weston was not interested in Caro, but in her? The idea was so tantalising, so beguiling, her heart skipped, her skin aching with longing as she remembered his strong arms, and allowed herself to consider how it might feel to be held in his embrace. How desperately she wanted that, she realised with sudden clarity, understanding in that moment how much she needed to feel loved, to feel safe and wanted, and like she was no longer alone.

They made their way along Regent Street, stopping at this window and that, and beguiled by the dazzling array of fashionable people out on the street. Mr Weston seemed to know many of them, and pointed out a few, the most notable being Charles Kean, the famous actor. Son of the legendary Edmund Kean, his productions at the Princess Theatre on Oxford Street were famous for his meticulous research into historical dress and settings.

"Oh, how I should love to see him perform," Aunt Connie lamented longingly, pressing a hand to her chest. "I've read so much about him and his performances, but we've seen nothing other than the travelling theatre shows that appear in the village during the summer months. They are most diverting, of course, but to see Shakespeare performed by such a man in a London theatre...."

Connie sighed and gazed after Mr Kean with a dreamy look in her eyes. Maggie pinched her aunt and gave her a stern look, quite certain she was angling to get Mr Weston to take them all.

"I'm sure that could be arranged," he said, smiling at Aunt Connie.

"Oh, no, Mr Weston, you have been too good, too patient already. We cannot, *will* not, impose upon you further," Maggie said in alarm, so afraid her sister and aunt would take advantage of his kindness that she glared at Connie and at Caro too, who was opening her mouth to protest.

Connie looked crestfallen but Caro stalked past Maggie, muttering 'killjoy,' under her breath. Maggie heard it, and she thought Mr Weston did too.

Aunt Connie hurried after Caro before she could get too far ahead, leaving Maggie with Mr Weston. She glanced up at him uncertainly, not wishing him to think ill of Caro for her complaint.

"She is so excited to be in London, she wishes to see everything all at once," Maggie said by way of apology. "It's just she's very excited and—"

"You do not need to make excuses for Caro to me," Mr Weston said, taking her hand and placing it on his sleeve. "It was you she was rude to, but really, there is no need to refuse my invitation. I promise you I should never have offered if I did not wish to accompany you. I've had a delightful time today, you know. It's fun seeing everything that is familiar to me for the first time through your eyes."

"I'm sure we must seem like bumpkins to you," Maggie said ruefully.

"Not at all. I think you are all the most charming companions a fellow could hope for."

He smiled down at her and Maggie gazed helplessly up at him, wishing she understood him, that she knew what it was he wanted from them, if anything. Perhaps he really was just a kind fellow looking after his neighbours, treating them as his friends, or was it Caro he wanted? Or did she dare hope…?

Perhaps he recognised the worshipful look in her eyes and realised his neighbour was an unsophisticated fool, for he looked away from her at once, his expression unreadable.

"Come along, Mrs Finchley," he said briskly. "The Parthenon Bazaar awaits if you have the stamina for it, and your aunt and Miss Caroline are getting away from us. We'd best catch them up."

Larkin cursed himself. What the devil was he playing at? He'd been lulled into foolishness by the pleasure he'd taken in the day so far. The three women were, just as he'd said, the most charming of companions and he'd enjoyed treating them and squiring them around town. But it was Mrs Finchley who captured his attention, Mrs Finchley whose beautiful profile he could not stop gazing at. No doubt it was all the fault of that blasted dream. It had returned to him nightly, each time a little different, each time allowing him to explore the adventure, and the woman, a little further. This morning, he had woken aroused and restless and longing to take her in his arms. He wondered if he was confusing reality with the woman that existed in his imagination, for she was everything that was passionate and welcoming, responding to his touch in a way that made him ache for her. It was this captivating creature whose hand he could not resist touching, just to see the colour rise to her cheeks, could not resist flirting with just a little, only to see how she reacted to him. Yet she was not his dream lover, but flesh and blood, and he was being cruel, for he did not mean to pursue her. Did he?

Suddenly he felt certain of nothing, his heart a confusion of longing and desire and the desperate need not to make another stupid mistake. Was he doing it again, forcing himself into a woman's life when she did not want him there as anything other than a friend? Were those blushes because his attentions embarrassed her? Suddenly, he felt uncertain of everything, of what he wanted, of what Mrs Finchley wanted, or needed.

Before Elmira, he'd been as carefree and pleasure-loving as any of his friends, despite his 'do gooding,' for which they often teased him. But he'd had no trouble with women, though he'd been a little more careful than some of his companions, understanding what consequences women bore more keenly than perhaps his friends did. Life had seemed a good deal simpler then, and so he had not questioned his feelings for Elmira or hers for him, which he ought to have done. Now, however, he did nothing, but question and the questioning only left him increasingly confused.

He was relieved therefore when they arrived before the Parthenon Bazaar, and he could stuff all his misgivings and anxieties into the mental cupboard where he put anything he did not wish to look at. For now, he wished only to live in the moment, to enjoy the women's company and take pleasure in the joy they found in shopping in such exciting new surroundings.

The Parthenon Bazaar had once been one of London's most fashionable theatres but had ultimately failed and fallen into disrepair. Since then, it had been lavishly remodelled and repurposed. The party walked inside under the porch and into an elegant vestibule with a display of statuary. Taking the stairs, they found themselves in a picture gallery but did not stay long to view the offerings, which they all agreed were a little humdrum and of no greater quality than they might find in local exhibitions around Norfolk. Eager to see more, they discovered the room led onto a gallery which housed a magnificent toy bazaar. Maggie gasped with delight and immediately set about finding a gift for Gideon whilst the Misses Merrivale gazed over the balcony at the floor below.

"Why, but it's enormous," Miss Caroline exclaimed, her lovely face lit with joy.

To his chagrin, Larkin noticed her exclamation had taken the attention of two young bucks who stood gazing up at the vision of loveliness with dim-witted expressions that made them look as if they'd each been struck in the head with a mallet. Miss Caroline did not seem to notice but her aunt did and pulled her niece away.

"Come and help Maggie find something for our dear Giddy, Caro. There's time enough to look downstairs afterwards."

Thus occupied, the ladies walked off and Larkin found his attention drift back to Mrs Finchley. She had moved to inspect an aviary where little birds chirped and hopped from branch to branch.

"At least these are alive," he remarked.

"Yes," she said ruefully, watching the pretty things flit back and forth with a considering expression.

"Are you thinking of buying one?" Larkin asked her.

"I don't know. What do you think?" she asked, turning to smile at him with such trust in her eyes that Larkin's heart felt squeezed in his chest. "I don't really approve of seeing them caged when they ought to be flying free, but when I was a girl, we had dogs and cats, not to mention all the chickens and ducks and a few pigs. Horses and ponies too, naturally, and yet Gideon can have none of that, for we are in a rented home in a city and only until the season is over. Then we shall have to move again, I suppose, and find something smaller and cheaper. We are not at the manor any longer and I really must get used to that. I keep forgetting, you see. Thinking that when this is done we can go home and… foolish, isn't it?" she said, such a depth of regret and longing in her voice Larkin moved to take her hand in his, only to remember himself and stop before he overstepped once again.

This was why he ought to get their home back for them if it was possible, though. He could not bear to know how much they missed it, and to realise how much Gideon would miss out on as he grew up.

"Not at all," he said. "You've lost something that has always been integral to your lives, your happiness. It is only natural that you mourn the loss of it."

Mrs Finchley nodded briskly and blinked away tears, smiling bravely instead and turning back to the birds.

"I think it is important for children to have the care of something. It teaches responsibility, and caring too, but this is all I can offer him. Except for perhaps a goldfish, but that seems a little dull in comparison."

"Perhaps if you bought two birds, and they had a decent sized cage, so they had space at least. It's got to be better than the inside of this shop, anyway," he pointed out.

"I don't think I can afford a large cage, too," she said with a frown. "Oh, dear. Perhaps it's not such a good idea. I shall only feel sorry for the poor little things and want to set them free whenever I look at them."

Larkin opened his mouth, about to say he'd build the cage for them, but closed it again. Not his family. Not his responsibility, he reminded himself. He really had to stop sticking his oar in.

"What about a train?" he suggested, guiding her to the back of the shop where he'd noticed a display of tin toys. He picked up a smartly painted train in green with red pinstripes and held it up to show her.

Larkin bent down and gave the toy an experimental push to see how it travelled over the wooden floor and Maggie laughed as the little train promptly flew towards the bannisters.

"Blast!" Larkin exclaimed and ran after it, snatching it up in the second before it dived off the edge to the shop below. He let out a breath of relief and turned to see Mrs Finchley watching with her hand over her mouth. She was laughing at him, the wretch, and doing a very poor job of hiding it.

"Oh, I-I b-beg your pardon," she stammered. "How quick you were!"

She went off again with a peal of laughter that made his heart feel lighter, even if she was laughing at his expense. How lovely she was, her eyes sparkling, the colour in her cheeks a delicate rose that he longed to capture in paint. More than that, he longed to reach for her, to pull her into his arms and kiss her senseless.

No. No, that was not going to happen. Not in a public place. Not in *any* place. Not ever.

The reminder made him feel oddly out of sorts and despondent, but he shook the sensation off and walked back to stand beside her.

"Well, it works," he said, finding a smile from somewhere.

"So it does," she said, gazing up at him with a look that reminded him of everything he had just promised he would not do. He glanced down at her. A mistake, as his gaze fell at once to her mouth, lingering on her plush lips, soft and ripe for kissing. She wanted him to kiss her, a little voice in his head told him, but he silenced it before it got him into trouble.

Instead, he walked back to the display of tin toys. "What do you think, then? Do you think the train is best? There are others?"

"I think he will love the train, especially when I tell him you nearly crashed it in the shop," she said, giving him a mischievous smile.

Despite his best intentions, the devilry in her eyes called to him, begging him to answer in kind.

"In that case, I shan't give it to you!" he said, holding the train up where she could not reach it.

"Oh, now, Mr Weston. That is hardly gentlemanly of you," she scolded.

"Who said I was a gentleman?" he replied, the words out before he could think better of them.

Stop! yelled a voice in his head. *Stop this now!*

Mrs Finchley looked around and discovered, as he'd already realised, that they were alone up here. She reached up on tiptoes and made a grab for the toy, but Larkin stepped back, holding it out of reach.

"Say you will not tell Gideon I did something so foolish," he demanded, his voice grave.

"I *will* tell him," she retorted, laughter and defiance shining in her eyes. She reached up again, lunging for the toy and overbalancing. She gasped, the toe of her shoe catching on an uneven floorboard and fell against him.

"Ooof!"

Larkin pulled her close, his intention only to stop her falling, but then she was in his arms, her warm, soft body pressed close to his, and his mind turned to treacle.

One hand still held the train, but the other was upon her waist, her deliciously shapely waist, while her breasts pressed against his chest. He gazed down at her, seeing her eyes widen as she realised how close they were. Larkin waited for her to push him away and scold him for taking advantage of her mishap, as she should, as she must do. Only she didn't. She simply stared up at him, and then closed her eyes, lifting her face to his.

Larkin swallowed hard, the little voice in his head suddenly shrieking at him that this was not what he wanted. Mrs Finchley was respectable, she'd have expectations, she'd need marrying. He'd have to be a father to Gideon!

"We ought to find Miss Caroline. There were two gentlemen ogling her rather too keenly for my liking. We don't want her to get herself into a difficult situation," he said briskly, all the time extricating himself from their embrace.

Mrs Finchley stiffened, moving away, her frame suddenly rigid where a moment ago it had been pliant and giving. "Of course," she said curtly, hurrying past him, but not before he noticed the burn of embarrassment colouring her cheeks.

Damn him to hell! Now he'd humiliated her, and no doubt hurt her feelings, too. *Well done, Larkin. Excellent work, you utter prat.*

Smothering a groan of frustration, he hurried after her.

Oh Maggie, you fool! You utter fool! How could you do such a pathetic, such a reckless thing?

All the way down the stairs, Maggie berated herself, shame and humiliation burning inside her so fiercely she felt too hot and longed to go back outside. She pressed her gloved hands to her cheeks, trying to cool them before anyone noticed. Before *he* noticed.

Oh, Lord, if she had spoiled Caro's chances and spoiled their friendship with a man of whom they had all become so very fond, she would never forgive herself. How could she be so selfish as to let her own desires wreck all their futures? Yet she had been growing ever closer to such foolishness all afternoon, but had she imagined the way he had spoken to her, the lingering glances and touches? Well, she must have, or perhaps he was just reacting to the encouragement she must have so blatantly given him. For a gentleman such as Mr Weston would never lead a lady on. It was her own foolish heart seeing things that were not there and her own selfish wickedness that had tempted her to practically throw herself at him. Since he had entered their lives, she had come to realise she was not so sanguine about living the rest of her days as a widow as she'd believed. She was lonely, and not only for friendship, but for the closeness one only found with a husband. Whilst her marriage had been fleeting thing, she knew that physical love, not to mention the comfort and companionship of such a union were not easily replaced with friends. Mr Weston was handsome and charming and so very kind and attentive to them; it was only natural that her feelings should warm to him after so long in mourning and after so much unhappiness. But to embarrass the man and betray her own sister by acting on those feelings was beyond the pale.

Ought she to apologise, she wondered? No. That would only highlight her dreadful behaviour and would be too humiliating to endure. Maggie felt certain Mr Weston's innate good manners would ensure he put her dreadfully bold behaviour aside. She only hoped it did not spoil everything for Auntie and Caro. For her own part, she would do her best to keep her distance from Mr Weston and take some time to remind herself that such an eligible fellow would hardly be interested in a penniless widow with a lively son to raise. Perhaps this was a blessing in disguise, in fact. She must check her feelings before they could grow out of proportion, and she fancied herself in love with the poor man.

So Maggie did her utmost to calm herself, outwardly at least, focusing on the bazaar and doing her best to look pleased with it. In any other circumstances, she would have been delighted, for it was a fascinating place. The ground floor held dozens of glass-topped counters, each displaying something interesting. Trinkets and jewellery, millinery and lace all jostled for attention beside gloves and hosiery and so much else it was quite overwhelming. Maggie caught up with her aunt and Caro, who exclaimed excitedly over all they had seen and, to Maggie's dismay, seemed to have made far too many purchases. In normal circumstances she would have remonstrated with them for their reckless spending, but as she had behaved far worse than they she did not feel she had the right to do so.

More counters stuffed with cutlery, sheets of music, pocketbooks and porcelain objects had to be inspected and remarked upon. They all sighed over darling little children's dresses, and in the next stall Maggie had to drag her aunt bodily away before she bought a cut glass ornament in the shape of a bird. Caro complained bitterly over the loss of their piano when she saw the variety of sheet music on offer, all of which was utterly useless to them now. There were children's books, however, and Maggie could not resist buying a copy of Tom Thumb's Picture Alphabet, a purchase she comforted herself was educational for her son and so not in the least frivolous. Then she remembered the train and did not know whether to be comforted or dismayed when she discovered Mr Weston had rejoined them and that he had purchased the train himself.

Mr Weston noticed her standing alone at the bookstall and walked towards her, looking as though he wished to speak, but Maggie turned away, hurrying to stand close to her sister and aunt once more. She had humiliated herself beyond bearing as it was, and if he was kind to her on top of that she would die. Instead, Maggie determined to repay him for the train and prayed that everyone else was feeling as weary as she was, if not so out of sorts, for she longed to go back to the house. She could not think of it as home, but at least Wallace and Mrs Moody and Gideon would be there, and Mr Weston would not be, and she might contrive to feel comfortable again.

It was another half an hour before Caro could be persuaded to leave, however, and only then when she was the proud owner of a splendid ostrich feather dyed a jaunty shade of green. Indeed, the display held so many feathers, all in extraordinary colours, that Auntie Connie was moved to wonder aloud if there was a bird left anywhere that wasn't entirely bald.

The journey back home was no quieter than the one going, despite everyone being fatigued by such diverting entertainments. Only Maggie was silent, though she tried her best to do her bit to attend to the conversation and appear at ease, whilst studiously avoiding Mr Weston's gaze. Once or twice, she thought he tried to catch her eye, but she refused to meet it, certain it would do her no good and only make an awkward situation worse.

If only he did not speak of it, perhaps in time they could forget it ever happened and be easy together again. For she realised she valued his friendship too highly to ever risk it again for feelings which she now knew were entirely one-sided. It had only been a silly daydream, after all, to think that such a man might take an interest in her, and she was sensible enough to put such romantic nonsense to one side. She might feel sorry for herself for a day or two, but that would pass as all things passed if one kept busy and did not dwell on what could not be changed.

When they finally arrived back at Berwick Street, Maggie congratulated herself on behaving very prettily, thanking Mr Weston most warmly for a wonderful outing and leaving him with perfect politeness, all without ever meeting his eye.

Chapter 12

Dearest Delia,

Thank you for your last letter. It was so good to hear all of Rex and Emmeline's news, and yours too. How lucky you are to have found a man like Muir Anderson. Your life sounds truly idyllic, and I am so very happy for you.

I beg you will forgive me for refusing to tell you where I am living, and to use such subterfuge in the sending and receiving of correspondence but I fear it is for the best. It has kept me hidden this long and I do not intend to reveal myself until the duke is dead. Only then will I believe myself safe.

I know that I have been wicked indeed, and stupidly reckless in writing that dreadful story, but I never expected it to be such a success, I swear. It was revenge for everything I have lost that motivated me, a way of soothing my own impotent rage, but now I see just what a fool I have been, for I have jeopardised my sanctuary. If only it had sunk without trace, as I expected it to do. What an utter henwit I was to think no one would recognise my description of Sefton and revel in his humiliation. I have tried to withhold the final chapters from publication, but only succeeded in delaying them a little, which seems to have increased the demand tenfold! I made a legal agreement which is binding, however, and must now honour it, come what may. At least the exercise was financially rewarding, something I may have cause to be thankful for when I find myself cast out in the cold when the truth about me is discovered.

I am living on borrowed time, I fear, and if things go badly, I may return to you sooner than you expect, if only for a little while, before I disappear again.

Please send Aunt Lucy and dear Rex all my love and kiss all my new nieces and nephews. One day I shall do so myself, I promise.

I miss you all and love you so much.

Your own, Genevieve x

—Excerpt of a letter from The Lady Genevieve Hamilton to The Lady Cordelia Anderson.

4th October 1850, Berwick Street, Soho, London.

Larkin stood on the street for a moment after the door had closed and cursed himself again. *Bloody, bloody, insensitive half-witted idiot!* He had behaved appallingly, giving Mrs Finchley reason to believe he had feelings for her, that he desired her, and then he'd cut her dead when she'd been brave enough to show she reciprocated. What must it have cost her to allow him to see her desire to be kissed, only then to have her bravery thrown back in her face? He felt sick, sick at heart and sick to his stomach, and he did not know what to do for the best.

She had given him the cold shoulder ever since, and he could hardly blame her for that. Perhaps it was for the best. Perhaps if he gave her some space, they could go back to being friends, for they *were* friends, he realised, and he hated to think he might have spoiled something that was important to him—to them both—by acting so thoughtlessly.

With nothing else he could do, Larkin went home.

5th October 1850, Berwick Street, Soho, London.

The next day Larkin rose late, in a wretched temper still, racked with guilt over what had happened the day before, a situation not helped in the least by the wickedly erotic dream that had woken him in the early hours, desperate with desire for the woman living just next door. In his dream, she had lifted her face to his, just as she had in the shop, but he had not denied her. Oh, no. He'd denied her nothing at all, exploring her lush curves intimately with his hands and mouth and awaking with his body shaking with lust and the certain knowledge such things were out of the question. He needed to get out more, he decided, and find himself a lady to spend some time with before he went mad. He'd taken lovers enough during the months when he'd taken to drinking and gambling wildly but had not had the heart to find himself a mistress. Now, that seemed an utterly foolish state of affairs and must be fixed as quickly as possible. For knowing Mrs Finchley might feel the same for him only made things ten times worse, and he found it impossible to go back to sleep, dozing fitfully until Barnes finally roused him with a tray sent up by Mrs Goodall.

"There's this, too," Barnes said, handing him a sealed note.

Larkin took it, noting how heavy it felt, and used the knife on his tray to break the seal. Out dropped some coins, and he frowned as he scanned the short missive.

Mr Weston,

Thank you kindly for the lovely outing yesterday. We all enjoyed it very much. Please find enclosed the money I owe you for Gideon's train.

Mrs Finchley.

His jaw clenched, frustration gnawing at his guts. The train had been a present for Gideon, and he'd told her as much, but he understood he had hurt her pride, and this was her way of salvaging it. He could not blame her, *did* not blame her, only himself.

"Are you still going out, sir?" Barnes asked.

Larkin put the note aside with the coins and nodded. "I am." He turned his attention to the breakfast Barnes had brought him and did not feel like eating it. Yet he would not compound his villainy by insulting Mrs Goodall, who was the most marvellous cook and who even Barnes seemed to have taken to with no fighting over what was whose territory.

Today he had a sitting with Tilly to continue his portrait. He would concentrate on that and not think about Mrs Finchley at all.

6th October 1850, Berwick Street, Soho, London.

Larkin woke on Sunday morning in much the same state as the day previous and his sense of déjà vu was only compounded by the arrival of yet another note, again heavy with coins.

Mr Weston,

Thank you kindly for arranging for your gardener to cut the grass and tidy our garden. I have enclosed the money I owe you for the work. I beg you will inform me if it is not enough.

Mrs Finchley.

Larkin sighed, pinching the bridge of his nose. This was how it would be from now on, he knew, with Mrs Finchley being scrupulously polite and observing all the proprieties and him forced to go along with it. Only days ago, she had burst into the kitchen, blushing and turned her back when she'd discovered him in only his dressing gown. The memory made him smile but was horribly melancholy too. He'd done this, just as he'd ruined things with Elmira. Perhaps if he'd not flirted and encouraged her to think of him as some heroic lover, Elmira might have been his friend and trusted him with the truth. Perhaps they would be friends still. Instead, he had messed up another friendship by not knowing what it was he wanted from it.

"Bloody idiot," he muttered, causing Barnes to look up from the drawer where Larkin's clean shirts were kept.

"Beg your pardon, sir?"

"Nothing," Larkin said gruffly. "Mrs Finchley paid for the gardener."

"Ah. I wondered if that was it," Barnes said with a frown.

"And so now, instead of doing her a kindness, I've forced her to pay for something she cannot afford."

Barnes nodded, looking chagrined. "A difficult one, if the lady insists upon paying. Perhaps there is some other small way we can make up for the cost?"

"Like what?" Larkin asked morosely.

"Gammon."

Larkin stared at his valet, wondering if he was being insulted.

"Gammon, sir," Barnes clarified. "You won that lovely big piece of gammon once, at cards, don't you remember?"

"Oh, yes. I gave it to my mother. That was ages ago," he protested, wondering where Barnes was going with this.

"Yes, sir," Barnes said with exaggerated patience. "But if you was to say you won a piece of gammon or a joint of beef, then they couldn't pay you for it, 'cause you hadn't paid for it either."

Larkin considered this. "That's not a bad idea, Barnes. Well done. I'm going to the club on Saturday next. You get something in ready and you can give it to them on Sunday morning. If you give it to Mrs Moody, she'll cook it for their lunch while they're at church, before they know anything about it, and then it will be too late."

"Very good, sir. I just noticed the ladies all going off to church a few minutes ago, actually. Will you be joining them?" Barnes asked with studied nonchalance.

"No," Larkin replied tersely. "I've work to do."

Barnes pulled a face. "Mrs Goodall won't like it, working on a Sunday, sir."

"Then Mrs Goodall can take the day off," Larkin retorted. "If it's good enough for her, I don't see the good lord can object to me putting some paint on canvas."

"Right you are, sir," Barnes replied and, correctly interpreting his master's mood, made himself scarce.

12th October 1850, The Sons of Hades, Portman Square, London.

Larkin made his way through the luxurious rooms of the club he owned with his friends, the scent of leather, polish, cognac and cigar smoke lingering in the air. It was early evening and there were few punters about, though he noticed one of the rooms they rented for private games was taken. At one time, he'd practically lived here, with only Leo spending more time among the comfortingly familiar rooms than he did. What had begun as a lark for them all, a place for them to escape their fathers' eagle eyes and behave badly, had become a successful enterprise, a joint venture where only men they deemed worthy could come and drink or gamble, do business, or simply put their feet up and escape whatever trials they wished to avoid.

Making his way up the stairs to the rooms put aside for the owners, Larkin's spirits lifted a little upon opening the door to the main office and seeing Leo at the desk.

"Lars! It's been an age," Leo said, setting aside the ledger he'd been perusing and getting up to greet him.

"Well, whose fault is that?" Larkin said, embracing Leo warmly. "You're getting fat, old man. Married life agrees with you," he teased, patting Leo's stomach.

"Get away with you," Leo said, laughing. "I'm as fit as a flea, and married life does agree with me. When are you going to set aside your bachelor ways and join us, eh?"

"Yes, come in, Lars, the water's fine," drawled a deep voice and Larkin turned in surprise to discover Jules sprawled in an armchair.

"Jules! You here too?" Larkin grinned as Jules stood and held out a hand.

"Well, Leo here said there was a game afoot. A dragon that needs slaying, or some such drivel."

"Well, he's right," Larkin admitted. "And I'd be glad of your advice. Your help too, if you're up for it."

"Let's have a drink," Leo suggested, lifting the cognac decanter that habitually sat on the desk and setting out three glasses.

Once Leo had supplied everyone with a healthy dose of brandy, Larkin explained about his new neighbours and the tragedy of the late Mr Merrivale's estate.

"I remember hearing about that," Jules said, shaking his head. "It was at The Crooked Penny, and a more justly named club there never was, for you're as likely to get cozened there or your throat slit as anywhere in London."

"That's what I'd heard too. I'd wager anything the game was rigged," Leo chimed in.

Jules nodded. "There was certainly a good deal of talk when it happened. Apparently Merrivale was half seas over and clearly out of his head with desperation. Even the clientele at the Penny, charming as they are, protested he was in no state to play, but Jenkins goaded the fellow so blatantly Merrivale was never going to refuse, what with the state he was in."

Larkin's jaw tightened at this revelation, though it was nothing more than he'd expected. He glowered into his drink, turning his glass back and forth in his hands. "Poor old Merrivale, fool that he was. He ought never to have been playing so deep with so many people depending on him, but he did and now he's left his family out in the cold."

"Are they in debt?"

Larkin shook his head. "I don't believe so. From what I gather, anything of value was sold to cover his creditors. The house and a few contents were all that remained, but that's what's of value to the ladies. It's their home and they mourn the loss of it. I just keep thinking how I would feel if Mitcham Priory was taken from my family by foul means, and I was powerless to get it back."

"Sticks in the throat," Leo agreed, his expression serious. "So, what are we going to do about it?"

"I'm going to win it back," Larkin said, more determined than ever to do it, to make amends to Mrs Finchley for the way he'd toyed with her affections. Though it pained him to admit it, he could not call it anything other than what it was. He had flirted with her, mildly yes, but she was a woman who was plainly vulnerable after everything she had endured. Every code of honour screamed at him that such women were to be protected, and he, of all people, had behaved badly.

Leo and Jules exchanged glances but, unlike Montagu, they did not imply he had lost his mind.

"How?" Jules asked.

"That's what I need you for. I've asked Montagu to find out what he can about the fellow, a Mr Jenkins. As soon as I hear from him, I'll know how to proceed, but I'm thinking of an exclusive invitation to a high stakes game. A fellow like this Jenkins would likely give his right arm for membership here, so such an invitation would be irresistible, don't you think?"

Leo nodded, smiling wickedly. "I do. And then we'll fleece him."

"I'll fleece him," Larkin amended. "But I'd appreciate your help."

"Then you have it," Jules said with his usual lazy smile. "I shall look forward to it. Haven't been to a game in an age. Can't say I've missed it, though," he admitted.

"How is the lovely Selina?" Larkin asked, amused that the once reckless rake had become such a devoted husband and father.

"Increasing, again," he admitted with a grin that showed how pleased he was by this news. "But don't put it about. I've not told my parents yet."

"Congratulations!" Leo and Larkin both exclaimed.

"Didn't know you had it in you," Leo added with a wink.

Jules snorted and rolled his eyes. "Stow it. Pour me another drink and let us celebrate properly. We'll have a hand or two before dinner and then take advantage of our own excellent chef. So long as I'm home before midnight, I'm in the clear."

Larkin laughed, shaking his head over his friend's curfew. "Will you turn into a pumpkin, or will Selina lock you out?"

Leo laughed and then coughed. "I said the same," he admitted ruefully, and Larkin mocked them both for being hen-pecked as he was supposed to do, but the words felt hollow, and he could not but wish he too had someone waiting for him to get home.

Chapter 13

Larkin,

I did a little fishing as you requested. Jenkins is, as you supposed, an unsavoury character. Rumours of cheating, fraud and violence abound and so I beg you to have a care if you decide to pursue your quarry.

For your information, it appears country life does not suit this estimable fellow, and he is in London at present. I am reliably informed he is staying at the Punch and Judy in Covent Garden.

For heaven's sake, keep your wits about you if you deal with the villain. For if you wind up in the Thames because of information I've handed over, I will never forgive myself, or you and your father will murder me.

—Excerpt of a letter from The Most Hon'ble Lucien Barrington, The Marquess of Montagu, to The Hon'ble Larkin Weston.

13th October 1850, Berwick Street, Soho, London.

Maggie looked out of the window with a sigh. London on a grim, wet day only made her homesickness all the keener. A wet day at the manor was an excuse to cosy up and read by the fire. Even walking down muddy lanes in the rain, with the wind blowing through the trees overhead, and knowing she would soon be warm and dry was a very different feeling from that she'd had today. Hurrying home from church, along streets filthy with refuse and surrounded by buildings, with the rain pelting them and the wind blowing them this way and that was not in the least bit pleasant. She felt certain that if they'd never had to leave their beautiful home, she would not now be feeling so very unsettled and dissatisfied. When she'd had the gardens and the home farm to attend to, there was so little time to consider her own heart. Now, she had far too much time on her hands, too much time to feel resentment over losing everything she'd loved, and then to feel guilty for her ingratitude when she was so much more fortunate than many.

As Maggie hung up her wet things to dry, so Sally would have one less thing to do, she smoothed down the skirts of her old day dress that had once been a favourite but was now faded and soft with too much wear and washing. It was comforting, though, to wear something so familiar, and no one would call on them today. No one had called upon them since that day out with Mr Weston, for they had not seen him since.

Maggie was not in the least bit surprised nor dismayed by this, she assured herself. It was simply this dreary weather and not having enough to do that made her feel as though she would run mad. Only poor Giddy was disappointed not to have seen his friend again and often asked after his 'Westie.'

As she made her way down the stairs, Maggie sniffed appreciatively at the delicious scent wafting from the kitchens and wondered what Mrs Moody was cooking. She was a remarkably thrifty cook, unlike Mrs Goodall, who had never had to economise to such a degree, even when they ought to have done, for Maggie's father had loved his dinner.

"Dinner is ready, missus," Priddy told her, before dashing downstairs to the kitchen.

Maggie nodded and made her way to the small dining room. It was a rather poky room, and the fire smoked when the wind blew from the west, so they only ate in here on a Sunday. The rest of the week, they preferred to eat by a small table by the window in the front parlour that got the morning sun, if there was any.

Today, Maggie found everyone awaiting her arrival with Gideon holding his knife and fork expectantly.

"Special din-dins," he said, with obvious excitement.

"Oh?" Maggie said, smiling at her son and smoothing down a cowlick that promptly sprang up again. "What's special about it?"

"Moody said special, with Yorky pudding," he told her eagerly.

"Yorkshire pudding," Caro corrected with a smile. "It certainly smells divine, whatever it is."

"Beef," Aunt Connie said, sniffing the air and giving a contented sigh. "That is certainly roast beef and Yorkshire pudding."

"Don't be silly, love," Maggie said, feeling bad for spoiling their excitement. "We can't afford such things as roast beef. Do you know what the price of a single, scrawny chicken is here? Oh, it makes me want to weep when I think of the fat birds we had at home," she said, and then scolded herself again for remembering things she'd do well to forget.

"Perhaps it's toad in the hole," Caro suggested, for their aunt looked crestfallen by the suggestion there was no roast beef and Yorkshire pudding. "We like that too, don't we, Auntie?"

"Eww!" Gideon cried, his face the picture of horror. "Not toads! Can't eat toads. Nasty, nasty, nasty—"

"No toads, darling," Maggie said hurriedly, before Gideon could make himself sick with the idea. "It's just a silly name for sausages. It's sausages in a Yorkshire pudding."

"Sausages?" he repeated suspiciously. "No toads?"

"No toads," Maggie assured him with a smile.

Gideon sighed with relief and, as the crisis was averted, Maggie turned to speak to her sister again, just as Mrs Moody came into the room, hefting an enormous platter. Upon it was a magnificent roast beef, surrounded by roasted potatoes and parsnips.

"Good heavens!" Maggie said in alarm, wondering if the woman had blown the entire month's budget on one meal. "What on earth—"

"Settle your feathers, Mrs Finchley," Mrs Moody said as she set it down on the table. "It's a present. Mr Weston had a bit of luck at cards yesterday, so Mr Barnes told me. Won a fine piece of gammon and this bit o' beef. Well, it's only him next door and he can't be eating all that by himself, so he's kept the gammon, seeing as he's partial to it, Mr Barnes says, but he said to give the beef to us. For Master Gideon ought to enjoy a good roast dinner, as he's a growing lad. What but that's nothing but the truth, I accepted, seeing as how you was all at church."

Maggie stared at the monumental piece of meat and then looked at her son, who was practically salivating as Priddy set down a vast Yorkshire pudding.

What could she do but accept the kind offer? Yet her pride recoiled against something that felt very much like charity. Luck at cards indeed, she fumed inwardly. This was his way of returning the money she had spent on paying him for the gardener. Maggie felt so annoyed by his high-handedness she felt sure a single morsel of beef would stick in her throat and was dismayed to be proven wrong. The meat was succulent and cooked to perfection, and she was not such a fool as to cut off her nose to spite her face.

So she tucked into the feast, finding pleasure in the happiness her family took in the rare treat.

Indeed, there was so much meat that Mrs Moody assured them they would have cold roast beef sandwiches for tea, and she would also make pies and grind what was left over for rissoles. They had also the pleasure of dripping on toast to look forward to, sprinkled with a little salt, which had been a regular Monday morning treat when Maggie was a child.

So they all ate far too much and retired to the parlour and sat by the fire, talking and sewing as Gideon played with his toy train on the floor. Maggie watched her son with a smile and let her aunt and sister's chatter lull her into a pleasant state of apathy as she considered all the ways she could return Mr Weston's charity to him without costing herself a fortune.

16th October 1850, Berwick Street, Soho, London.

It was midweek before an opportunity presented itself to Maggie. The sun was shining and even contained a little warmth which felt lovely upon her back as she took Gideon outside to play in the garden. He had driven everyone distracted during the past week of rain, thundering up and down the stairs, climbing on furniture and generally causing chaos as the confines of the small house chafed at him. Maggie found herself torn between impatience for his naughtiness and sorrow, as she understood how much energy he had and how badly he needed to run about and play. At the manor they'd had so much space, and so many trees to climb—and muddy clothes had been far easier to deal with when a laundry room and plenty of staff were at their disposal—but there was no sense in retreading that well-lamented path. The manor was gone. That was all there was to it.

As Gideon ran up and down, alternately kicking and throwing his ball, Maggie had to admit that the gardener had been a godsend. He'd done a marvellous job cutting the grass back and removing the encroaching brambles. Though she could ill afford the cost, she couldn't regret paying for the work, because it gave Gideon somewhere to play.

"Catch, Mama!" Gideon said, and flung the ball towards her in a haphazard manner.

Maggie laughed, reaching to catch it, but just missing.

"Nevermind. Try 'gain," Gideon said encouragingly, running to pick the ball up again.

This time he stood closer to her and threw it again, but it went awry somehow, and Maggie missed it once more.

"No, Mama. Must catch like this," Gideon said gravely, showing her the way he stood with his hands at the ready. "Westie showed me how. I'm good at catching. I show you."

He handed her the ball back, and Maggie threw it to him. He caught it deftly and gave a whoop of triumph, running around waving the ball over his head.

Maggie's throat tightened. If Gideon had a father, he would teach his son such things, how to play cricket and catch a fish, and all the things that fathers were supposed to do with their male offspring. All Gideon had was the kindness of a neighbour, and she'd spoiled everything by acting like a bold little madam, in the middle of a bazaar no less. The memory caused every part of her to stiffen with regret and humiliation. The first tense pulses of a headache throbbed at her temples.

Gideon had run off farther up the garden and Maggie hurried after him, worried in case he escaped next door, but she found him sitting on the lowest branch of an apple tree, munching on one of the many apples littering the ground. The branches overhead were laden with them too. At once, Maggie hurried back to the house to ask Mrs Moody for a basket. Gideon helped her fill it, which he thought a great game for about five minutes before he returned to playing with his ball. Still, Maggie had a fine haul of fruit, which she lugged back to the house.

"Heavens, there's plenty there. I'll make a nice apple pie," Mrs Moody said, looking pleased at the sight of the overflowing basket. "And a crumble tomorrow, and I can make apple cake."

"There's lots more too," Maggie said happily, emptying the basket into a large bowl and setting the rest on the table once it was full. "Do we have any jars?"

"Yes. I discovered loads of them in the scullery. Dozens of the things, there are," Mrs Moody said, looking at Maggie in surprise. "You're going to make something?"

"Yes!" Maggie said, feeling pleased with herself. "Apple butter. I often used to make it, and jams and preserves too, when we lived in the country. I like such jobs."

Mrs Moody nodded her approval, as Maggie picked up the basket again.

"Come along Gideon, back outside with you," she said, and smiled as her son ran out of the door ahead of her.

19th October 1850, Berwick Street, Soho, London.

Larkin set down his brushes and stretched the tense muscles in his back before stepping away to look at the painting of Tilly. He had brought the large canvas home in a carriage so he could work in his studio to finish it, now he felt satisfied with the likeness. Capturing the texture and the way light and shadow fell upon the various fabrics the child wore was a challenge, and he preferred to do this in his own studio. Mrs Harris had lent him the dress for reference, and he'd arranged it over some cushions to approximate the same pose. He considered the silk of the pretty gown and smiled, proud of the lightness and the soft gleam he'd given it. It was certainly the best thing he'd done so far and, once people saw it, even more of the great and the good would clamour for him to paint them.

He walked to the window and looked out, finding himself wishing Gideon would pop up like he had so often before that fateful outing to Regent Street. He supposed Maggie must be standing watch over the boy, determined he would not go wandering next door again. The thought made him unaccountably melancholy, which was ridiculous. Gideon might be an engaging scamp, but Larkin had no desire to play babysitter.

His next project would be Miss Caroline, he determined, returning to thoughts of his future career and putting all else aside. If Maggie wanted the girl to find herself a worthy husband, such a portrait would do her a great deal of good, and capturing the unknown beauty would certainly give him credit for having discovered her. More importantly, any romantically minded young man would take one look at the divine Caro captured upon canvas and fall instantly in love, he thought with amusement. He wondered if Maggie would refuse to allow him to paint her sister but knew at once she would not. Maggie would endure any discomfort to ensure her aunt's and her sister's happiness. Of this much, he was certain. His only difficulty would be ensuring she did not feel the need to repay him.

Deciding he needed a break, Larkin made his way down the stairs to the kitchen in search of coffee and cake and entered the kitchen to find Barnes looking at a table laden with glass jars.

"What's all that?" he asked as his valet looked up.

"Apple butter," Barnes said with a grin. "Mrs Finchley sent it over as thanks for the beef."

Larkin laughed despite himself. "Oh, the devil. I ought to have known she wouldn't let me get away with that."

"Aye, a proud one is Mrs Maggie," Mrs Goodall chimed in, looking at the jars with approval. "It'll be good, for she always had a fair hand for such things, but what we're to do with that much of it, I do not know. You'll be eating apple butter until next Michaelmas, you ask me," she said with a snort.

"You've been with the family a long time," Larkin observed, giving Barnes a look that encouraged him to make himself scarce. His valet was nothing if not quick-witted and returned a nod before leaving the room.

"Oh, since before Maggie was a twinkle," she said amiably. "Mr Merrivale was such a card, always laughing and joking, it was a happy household. Even after Maggie's mama passed, he always made sure to pay her attention. Doted on her, he did. Then he married again, to Miss Caro's mama. Well, she was a little doll. The sweetest natured lady you ever met, and so lovely, though Caro is even more beautiful, if you ask me. But when she died, the heart went out of the master. He still doted on his girls and always paid for new gowns and brought them gifts, even when he'd no money to do so, but he wasn't present, even when he was there, if you understand me?"

"I do," Larkin said, accepting the cup of coffee she poured him and a generous slice of fruit cake. "He was mourning."

"He was, and it affected his brain, I reckon. Had to be that, for marrying that awful woman was the worst thing he ever did. Well, save for topping himself. We was going on very nicely, you see, for Maggie had practically been running the household beside me since Caro's mama died. Couldn't have been more than eleven, I reckon. But she's got her head screwed on. Leastways, I thought she did until she married Captain Finchley."

"Oh?" Mr Weston said, his ears pricking up.

"Wet blanket, he was," Mrs Moody said, pursing her lips with disapproval. "I don't know what old Merrivale was thinking to allow it when they'd only known each other days. But like I said, he wasn't thinking, not about what was best for Maggie, anyhow. Though it is wicked of me to say so, she's lucky she's been given a second chance, for it would never—"

Mrs Moody gasped and clapped a hand across her mouth in horror. "Oh. Mr Weston!" she exclaimed. "Hark at me, rattling on about private things and I never… *never* gossip about my family. How did you get me to speak so?" she demanded, looking at him accusingly.

Larkin held up his hands in a peaceable gesture. "I said nothing, Mrs Goodall, I only listened, but you may rest assured I would do nothing to hurt Mrs Finchley or any of them. I, like you, worry for them, but I am in a difficult position, being a single man. If I pay them too much attention, people will talk. Yet, I would help them however I could."

Mrs Goodall gave him a long, hard look and then nodded. "Aye. You're an honourable fellow, I reckon. Mr Barnes told me about Gideon making a nuisance of himself and what you did, playing with the lad and then making introductions for Miss Caroline and getting the gardener to tidy their place up. You did them a great kindness when you'd no need to. That piece of beef, too. You never won that—and don't tell me you did, for I saw the receipt for payment."

"You've caught me out," Larkin said with a smile. "And it seems Barnes is not as discreet as I assumed. But you're right. I only want to help, but Mrs Finchley is set on thwarting me too, it seems," he remarked ruefully, gesturing to the jars of apple butter.

"Ah, well. That's not so bad. Keep her on her toes, it will. Boredom is what will drive poor Maggie out of her wits. She's a managing sort of female, born to run a large household, and sitting about doing nothing will drive her distracted."

Larkin considered this and had a sudden vision of the lady standing side-by-side with his mother at Mitcham Priory, organising one of the many large charity events she put on each year. He started in shock, pushing the image away and wondering what the hell he was thinking. Yet instinctively he knew his mother would like and approve of Mrs Finchley, and a strangely unsettling sensation gnawed at his guts. No. No, that would not do at all, he told himself, and buried the image down deep where it would not trouble him again.

28th October 1850, Berwick Street, Soho, London.

"I'll go!" Maggie called as the door knocker sounded, for Priddy was upstairs changing Gideon after an *incident* with jam tarts in the kitchen, and Wallace was filling the coal scuttles.

Priddy was such a tiny little dab of a girl, they could not expect her to lug the heavy coal scuttles about. Maggie had tried to get Wallace to allow her to do the dirty job, which was far beneath his dignity, but he'd become quite cross with her, so she'd been forced to retreat.

It had been well over three weeks since she had seen Mr Weston, and she had become accustomed to the idea that she was safe from doing so, which only made it all the more shocking to find the man himself standing on her doorstep. He removed his hat politely and bowed, smiling with his customary warmth, just as if he'd not witnessed the most embarrassing and shaming moment of her life the last time they'd met.

"Oh!" Maggie said stupidly, at a loss for anything more useful to say.

"Good morning, Mrs Finchley."

"I-I didn't expect you," she said, and then cursed herself, as it sounded like an accusation. "I mean, good morning, Mr Weston." Though far more polite, the words still sounded stiff and most unwelcoming, but he appeared undaunted and stood waiting.

Drat the man. She really, *really,* did not want to invite him in.

"Was there something you wanted?" she asked, refusing to give way.

"Yes," he replied, but said no more.

Well, now he was being difficult on purpose. "Are you willing to share the information or am I to deduce it myself?" she asked, softening the acerbic words with a polite smile. "Morse code, perhaps?" she suggested, and then wanted to bite her tongue out. Mr Weston had not done the least thing wrong. She was the one who'd behaved badly, not him. It was just that seeing him unexpectedly had put her in such a dither she was cross with him for making her feel foolish.

"We could try, but I'm not sure I'm very proficient," he said apologetically, though amusement lurked in his eyes.

Maggie sighed and shook her head. "Forgive me. That was appallingly rude. Please, do come in, Mr Weston."

She led him to the front parlour and sat down, waiting. Mr Weston entered, careful to leave the door ajar in case she assaulted his person again, she noted cynically, and sat at her invitation.

"Will you take tea?" she asked, praying he would not.

"No, thank you. I will not keep you long. It is only that my latest commission is almost completed, and I wished to discuss the possibility of painting Miss Caroline."

Maggie's heart gave a jolt. Well, here was a reminder, as if she needed one, of just why Mr Weston had taken such an interest in them. For Caro's sake, she must put her own hurt pride aside and do what was best for her sister.

"I believe you know our financial situation, Mr Weston," she said bluntly, for there seemed little point in not being certain of what he was offering.

"I have no intention of charging you," he said, his expression more serious now as he lifted a hand to forestall any comment she might make. "And before you suggest otherwise, this is a mutually beneficial exercise. The portrait of such an unknown beauty will cause a stir among the *ton* that will not only promote my work but will do much to enhance Miss Caroline. If the portrait is exhibited before she comes out, every other young miss will plague their fathers for a similar work and I guarantee all the young eligible men of the *ton* will be in love with her before she sets foot in a ballroom."

"And many of the ineligible and less than respectable men too," Maggie added with a frown, though she could not deny the truth of his words, nor would she deny Caro this opportunity, yet she feared what such celebrity might do to her sister, who was rather shy by nature.

"I assure you that having Lady Montagu as her sponsor will make even the most hardened libertine think twice. Montagu would tear them apart," he said with a smile.

"I had not considered that," Maggie said, admitting herself relieved. "Very well. When would you wish to begin? And where? For she cannot be seen to be visiting a bachelor household, even with a chaperone. I won't have anything tarnish her reputation."

"Quite so, which is why I have arranged to use the same room in Montagu House that I used to paint Miss Barrington. Lady Montagu was delighted at the prospect of seeing you all again. So you and your aunt could take turns to sit with Miss Caroline or visit with Lady Montagu. I hope this is satisfactory."

It wasn't in the least satisfactory if it meant Maggie had to spend extended periods of time in company with Mr Weston, but she could hardly say so. She reminded herself he was a professional artist and took his work seriously. He would be too caught up in capturing Caro's beauty to pay her any mind. If she took a book, she might return the compliment too, she thought with a stab of amusement. Unless he began flirting with Caro. That was such an appalling prospect she felt herself blanch, but she was being ridiculous. Mr Weston was far too much of a gentleman to flirt with her sister in front of her.

"Mrs Finchley?"

Mr Weston's enquiry pulled her from her anxious musings and Maggie scolded herself for sitting in silence for so long. Lord, but he must be getting the idea she was not only no better than she ought to be, but a halfwit too.

"I beg your pardon. I was only considering the ramifications of such a sitting, but I believe that is satisfactory," she replied, appalled by how stiff and unfriendly she sounded. Once again, she reminded herself the situation was only awkward because she had made it so and tried to look less ill at ease. "I appreciate what you are doing for my sister," she added, managing to sound a degree less frigid with disapproval.

At that moment, the door burst open, and Gideon ran into the room.

"Westie!" he exclaimed, and threw himself at Larkin with such force he toppled him back against the sofa.

Maggie stood, horrified, and about to haul her son off the poor man, but Mr Weston only laughed, his big hands grasping the little boy by the waist and holding him up in the air, staring up at him as Gideon squealed with delight. "Why, you little rogue! How big you are. I'll bet you've grown a full inch since I saw you last."

"Big, big!" Gideon chortled happily as Mr Weston straightened and set the boy on the floor, giving Maggie a sheepish smile.

"I beg your pardon. It's just it's been rather quiet without Gideon appearing out of the blue at odd moments."

Maggie wrung her hands together, feeling instantly at fault. If she had not behaved badly, Mr Weston would not be forced to stay away in fear of her throwing herself at him again. Indeed, when she came to think of it, it was a wonder he dared to call on her at all.

Perhaps something of her chagrin showed on her face for Mr Weston, looked at once concerned. "I hope you have not felt the need to keep him away. Whilst I must work for much of the day, I can always spare a little time for this young scamp, if you do not mind it?"

Maggie swallowed hard, refusing to allow herself to become maudlin for the loss of something she'd never had. She must do what was best for Gideon and the fact remained, he needed a masculine figure in his life. If Mr Weston was kind enough to give up his time for her son, she could not be so cruel as to refuse for the sake of her own wounded pride.

"You are very good, as always, Mr Weston," she replied, fighting a catch in her voice, but apparently not well enough as his gaze softened, and he took a step towards her.

"Mr Weston! Why, I did not hear you come in. Maggie, why have you not ordered tea for our guest?" Aunt Connie said as she burst into the room, beaming at Mr Weston as if he were a long-lost relative.

"Indeed, Mrs Finchley very kindly offered me refreshments, but I am not staying, Miss Merrivale. If you will excuse me?"

"Oh, so soon?" Aunt Connie lamented, but waved him goodbye as Maggie dutifully followed him to the door.

"I can see Westie again soon?" Gideon demanded plaintively, tugging at her hand.

"Yes, darling. I'm sure you will," she said soothingly.

"Why don't you come to tea tomorrow, Gideon, if your mama says you may?" Mr Weston offered, though he looked cautiously at Maggie as if expecting a refusal.

"Mama!" Gideon exclaimed, bouncing on the spot.

Despite the turmoil of her own feelings, Maggie could not help but smile. "Gideon would be delighted to attend, Mr Weston. If you are certain it is not too much of an imposition."

"Not in the least. I should be happy to see him. At four o'clock, then?"

"Yes, thank you. I shall ask Wallace to escort him. To the back door, if you don't mind it?"

"Of course not. We can't set all the curtains twitching, can we?" he replied with a boyishly crooked grin that seemed to strike a painful dart to her chest. "Well then, Master Gideon, I'll see you tomorrow, and before you ask, yes, I'll make sure there are lots of cakes."

"Cake! Cake!" Gideon chanted and ran back into the house. "Caro! Caro! I having cake with Westie!"

"Thank you," Maggie said as Mr Weston nodded at her, then turned and walked away.

Chapter 14

Larkin,

Our quarry has taken the bait.

I need not tell you this is all highly irregular and if any suggestion of duplicity or fraud was to attach to the club, it would do us no good at all. So to allay suspicion, the competition Jenkins has entered has several games to get through, with the winner sitting at the 'high table' with us. We've invited a few others on the waiting list for membership, so all appears legitimate. Not that we will be cheating, obviously, but we must ensure Jenkins wins, which is not exactly the usual way of things. It will be interesting to watch him play and see if he cheats or not and if he has any tells. Both Pip and Ash have agreed to play him and take notes, obviously Jules and I will take our turn.

The date for the last game has been set for November 12th. I hope you'll be ready for him. I might be a touch overdramatic, but I suggest you burn this missive.

—Excerpt from a letter from Mr Leo Hunt (Son of Mr Nathanial and Mrs Alice Hunt) to The Hon'ble Larkin Weston.

29th October 1850, Berwick Street, Soho, London.

Larkin looked across the table to Gideon, who was licking jam off his fingers.

"Was that good?" he asked the boy, amused.

"'Licous," Gideon replied solemnly.

"I believe you mean *delicious,*" Larkin corrected, to which Gideon nodded vigorously.

"Yes, what I said, 'licious."

Larkin laughed and nodded at Mrs Goodall to take the cake away. "I think he's finally full."

"He did a fine job, all those sandwiches and two good slices of cake, and didn't touch the sides," Mrs Goodall said with approval.

"No more?" Gideon asked, looking a little crestfallen to see the scrumptious ginger cake taken away.

"I think you'll burst if you eat more, and your mama will not be pleased if I make you sick. You can take some home for tomorrow, though. Look here, how about doing some drawing?" Larkin suggested, passing the paper and pencil over that he'd brought down ready for the boy.

"You draw too?" Gideon asked.

"Certainly, I will," Larkin agreed, watching to see if he held the pencil correctly and smiling as the lad began his first artwork. Satisfied he was in the company of a proficient artist, Larkin began a series of pictures he planned to give to Gideon to colour in.

"What are you drawing?" he asked, looking over Gideon's shoulder.

Gideon immediately grinned and hid his picture, leaning over it. "Don't look! Surprise," he insisted.

Larkin laughed and returned to his own work. A moment later, he felt eyes upon him.

"What are you drawing?" Gideon asked.

"A frog on a lily pad, holding an umbrella," Larkin said, chuckling at the delight in the boy's eyes.

"Show me!"

Obediently, Larkin turned the page, and Gideon gazed in wonder at the drawing. "Very good drawing, Westie," he said, giving him an encouraging pat on the arm. "Well done."

"Thank you," Larkin replied gravely, and the two artists returned to their work. Ten minutes later, Gideon pronounced himself finished.

"For you," he said, handing the paper to Larkin.

Larkin thanked him and held the paper up and stared at the picture with the oddest sensation kicking about in his chest.

"That's you, that's me, and that's mama," Gideon said helpfully, pointing at each of the figures holding hands and wearing big smiles. Gideon was in the middle, with Larkin and his mother on either side. He'd made Larkin a towering figure with a massive head, enormous hands with rather too many fingers, and the biggest smile of all of them.

"Like it?" Gideon asked uncertainly, watching Larkin's expression.

Larkin immediately pasted a smile to his face to cover the turmoil the child had wrought on his peace of mind. "Of course I do! It's a wonderful drawing. You'll be a great artist if you keep this up. Thank you, Gideon."

Before he could put the drawing away, Mrs Goodall looked over his shoulder and saw the image Gideon had drawn.

She smiled sadly. "Poor boy wants a da," she said softly, patting Larkin's shoulder and sighing.

Larkin gave Gideon a new piece of paper, tucking the drawing he'd been given safely away. "Perhaps you should draw something for your mama," he suggested, wondering a little anxiously what the boy would do next.

"Yes," Gideon agreed.

"What are you drawing, then?" Larkin pressed, putting aside his latest of a fox wearing a top hat and beginning upon one of a train.

"Pony," Gideon said, not looking up.

"A fine choice," Larkin agreed, and then wondered if the boy hankered for a pony of his own. What was he saying? Of course he did. What boy didn't want his own pony, and if they lived at the manor, perhaps such a thing might be possible. With no expensive rent to pay, and likely a small income from the land too, their lives might be entirely different. Though he had been determined before, Larkin was now entirely resolved to ensure they got their home back.

"Look!" Gideon held up the drawing.

The pony had a very large head and a very small body and legs like a daddy longlegs. The mane was certainly exuberant, as was the tail, and Larkin thought it entirely charming.

"He's a very handsome pony," he said, smiling at Gideon. "Does he have a name?"

"Bertie," Gideon replied promptly. "He will live in the garden, and I'll feed him apples and carrots."

"Oh, bless the poor child," Mrs Moody said with an emotional sniff, dabbing at her eyes with her apron.

Larkin frowned, not finding this entirely helpful when he was already all at sea. He wanted to go out that second and buy a pony and a puppy and anything else the dratted boy wanted and why should he feel so blasted responsible? Mrs Finchley and her son were not his concern, he reminded himself. Yet he'd made them his concern and, more to the point, no matter how much he fought the idea, he *wanted* them to be.

30th October 1850, Berwick Street, Soho, London.

"The theatre?" Maggie looked from Caro to her aunt, perceiving the glow of happiness and excitement with a leaden sensation in her stomach. "But—"

"Oh, don't!" Caro cried, springing up from her seat on the sofa where they'd just settled to take tea. "Don't start giving us dozens of reasons we must not enjoy ourselves for once. I am so dreadfully bored, and I hate this horrid house. I miss my piano and my friends in the village and going for rides in the countryside, and at last something good has happened, so don't you dare tell us we may not go!" she exclaimed, and flounced out of the parlour, slamming the door behind her.

Maggie blinked in shock, too surprised by the outburst to say a word.

Cuckoo, cuckoo, cuckoo!

"Oh, do hush, Cecil!" Aunt Connie said in exasperation. "Poor Caro. I think it is finally sinking in that we can never go back home. To begin with, I believe she viewed it as rather an adventure. Like a heroine in a novel. But now she knows this is to be our life, that we cannot go back, and it's hit her hard. Don't take her words to heart, Maggie. She doesn't mean them."

Maggie nodded but knew there was some justification for Caro's anger. She had been about to say that they were in mourning and must not go, but that was not her true motivation. She'd have grasped at any excuse to refuse and that was wicked of her. To deny her aunt and her sister such a treat because she was a fool was selfish and weak, things she had never before believed of herself. But she was realising a good many truths about her own character and none of them seemed to be very flattering.

"If Mr Weston is so kind as to invite us, then of course we shall go. We shall already cause a scandal because of Papa's actions, and there is no point in not beginning as we mean to go on, I suppose," she said calmly, setting down her teacup. "If you will excuse me, Auntie, I have rather a headache. I think I shall lie down for a while. Please reassure Caro that I will not refuse the invitation."

Wearily, Maggie climbed the stairs and lay down on her bed. She had spent much of the afternoon making adjustments to Gideon's clothes, hoping desperately they might last another month or two before he outgrew them for good. He certainly needed new socks, for the ones he had were now more darn than sock and she worried they would rub his toes. Yet more expense, and entirely inescapable.

Outside, she could hear the clatter of cartwheels and hooves and people chattering as they went about their day. She stared up at the ceiling, absently noting a small stain she did not think had been there before. All the rain and wind they'd had earlier in the month must have made a tile slip. Not that she cared. It wasn't her house, she reminded herself. She would never have her own home again, only a series of increasingly cheap rented places as her income dwindled.

"Stop it," she chided out loud. Feeling sorry for herself would help no one and fix nothing.

Caro would have a splendid season and fall madly in love and make a fine match. Her husband would be wealthy and kind enough not to allow his new relations to fall into poverty, and he would help Gideon get into an excellent school. Perhaps that husband would be Mr Weston, for surely, he was bound to fall in love with her whilst he painted her beauty. What man could resist such innocent loveliness? And Maggie would be happy for them both. There. Everything was rosy.

Despising herself for her weakness, Maggie turned on her side and stuffed her fist into her mouth, sobbing silently for all the things she had lost, and all the things she would never have, and for a man who might just be the answer to a prayer... just not hers.

2nd November 1850, Berwick Street, Soho, London.

As she might have expected, Maggie endured a household in an uproar of excitement, as Caro drove poor Sally to distraction, trying to decide what she ought to wear for her first proper evening out as an adult.

Sensing that even Sally's patience was being tried, Maggie stepped in.

"Caro, darling. You are too young to remember, but I recollect very well coming to town with your mama and watching her ready herself for the theatre."

"You do?" Caro exclaimed, immediately diverted. She sat down on the bed, regarding Maggie eagerly.

"I do," Maggie said with a smile and sat down beside her, taking her hand. "And your mama told me there was one very important rule that must always be observed. For one goes to the opera to be seen, but one goes to the theatre *to see*. For the opera, you may dress as lavishly as you like and pour your jewellery box over your head for good measure. The theatre, however, is not the place for too much ostentation, and a stylish promenade dress is far more appropriate than full evening dress."

"Truly?" Caro looked rather disappointed.

"I fear so," Maggie said with a sympathetic smile. "Consider also that you have not yet been presented. We will have enough scandal attached to our names, plus censure for not wearing mourning for a full year. I believe it might be prudent to be a little more circumspect and not make spectacles of ourselves. What do you think?" she added, disinclined to once again be thought of as the voice of doom.

Caro nodded with a sigh. "Mama was always the height of fashion, Papa said, so I must bow to her judgement. I would not wish people to think us outrageous or… or *fast,*" she added, whispering the word as if it were too awful to contemplate out loud.

"I think you are very wise," Maggie said, patting her sister's hand, relieved the sartorial crisis had been averted.

Still, despite such constraints, the Merrivale ladies contrived to look splendid indeed, and not at all as if ill fortune had dealt them a heavy hand. As they were to be in public, they had all erred on the side of caution and chosen darker colours. Aunt Connie was once again in a deep purple, which was her favourite shade, and Caro in a lighter lilac grey that flattered her pearly complexion and glossy raven hair. Maggie had chosen a dark blue taffeta robe. The corsage, made entirely of small, close folds, fit her slender form like a second skin. The sleeves were narrow to the elbow where they widened, falling open with deep lace ruffles: a pretty, extravagantly feminine touch which echoed the deep flounces on the skirt and worked well against the simple severity of the bodice. After congratulating each other on looking ravishing, they congregated in the front parlour to don their cloaks and await Mr Weston.

The gentleman arrived at the appointed hour, admired them all with appreciation, and escorted the ladies out into a crisp November night that promised frost would greet them on the morrow.

"Have you seen this play before, Mr Weston?" Caro asked, her delight in the coming evening making her lovely face glow and her eyes sparkle. Maggie wondered ruefully if any young man attending this night would see anything that happened on stage or would spend the entire evening gazing at her sister.

"I have not," Mr Weston replied with a smile. "But my friends recommended it. I know a little of the plot, however."

"Oh, do tell," Connie exclaimed, looking every bit as thrilled as Caro.

"Well, as you have no doubt guessed, The Templar is tale of one of the Knights Templar. The story is that of Sir Guy de Lusignan, who is betrayed by his own order and falsely accused of crimes he did not commit. We follow Sir Guy's story as he seeks to clear his name and restore his honour. I believe he must contend with a scheming bishop and a ruthless rival, and it is a thrilling production by the masterful Charles Kean. I am told the costumes, and the scenery are especially fine."

Caro clapped her hands together. "How marvellous. Is there much fighting?" she asked eagerly, rather to Maggie's surprise.

"I suspect there may be some sword fighting," Mr Weston replied, amused.

Auntie Connie and Caro exchanged glances of delighted anticipation at such blood thirsty delights and Maggie glanced at Mr Weston to see him grinning appreciatively.

It was a short journey to Oxford Street, and they soon arrived outside the grand Renaissance building that was the Princess's Theatre.

"This used to be the site of the former Royal Bazaar," Mr Weston explained as he led them inside. "It burned down in 1829 but was rebuilt and opened as the Queen's Bazaar and exhibited paintings and dioramas. Then it was made over again and opened as the Princess's Theatre."

Maggie nodded, interested and touched by how ready Mr Weston was to entertain them and ensure they had a wonderful evening.

"My friend, Lord Blackstone, has kindly lent us his box for the evening," he told them as he guided them through the foyer and up the stairs.

"The Marquess of Blackstone," Aunt Connie said with interest. "He is the son of the Duke of Bedwin, I believe?"

"That's right. This way, ladies."

They followed Mr Weston up a grand staircase which was apparently for the private use of those who had a box, which Maggie appreciated, for it was far quieter than the crush of people making their way up the main stair. Aunt Connie's and Caro's eyes were on stalks as they gazed around at the fashionable crowd and the magnificent surroundings and the two chattered happily as they ascended.

The Marquess of Blackstone's private box was undoubtedly one of the best being closest to the stage and gave them the perfect vantage point to view both the performance and the audience. Caro gasped in awe as she gazed upon the profusion of red velvet and gold tassels, the lavish embroidery and beautiful paintings over every surface, with gilding everywhere. She took the seat on the far right of the box, with Aunt Connie beside her.

"How sumptuous it is," Caro said, looking quite overwhelmed as she sat, stroking the lush velvet upholstery of the chair she sat upon. The box also contained champagne on ice, crystal glasses, a jug of orgeat, a large bowl of fruit, and a selection of petit fours.

"Why, Mr Weston, this is delightful. Thank you so much for arranging such a treat for us," Aunt Connie said, turning to Mr Weston, who sat beside her.

Caro was quick to follow. "I've never been so excited in my life," she confessed, her lovely face flushed with pleasure. "Thank you so very much."

Mr Weston smiled warmly at them. "It's entirely my pleasure, I assure you. I only hope you enjoy the performance."

"Oh, we will," Caro and Auntie chorused, settling themselves expectantly.

Mr Weston turned back to Maggie, who was sitting on his left. "Is everything to your satisfaction?" he asked, his voice soft.

Maggie nodded, smiling at him, for what else could she do? He was so very kind to them, and he seemed to be so very good as to not hold her shocking behaviour against her. If only they could go back to how things were, she promised herself she would be content to be his friend. "It's beyond any expectation, and you've made Caro and my aunt so very happy. I cannot thank you enough."

"What about you?" he asked, holding her gaze, his expression intent. "Have I made you happy?"

Maggie's heart leapt, a flush creeping up her throat to her cheeks. *Stop it*, she told herself, determined not to read too much into the comment. She had made a fool of herself once before. She would not do so a second time.

"What is there to be unhappy about in such a wonderful theatre, with an evening's entertainment before me?" she replied carefully. "It is all perfect."

Mr Weston regarded her for a moment longer, but seemed satisfied, and turned away as the curtain rose and the play began.

2nd November 1850, Princess's Theatre, Oxford Street, London.

They remained in the box during the interval, at Maggie's insistence. Whilst she would not for the world spoil Caro and her aunt's pleasure, Caro's reputation had to be protected, and she had not yet been presented, and ought still to be in mourning. Far better to keep a low profile until the season began. However, that did not stop people coming to visit them, curious to discover who Larkin's guests were.

Larkin was handing around drinks to his companions, who had risen to avail themselves of the petit fours when the first visitors arrived.

"Evening, Lars," drawled a refined, lazy voice and Larkin looked up, amused to see Lord Harry Bedwin, with his close friend and companion, Mr Charles Abner. Both young men, around eighteen years of age, wore the studied swagger he recognised too well from his own youth. Affecting the appearance of world-weary cynicism, they appeared far too nonchalant when their eagerness to meet Larkin's beautiful young guest was obvious.

"Harry, Charles, how do," Larkin replied, grinning at Harry, who he'd known since his birth. "You are both looking fine as fivepence," he observed, quirking an eyebrow at Harry's bright red tartan waistcoat.

"Thank you," Harry replied calmly, ignoring the hint of sarcasm that Larkin knew had not escaped him, and taking the comment at face value. Harry was nothing if not good-natured and knew how to take a bit of ribbing. "I saw Mr Anson on my way here and he admired it, too."

"I never doubted it," Larkin replied with a laugh, and then decided he had best put the two young men out of their misery and do Miss Caroline a kindness, for both were exceptionally eligible, Harry especially, being the younger son of a duke.

"Lord Harry, Mr Abner, might I make known to you, my guests? Mrs Finchley, Miss Merrivale, Miss Caroline Merrivale. Ladies, I present Lord Harry Bedwin, and Mr Charles Abner."

The ladies all curtsied very prettily but, despite the boy's impeccable manners, it was clear the young men had eyes for no one but Miss Caroline. The girl, suddenly shy in the company of two such magnificent, handsome, and obviously eligible young men, blushed and stammered out a few rather awkward replies. Her inarticulate responses seemed not to faze her admirers, however, who hung upon her every word.

Feeling eyes upon him, he looked up to see Mrs Finchley watching him intently and smiled. She started and looked hurriedly away, which made him curious to know what she had been thinking. Leaving Miss Caroline to her aunt's chaperonage, he moved to where the lady stood, looking down upon the comings and goings of the audience below.

"Do not fear. Lord Harry and Mr Abner are most respectful young men, despite their rather raffish airs. You have nothing to fear. Indeed, they are exactly the kind of young men who can do your sister's consequence nothing but good."

Mrs Finchley looked at him and nodded thoughtfully before returning her gaze to the crowd milling beneath.

"Perhaps we might arrange to meet them for a walk in Hyde Park if the weather remains fine?" he suggested. "Miss Caroline might feel a little more at ease in a less formal setting. It would be good for her to have some familiar faces when she makes her come out."

"That is an excellent notion and, as ever, most thoughtful, Mr Weston," she replied with a polite smile that did not quite reach her eyes.

Larkin studied her, feeling increasingly ill at ease himself. He had hoped this evening would be a way to smooth the tension between them, but it was plain she was still very much on her dignity. He cursed himself again for his clumsy handling of a woman who was so painfully vulnerable it made his heart hurt. He had spoiled a friendship he had valued more than he'd realised in his hurry not to give the wrong impression. Except he was coming to realise it had not been the wrong impression. Not entirely, at least.

Though the idea of it made him horribly uncomfortable, he owed her honesty if nothing else. If he showed her his own vulnerability, she might realise he had not been rejecting her out of hand, but was only afraid he could not trust his feelings. The walk in Hyde Park might be an opportunity for him too, to speak privately with her, without fear of being overheard.

In the meantime, he could only do his utmost to assure her of his continued regard. His gaze returned to her profile and his fingers itched to capture her pose. How beautiful she was. A critic might suggest her nose was a touch too long for perfection, but

Larkin thought it added refinement to her bearing, a slight aloofness to her demeanour that was highlighted at present by her coolness towards him. Her mouth, conversely, was wide and lush, made for laughing and passionate kisses, and it stirred his blood to consider he might know how she tasted if he'd not been such a lamentable prat.

Suddenly aware of his scrutiny, she looked sharply around and coloured as she found him watching her.

"I believe the curtain will rise shortly," she said, and turned away, returning to her seat.

Discovering himself dismissed, though he thought there was time yet before the performance began, Larkin took the hint and returned to her aunt and Miss Caroline. He suggested the meeting in Hyde Park the next day, to which her two admirers readily agreed, and he had barely got rid of them before Ashton Anson arrived with his wife, Lady Narcissa.

Once more, introductions were made, with Ashton and Lady Narcissa greeting the ladies warmly. Ashton immediately took to Aunt Connie, who was likewise impressed and began flirting with his friend outrageously.

"But don't we make a handsome pair," Ashton remarked, for his waistcoat was the same deep purple as Miss Merrivale's gown and lavishly embroidered in black silk.

"Quite stunning," Aunt Connie agreed with obvious sincerity. "I have rarely seen a man who could stand beside me and not fade into the background, but you, Mr Anson, are far too beautiful to ever be outshone."

"Auntie!" Miss Caroline squeaked, blushing with mortification, but Ashton only grinned appreciatively.

"Finally, a woman who values all my best qualities," he said, taking Miss Merrivale's hand and bowing low. "I am your servant, madam."

Aunt Connie chuckled and tapped his arm playfully with her fan. "Wicked fellow. I know your tricks, so don't go trying to make a conquest of me. I am far too old for your tarradiddles. My servant, indeed!"

"But I am," Ash said mournfully, pressing his hand to his heart. "Only command me and I shall obey."

"Very well, I command you to waltz with me at the very first opportunity," Connie retorted, the gleam of challenge alight in her green eyes.

Miss Caroline moaned softly and looked as though she wanted to be anywhere but here. Mrs Finchley, however, whom Larkin might have expected to step in and restrain her aunt's more outspoken behaviour, seemed curiously silent, which only made him more concerned for her state of mind. Happily, Ash was enjoying himself enormously and Narcissa, too used to her husband's sense of humour, watched with an indulgent smile.

"I accept your challenge. You may pencil me in, and then my honour will be redeemed," Ash replied gravely.

"Come along, you dreadful creature," his wife said, looking at him with fond amusement. "I had best stop you from plaguing these poor ladies and return us to our seats. I believe the next act is about to begin. You must call upon us soon," Lady Narcissa insisted as she dragged a reluctant Ash from the box.

"You may depend upon it," Aunt Connie replied gaily, waving a coquettish hand at her new friend as he was pulled away.

"Auntie!" Miss Caroline said, her tone reproving as she stared at her aunt as if she'd never seen her before.

"What?" Aunt Connie said innocently and returned her attention to the stage.

The rest of the evening proceeded enjoyably. The production was excellent and most exciting, and the Misses Merrivale filled the journey home with delighted chatter about the performance, about their new acquaintances and the pleasure of knowing they would meet the handsome young men again tomorrow. Their joy was contagious and therefore contrasted sharply with Mrs Finchley's silence. She watched her family with quiet amusement, but sorrow seemed to linger in the air around her, not that her sister or aunt remarked upon it.

Larkin wondered if he was being arrogant to assume that sorrow was his fault and promptly chastised himself. For Mrs Finchley had reasons enough to mourn, and his thoughtless behaviour was only a part of that. Perhaps the final straw, he thought bitterly, and promised himself he would do whatever it took to make her smile and see her eyes sparkle once more.

Chapter 15

Larkin,

Jenkins played his first game last night and won with no intervention necessary. He's a decent player and I would swear on this occasion, he did not use any underhanded methods. Still, the competition was not of the highest standard so we will see how he performs in the next round.

I will say he's an uncouth devil and I would not trust him as far as I could throw him. We need to proceed carefully, for I think he's sharper than he appears, and we would be foolish to underestimate him.

—Excerpt from a letter from Mr Leo Hunt (Son of Mr Nathanial and Mrs Alice Hunt) to The Hon'ble Larkin Weston.

3rd November 1850, Hyde Park, London.

Larkin watched with amusement as Lord Harry and Mr Abner vied for Miss Caroline's attention as they walked beside the Serpentine. Bathed in sunshine and set against the sparkling water, the three made an exceptionally lovely picture.

"They look like they've stepped out of a fashion plate," Larkin observed with a smile.

"I should catch them up," Mrs Finchley fretted, noticing that the three young people had got some distance ahead of them.

"I'll go, dear," her aunt said at once. "You're looking peaky this morning and ought not exert yourself. Perhaps Mr Weston would be so good as to lend you his arm," she suggested, giving Larkin a fiercely direct look that surprised him.

She stopped short of waggling her eyebrows, but only just. Amused, Larkin realised he was being given the perfect opportunity to speak to the lady alone, whilst being warned not to waste his opportunity. Or else, he suspected.

Before her niece could utter a word of protest, Miss Merrivale hurried off, her cloak and skirts billowing as she went.

Mrs Finchley glanced up at him, colour in her cheeks he thought was not entirely due to the crisp winter air, and certainly not to the sunshine which was welcome but held little warmth.

"I'm afraid she's never been terribly subtle," Mrs Finchley lamented, confirming his suspicions, her mortification plain. "Please do not feel obliged to remain beside me. I cannot think what she meant, but I am quite well and need no support."

"On the contrary, you need a good deal of support and have not had enough for some time," Larkin replied firmly, taking her hand and placing it on his sleeve.

"Really, Mr Weston," she said impatiently. "Why do you insist on dallying here? I know a man of your age and experience does not consider those young puppies any competition, but Caro is an innocent with so little experience of the world. She might conceive a foolish *tendre* for one of them and that will make your suit much harder, I assure you."

Larkin stared at her in consternation. "My dear Mrs Finchley," he said, hardly able to believe his ears. "Forgive me for my impertinence, but what the devil are you talking about?"

She stopped, glaring up at him with such impatience flashing in her eyes, he wondered if she would stamp her foot. "As you seem determined to pretend ignorance, then I shall be blunt," she said curtly. "If you wish to court my sister, you'd do well to go right this minute and stop her forming some childish infatuation for one of those young dandies."

Larkin gaped at her, too astonished to speak. Finally, he laughed and shook his head, gazing at her in wonder. "Is that what you think? That I've been dangling after Miss Caroline?"

"I would not say dangling," she retorted in confusion, her brows knitting. "For you have hardly been assiduous in your attentions, which, for a man of your stamp, seems very remiss, but I've seen the way you look at her, and I am *not* a fool."

"No, that you are not," Larkin replied, torn between laughter and real annoyance. "But if you have laboured for a moment under the impression I wish to court your sister you are a very long way from the truth."

Her mouth opened and closed and opened again and she seemed on the verge of giving him a blistering set down. Curiosity won out. "But I have watched you, seen how deeply you admire her," she said again, as if by repeating the statement she might make it true.

Larkin considered this and had to admit he might have given her cause to believe he was interested in Miss Caroline. "She is the most beautiful girl I've ever seen in my life," he admitted, knowing he had been captured by the girl from the start, but not for the reasons she assumed. "I'm an artist, Mrs Finchley, and I cannot wait to try my hand at capturing such perfection of face and form, but Miss Caroline is a child, and I am a man of four and thirty.

Whilst I am certain she is an amiable girl, I have not the slightest interest in making her my wife."

"Y-You don't?" she stammered, clearly finding this hard to believe.

"I don't," he agreed, his tone firm. "If you want my opinion, your sister is a very long way from being ready to be any man's wife, and eligible he may be, but Lord Harry will certainly not be allowed to wed until he reaches his majority. I do not know Mr Abner's parents, but they'd be damned fools not to do likewise, and before you eat me, it has nothing to do with Miss Caroline and everything to do with the fact they are all barely out of the schoolroom."

Mrs Finchley let out a breath that did not seem entirely steady. "I know," she said, her expression bleak. "And I wonder if I have made a dreadful mistake in bringing us all here. The expense has already been far more than I anticipated, and to what end? It will be her one and only season and may raise hopes in her breast that I cannot then make good on. She will not return next season like all the other girls, with a little more polish and experience, for our finances will not stand it. I had thought that if a kind man like yourself, who would be patient with her, was to marry her, then perhaps it would not be so bad, but I see now that I have been a fool, just as you so correctly observed," she added bitterly.

"Now, none of that," Larkin said, making her look up with his sharp tone. "You are no fool and we both know it, so I shall hear none of this self-deprecation."

"Oh, but I am, and you certainly do know it," she returned, blushing hotly this time. She tugged her arm from his sleeve, but Larkin grasped her hand, making her gasp in shock.

"Let go before someone sees," she said in a fierce undertone, glancing around to see if they were observed but there were few people walking in the cold today, despite the sunshine.

"Please wait," he said, praying she would not leave before he'd explained himself. "Just give me a few minutes, then, if you wish to cut me dead ever after, you may do so with my blessing."

She stiffened, her expression furious, but did not fight him, taking his arm again, albeit reluctantly, and they carried on walking. The others were far ahead of them now and there was no chance of anyone saving her from his determination to speak.

Suddenly anxious, Larkin wondered if he was doing the right thing or simply exposing himself to more heartache. The thought was terrifying, yet he was not a coward, and he would not let a chance for happiness slip through his fingers, only to regret it later.

"I suspect it is no secret, but the reason I behaved so badly in my recent past was because I had my heart broken." Larkin waited for the moment when he regretted the words and felt mortification for having admitted it to her, but as he looked down and saw nothing but empathy in her eyes, he knew he was not mistaken. "It was entirely my fault," he added with a smile. "I realise now I have a fatal flaw, the desire to be heroic in some small way. I own a property with my friends, named Gillmont. It is a home for women who have been ill-treated by men, by life, and gives them shelter. I have personal reasons for being aware of the plight of such women —not as a result of my own behaviour," he added hurriedly.

"I never thought that," she said, her voice unexpectedly warm. Her approval eased his nerves, and he carried on.

"Elmira was one of those women and, like with Miss Caroline, to begin with I was captured by her beauty, by the combination of strength and fragility. She became my muse, my heroine, and I put her on a pedestal. A place, I might add, that she had no desire to be," he said ruefully. "We became close, and I believed I knew her, but I saw only the surface, what I wished to see and believe, and she allowed it. When I discovered she had not been entirely honest with me, I was devastated. But I realise now that I had been rudely awoken from a dream of my own making and, if I had been paying attention, I would have realised I was being a fool."

She was silent for a long moment, and he walked beside her, fretting he had been too frank, and she thought less of him for confessing his idiocy.

"I believe we have a good deal in common," she replied finally, and looked up at him, pain in her eyes. "I believe I fell in love with the idea of my husband, and not the man himself. He was so very handsome, and sweet and kind, and I was young and foolish and swept away by the romance of it, falling in love with his splendid uniform and his bravery at going away and fighting a war in a foreign land. The two weeks we had together were idyllic, and I want to believe that we would have grown together, and come to love each other deeply in time, but I cannot help but worry that if he had returned, I would have been a terrible wife to him. I fear sometimes that we were so ill matched I would have made him wretched. That truth plagues me, for sometimes it makes me feel I had a lucky escape, that I am relieved he is dead, and that is a terrible thing to live with."

Larkin heard the pain in her voice and wished he could take it away but did not know if could find the words. "If he had lived, you would have been glad, and you would have done all in your power to make him happy, no matter how ill-matched you were," he said carefully, wondering if he was making things worse. "It is not your fault that fate intervened, it is simply the outcome with which you must live. I can understand your guilt, but I think you are too hard on yourself and ought to allow yourself the chance to be happy again, no matter what the truth of your feelings might have been if the outcome had been different."

She let out a soft sound and covered her mouth with her hand. To his horror, he realised she was weeping.

"Forgive me. I'm a damned clumsy oaf and I keep saying the wrong thing," he said desperately.

"No." She shook her head, gathering herself and taking a deep breath. "No. You are kind, as you always are. Thank you."

Larkin nodded but knew there was still much to say. "That's why I didn't kiss you."

Her breath caught and she stared up at him, tears still glittering in her lovely eyes, shocked that he'd spoken of that desperately awkward scene and not continued to pretend it had never happened.

"Not because I didn't want to," he ploughed on, determined that this time she did not misunderstand him. "But because I did not want to make another stupid mistake and ruin a friendship I valued very highly. I was afraid my feelings were not to be trusted, and the truth is, I still don't know exactly what it is I feel, or want, but I need you to know that I hold you in the very highest esteem and I would not trifle with you. I know what it is to have your hopes raised and then dashed, and that is why I pulled back, despite already having done a good deal to encourage you to believe I had feelings for you. I was a clumsy fool, and I have regretted it for every second since that moment. Can you forgive me?"

She gaped at him, looking so utterly bewildered by his words that he had to smile.

"Is it so very shocking?" he asked her softly.

"Yes," she managed and gave a startled little laugh. "I thought I had misunderstood, read too much into your words, but—but I had *not*?" She continued to stare at him, searching his face for confirmation.

Larkin covered the hand that was now clutching at his sleeve and smiled. "You had not."

She blushed and looked away and then glanced at him again but could not hold his gaze.

Larkin waited, hoping she would say something, but he seemed to have stunned her into silence.

"I do forgive you," she said, after an interminable wait that made him wonder if he'd said the wrong thing again. "But I must also beg that you forgive me. I have been very rude to you and that was dreadful of me in the light of all the very great kindnesses you have done for my family."

"Your contempt was very well deserved. I promise you I never reproached you for it. But the question is, Mrs Finchley, what now? Will you continue to be my friend? Do you trust me enough to consider the possibility we might be more than that in time?"

"I do," she said, without a moment's hesitation and then smiled, as it was his turn to look startled. "I do," she said again, staring at him this time. "And I want you to know I have told you the entire truth about myself. I'm not hiding any secrets that you will uncover later or pretending to be something I am not. I wouldn't know how. I'm afraid I'm simply not that interesting," she added with a laugh.

Larkin let out a breath, feeling strangely liberated, the weight of guilt and regret that had burdened him falling away. "I'll be the judge of that," he replied warmly.

They continued walking in companionable silence, occasionally exchanging glances that seemed to contain a good deal more communication that either of them was ready to express in words just yet.

3rd November 1850, Berwick Street, Soho, London.

Maggie walked home with her hand upon Larkin's arm, feeling as though she were floating on a cloud. The sunshine had fled, but to her the world around them seemed sunny and bright and full of promise. She kept stealing glances at the man beside her, hardly daring to believe she had not dreamed the entire thing. A shaft of terror pierced her heart as she wondered if she was actually at home in bed and this just the working of her desperate imagination. But no, his arm was solid beneath hers, the chilly wind stung her cheeks and tugged at her bonnet, and Caro and Connie's lively chatter continued nonstop behind them until they arrived at their front door.

"Thank you so much, Mr Weston. We had a delightful walk," Maggie said, feeling suddenly shy as his eyes met hers.

"We must do it again," he suggested.

"Oh, yes, Maggie! Do say we can," Caro broke in before she could answer. "On Wednesday?"

"Certainly. Wednesday is perfect," Mr Weston agreed, giving Caro a conspiratorial smile. "I shall see you then."

"Providing it doesn't rain," Maggie pointed out, some cautious part of her determined to keep hold of her good sense and not be utterly foolish.

"Good afternoon, Mrs Finchley, ladies," he said, raising his hat to them before carrying on next door.

Hurrying into the warmth of their own house, they cast off cloaks, gloves, and bonnets and hurried to congregate by the fire to wait for the tea Wallace promised to bring them.

"Thank you, Maggie," Caro said, moving to hug her sister. "I had such a lovely time. Lord Harry and Mr Abner are very kind gentlemen and such fun. I am so glad to have met them."

Maggie kissed her sister's cheek. "You're welcome, dear," she said, wondering if she ought to give Caro a hint about not getting her hopes up and looking too high, but it seemed cruel to spoil her cheerful mood and so Maggie held her tongue.

"You're looking much more the thing," Aunt Connie observed with a sly smile. "I knew a walk and taking Mr Weston's arm would put the colour back into your cheeks."

"It's simply the fresh air," Maggie said, not yet ready to confide in her family about her conversation with Mr Weston. She wanted to sit quietly with the words and recall every one, holding them close to her heart and examining each of them until she was entirely certain she had not made the entire thing up, for it seemed too fantastically wonderful to be true.

Mr Weston, handsome and wealthy, fashionable and eminently eligible, held her in the very highest esteem. He had *wanted* to kiss her! That knowledge made her cheeks burn with the anticipation that he might actually do so if she gave him the chance. Her heart did the oddest little dance in her chest. Maggie busied herself with the tea tray that Wallace set on the table and kept her head down so no one would notice how flustered she was.

Wallace cleared his throat, though, and she was forced to look up.

"I beg your pardon, Mrs Maggie, but I read something in the newspaper today that gave me pause. I thought you ought to see it."

Frowning, Maggie reached for the clipping, which he handed to her, and she read the words with growing disquiet.

Ten Pounds Reward Offered,

For information concerning the whereabouts of Miss Connie Merrivale. Information to be addressed care of Mr P Chambers. Ridgeley House, Belgravia, London.

"Whatever does it mean?" Maggie asked, before handing the correspondence to her aunt.

"At first I thought it was that devil, Jenkins, trying to track you down, for I saw another notice asking for information a month back," Wallace said, his expression grave.

"Good heavens!" Maggie exclaimed.

Caro gasped and came to sit beside her, clutching her hand. "Maggie?" she said fearfully.

"Don't you worry, Miss Caroline," Wallace said staunchly. "That wicked fellow won't be troubling you ladies, not while there's breath in my body."

"Thank you, dear Wallace," Maggie said warmly, touched by his sincerity. "We know we may always depend upon you."

Wallace's gaunt face turned slightly pink, but he squared his shoulders, pleased with this confidence in him.

"What did that notice say?" she asked, troubled by the idea the horrid man had not yet given up his notion of marrying Caro.

"That he was your distraught uncle, or some such nonsense. Well, we all know that's a fat lie, for your only uncle didn't care a fig," Wallace said crossly. "But this one is different. That's a fine address and a well above that crook Jenkins' touch, I assure you, and then there's the reward, which that devil could never pay and would never offer, he's that mean."

Maggie considered Wallace. He was entirely sincere in his devotion to their family, for ten pounds was an unheard of fortune and he could easily have taken advantage of the offer. She promised herself there and then, if ever she could do so, she would ensure that Wallace was rewarded for his loyalty.

Maggie looked at her aunt, who was studying the notice with consternation.

"But why me? I don't know a soul in London any longer, I've certainly no recollection of a Mr Chambers," she added thoughtfully, and then brightened. "Perhaps it's an old friend seeking me out. Ten pounds seems an extraordinary amount, though, even for me! Why go to so much trouble now? If they wanted to see me so much, why have they left it so long? Better late than never, I suppose," she said with a frown.

"Should we reply, then?" Maggie asked, with a tremor of unease.

"No. No, I think we should call at the address. If someone wishes to see me, then I would like to know why," Connie said firmly.

Cuckoo, cuckoo, cuckoo, cuckoo!

"Oh, Cecil, do be quiet. I'm sure it's nothing to fret about, my dear. Don't get yourself all agitated," Connie told the clock with a sigh. "He does worry for me," she added in an undertone to Maggie.

"Well, I'm not at all sure he doesn't have a point," Maggie replied, wondering at her own sanity for agreeing with the sentiments of a cuckoo clock.

"Well, I'm sure if we asked him, Mr Weston would accompany us to ensure we are not being tricked or taken advantage of," Connie said, her eyes twinkling with mischief as she looked at Maggie.

Maggie stared back, wondering just what it was her aunt knew. Still, having such a good excuse—a good *reason* to see Mr Weston again did not seem a terrible trial.

"I suppose he might," Maggie allowed, and avoided her aunt's gaze as she handed her a cup of tea. "I shall ask him when we go for our walk on Wednesday."

"Oh, Maggie, could you not ask today or tomorrow?" Connie said crossly.

But Maggie shook her head. She thought Mr Weston needed a day to consider everything he'd revealed and to ensure he did not wish to take any of it back. For her part, she wanted nothing more than to run around to the back door of his house, pound upon it and demand he kiss her at once. Which also seemed an excellent reason for keeping away for a little while, in case she did something entirely inappropriate again and gave him a disgust of her.

"Wednesday," she said firmly.

Any further argument was cut short as Gideon burst into the room. "Mama!" he said. "Look, look at my pictures."

Maggie took the crumpled sheets from him and her heart swelled as she saw the drawings he had coloured in, drawings that only Mr Weston could have done for him. She smiled as she looked upon the fox wearing a hat, and a boy that looked very much like Gideon riding a fat pony.

"They're wonderful, darling. How clever you are."

"I'm an artist," he said proudly. "Westie said so."

Maggie hugged her son to her and kissed his tumbled blond curls.

"You are quite wonderful," she told him, silently adding that Mr Weston was quite wonderful too.

Chapter 16

Reward of Fifteen Pounds.

For any information pertaining to the whereabouts of Miss Constance Merrivale. Information to be addressed to Mr P Chambers. Ridgeley House, Belgravia, London.

—Excerpt from a notice in the London Morning Chronicle.

6th November 1850, Hyde Park, London.

"And then this one appeared this morning," Mrs Finchley said, holding out a second cutting for Larkin to look at.

Larkin held the small clipping carefully as the chill breeze tried to snatch it from his fingers. Aunt Connie was walking ahead with Miss Caroline, who had *quite unexpectedly* bumped into Lord Harry and Mr Abner.

"Fifteen pounds this time?" he exclaimed in surprise. "Whoever it is seems to be impatient to find her."

"Wallace does not believe it is Mr Jenkins, but we do not know who Mr Chambers is. Wallace believes he is merely a steward or the like, working on their employer's behalf," she said, looking to him for confirmation of this.

"I would agree. Not at all in Jenkins' style to offer such a lavish reward from what we know of him, and *Belgravia?* I don't see how he could manage that. Those houses are worth a fortune."

"That's what Wallace said," she replied, looking relieved. "But Auntie is determined to visit and discover for herself who is behind it."

"Would you like me to come with you?" Larkin asked, aware of her anxiety.

"Oh, yes! Yes, I would very much," she said at once, and then looked appalled at her own enthusiasm. "I mean—"

"Oh, no," Larkin teased her. "Don't back down now. I am feeling very pleased with the fervour of your reply. I beg you will not burst my bubble so soon."

She laughed a little self-consciously and shook her head. "I don't know how to do this," she said with chagrin, gesturing between the two of them. "I'm not sure I ever did."

"Do what?" Larkin asked innocently.

She sent him an impatient look and huffed, which just made his smile all the broader. He leaned down close to her ear and whispered.

"You're doing wonderfully well," he said, delighted when she gave his arm a playful smack.

"You're a dreadful tease," she complained, but did not look displeased by the fact.

"When would you like to visit this mysterious person, then?" he asked. "I could take you this afternoon, if you'd like."

She frowned. "I thought you wished to begin Caro's portrait today?"

"I do, but I suspect your aunt will fret herself to death and you too, if we do not go at once."

Mrs Finchley nodded. "She's on fire to see who is so anxious to find her. I've had the devil's own job making her wait until today to show you and see if you would accompany us."

"Then today it shall be."

6th November 1850, Ridgeley House, Belgravia, London.

Later that afternoon, they stood looking up at the white stuccoed magnificence of Ridgeley House. The houses here were relatively new, having been built only ten years earlier, and boasted many modern conveniences. Though none of them could think of who they might know who could afford such an elegant mansion, the ladies steeled themselves to discover the truth as Mr Weston led them up the stairs under a marble portico. The door magically opened before they could apply the knocker, to reveal a grand butler who asked them their business.

Larkin handed the man his card, adding, "And this is Miss Connie Merrivale, who I believe Mr Chambers has been looking for? Is this his house, perchance?"

"Mr Chambers is steward here at Ridgeley House," the butler intoned, with the suggestion that he was doing them a great favour by confiding this information.

Maggie could only feel relief at Mr Weston's presence, for he seemed merely amused by the butler's self-importance whilst Maggie feared she might not have held up under his stony-faced grandeur.

"Then whose house is it?" Aunt Connie demanded, clearly no more cowed by the butler than Larkin was.

"It's mine," spoke a gruff voice with a pleasantly rough edge that spoke of a man who was not of the upper classes.

As one, they turned and regarded the man who was tall and massively broad-shouldered. He had the look of an ex-boxer, with a broken nose and hard features, steel grey hair and shrewd blue eyes. He looked from one to the other of them as he spoke. "I assume you are here to collect the reward? Well, I tell you now, I shan't pay over a penny until I find Miss Merri—" He broke off, frozen on the bottom step of the stairs as he gazed at Aunt Connie in disbelief. "Can it be?" he said in wonder. "Connie?"

"Cecil!" Aunt Connie shrieked in astonishment and promptly fainted with all the elegance of a dying swan, skirts and petticoats fluttering as she fell upon the polished marble floor.

"Connie!" The man ran with surprising speed, falling to his knees beside their aunt, before anyone could gather their wits and do likewise. With the reverence of a man touching a goddess for the first time, he lifted her into his heavy arms and, with astonishing ease, carried her into the drawing room, the seams on his beautifully tailored coat looking close to splitting as his muscles bulged.

"Cheevers, smelling salts at once, and bring the brandy," he ordered.

The force of his order had a galvanising effect on the high-handed butler, who abandoned his snooty demeanour and practically ran to do his bidding.

Too astonished to do otherwise, Maggie, Caro, and Mr Weston hurried after the man whom Aunt Connie had identified as her long-lost love.

"I didn't think he was even real!" Caro squeaked, so overcome she clutched at Maggie's hand like a child. "I thought she'd made the entire thing up!"

"I'm afraid we all did, love," Maggie said, as stunned as her sister by the turn of events. "And I'm rather afraid that's Papa's fault, for he insisted it wasn't true whenever I asked about the man."

Too overwhelmed to ask the man questions, and feeling it was for Connie to do so, Maggie hushed any further speculation on Caro's part and hurried to see to their aunt.

"Oh," Connie moaned from her recumbent position on a beautifully upholstered chaise longue. Her green eyes seemed hazy as she blinked, her gaze settling upon Maggie. "Oh, Maggie. I had the most peculiar dream," she said and then looked around her, realising she was not at home.

Maggie hurried to sit beside her as Connie sat bolt upright, the colour draining from her face.

"Easy now, darling. You've had a dreadful shock," she said, gratefully accepting the smelling salts from Cheevers, who immediately set about pouring a glass of brandy.

"We'll all have one of those, and none of your stingy measures, you old grubworm, fill 'em up," ordered his employer.

"Yes, sir," Cheevers said, looking faintly alarmed and doubling the amount he'd already poured.

Maggie held Connie tightly as she stared at the man issuing commands and filling the room with his magnetic presence.

"Cecil?" Connie said again, clearly unable to believe it was possible.

"In the flesh, my darling," he said ruefully. "And you are as beautiful as the last time I saw you. I swear you've not aged a day."

"B-But you're dead," Connie said in confusion.

The man's face darkened. "I've always wondered what your blackguard of a father told you about me. It killed me wondering if you despised me all these years for abandoning you."

"Oh, no," Connie said, her expression softening as she gazed up at the man's stern features. "I never doubted you for a moment,

Cecil, I felt certain the only thing that would keep you from me was death."

There was a taut silence as Connie considered her own words. Sitting up straighter, she glared at her beloved. "Which rather begs the question of where on earth you've been all this time?"

"There's my girl," he said, grinning appreciatively and looking a little sheepish. "Well, it's a long story, Connie, my sweet, but if you're willing to hear it, I'm about bursting to tell you."

"Perhaps we might order some tea and sit down and discuss matters," Maggie suggested, taking the glass of brandy Cheevers had distractedly placed in Caro's hand and giving it back to him.

"Tea!" Cecil clapped a hand to his head. "Please excuse my manners. I'm afraid I'm unused to such fine company. Cheevers, tea for the ladies, and cake too. Make sure there's ginger cake, mind."

Connie glanced at Maggie, putting her hand to her heart as if it were trying to escape her chest. Maggie, knowing well that ginger cake was Connie's favourite thing in the entire world, understood at once. He had remembered.

Tea was promptly supplied, alongside the most comprehensive and lavish display of cakes, biscuits, sticky buns and éclairs that any of them had ever seen. Whoever this Cecil really was, he did not do things by halves.

Once Maggie had served tea, with Cecil preferring to stick to brandy, everyone looked at him expectantly.

"Well," he said, his rough-hewn, though not unappealing, countenance gaining a ruddy hue at their attention. "I've waited and prayed for this moment for so long, I hardly know where to begin."

"At the beginning," Maggie suggested, aggrieved on her aunt's behalf that the man was not dead but had stayed away for so long. He'd better have an excellent story to tell, or she'd have a few words for the wretch that he would not soon forget.

Connie clutched at her hand but seemed incapable of tearing her gaze away from Cecil, which was hardly to be wondered at.

"That night we were supposed to elope," Cecil said, his attention focused entirely on Connie. "Your father caught me before I could get to you. His men knocked me out cold, and the next I knew I was on a ship, bound for India."

"India!" Connie exclaimed, horrified. "Oh, Papa! How could he do such a wicked thing?"

Cecil shrugged. "I weren't good enough for you, love. I knew it, and he knew it too and didn't like it any. In his position, I might have done the same thing."

"But *India*!" Connie wailed. "And he t-told me you were dead!" she said, dissolving into tears. Cecil surged to his feet, looking as if he would gather Connie into his arms, but a warning glance from Maggie held him in place and he sat awkwardly.

"Don't cry, love," he begged. "You know I can't bear to see you cry."

Gallantly, Connie pulled herself together, blowing her nose noisily on a dainty lace-edged handkerchief before facing him again with dignity. "Do carry on," she said calmly.

Cecil nodded and took a large swallow of his brandy. "Well, I was put ashore without a penny to my name and no clue of how to get one. India is like nothing you've ever seen or could imagine, love. The heat is like living before the open door of a furnace, and the rain in the monsoon season is enough to make you believe the good lord is trying to wash the land off the face of the earth. Well, I can tell you I was buggere—that is, I was without a feather to fly with and totally at a loss. Heartbroken for you and what you must be thinking of me, homesick and scared to death. For a few months I barely survived and almost succumbed to lie down and die. But that would mean the old bastard had won, and I couldn't endure that. So I determined I would find my way back to you somehow, and not only that, I'd be a powerful man with blunt enough that he could not turn me away out of hand."

Maggie looked around at their magnificent surroundings and smiled. "It seems you succeeded."

He grinned at that, and Maggie saw in that smile everything that Connie had ever said about her lost love, his charm, his kindness and amiability, his love of fun and his sense of the ridiculous. Despite her lingering suspicion, she could not help but warm to this bluff, candid fellow and believe he truly loved her aunt still.

"I had a bit of luck," he agreed modestly. "But I don't want to give you the impression I've been living the high life all this time, Connie, love. The truth is I scraped a living for years and I lost heart. I knew a beautiful woman like you would have been snapped up long since and I believed I'd lost my chance at happiness. So, until four years ago, I was still just an ordinary fellow, working all hours to make his way until I had the biggest stroke of good fortune. An old English fellow I'd been friends with for years knew his time was up. Well, I'd had the chance to do him a few good turns on occasion, and seeing as he had no family, when he passed on, he left me his business. It was a decent business too, but being a bit long in the tooth, the fellow had failed to see how it might be expanded."

"What nature of business, might I ask?" Mr Weston cut in, for which Maggie was grateful, having wanted to know the same thing.

"Ah, nothing nefarious," Cecil replied, wagging a meaty finger at Mr Weston but looking at him approvingly. "I don't hold with transporting slaves, nor opium, nor anything of that nature, so you can rest easy. I do some general trading, and dabble a bit in precious stones, but fine textiles are my line. John Company can't get enough of the stuff."

"John Company?" Caro asked Maggie in an undertone.

"The East India Company." Maggie explained, before turning her attention to Cecil. "And so you are still in trade?" she asked politely, careful how she spoke for fear of him hearing condemnation in the words.

"No," he said, his eyes twinkling with satisfaction. "John Company made me an offer for the business, and though I weren't daft enough to let them have it for the measly price they offered, I secured a very advantageous deal with them that meant I'm a disgustingly wealthy man. Then, as if all my dreams had come true at once I read about your brother dying in the scandal sheets and it referred to you as *Miss Constance* Merrivale. Well, you can't imagine the joy I felt in reading that Connie love. The ink on that contract wasn't even dry before I was on my way here, coming home to find my darling and give her everything I ever dreamed I might. For she deserves to live like a princess, and if she'll give me the chance, I mean to see that she does."

He looked to Connie, who still appeared entirely dazed.

"What do you say, Connie, my love? Can you forgive me for not coming sooner? Will you give me the chance to make it up to you?"

Connie's lips trembled, and she pressed them together tightly, but she gave a nod of her head that made the man beam with pleasure. "Did you wait for me, love? Is that why you never married?"

"Of course I didn't wait for you!" Connie retorted, his words provoking her enough to shatter the spell she was under. "I thought you were dead, you halfwit! But I could never marry another, for you took my heart with you when you went."

Unable to help himself, even with Maggie hovering protectively at her aunt's side, Cecil got to his feet and went to her, falling to his knees before Connie and taking her hands. He kissed each one, gazing at her with such awe Maggie blushed and wished herself elsewhere, but they could not leave Connie alone with the man.

"I never married either, love, for the same reason. So you can imagine my disappointment when I went to the manor and found you gone, the house all shut up. I asked your neighbour, Mr Woolgar, but he wouldn't tell me a thing, so I tracked down Rachel, who used to work in the kitchens, and she told me you'd all fled. I was horrified and ever more determined to find you. I'm so sorry about what happened, love. Losing your brother and the manor all at once must have been a blow to you."

"It was," Connie said, blinking hard. "But, Cecil… oh, I hardly know what to think. It's… It's too much to take in."

She looked at Maggie, who nodded. "I think it is. If you will excuse us, Mr—?" She broke off, having forgotten his surname if she'd ever known it.

"Thompson," he replied.

"Mr Thompson. I believe you can see my aunt is rather overcome. Perhaps you might call upon us tomorrow afternoon once she has had a little time to recover her composure?"

"Of course," Mr Thompson said, squeezing Connie's hands and getting to his feet. "I'm a clumsy brute, I know, but I'd do nothing to distress Connie. Not for the world."

This did much to reassure Maggie about his character and his intentions, and so she thanked him warmly for his understanding, allowed Mr Weston to supply directions, and the family guided a stunned Connie back out to their waiting carriage.

"You *will* come tomorrow," Connie said, something between disbelief and terror in her eyes as Cecil stood by the open carriage door.

"My love, now I know you can forgive me for everything, I would follow you to the ends of the earth. I'll be there tomorrow, and the next day, and the one after if you wish it. I'll never leave your side again, unless you command me to go."

"Oh!" Connie said, and buried her face in the handkerchief Mr Weston had thoughtfully supplied her with as her own was sodden. Then Mr Thompson closed the carriage door, and they jolted into motion. Connie looked up then, almost pressing her nose to the glass as she watched Mr Thompson waving at her, until finally he was out of sight.

6ᵗʰ November 1850, Berwick Street, Soho, London.

"Come, Auntie, a nice little nap will do you the world of good," Caro said as she accompanied Connie up the stairs, leaving Larkin with Mrs Finchley in the hallway below.

"Well," Mrs Finchley said, tugging on the ribbons of her bonnet. "I feel like I've been plunged into a delightful melodrama. I only hope everyone lives happily ever after."

"I think there's every chance," Larkin said. "I confess I rather like Mr Thompson. He seems a genuine fellow, but if it will put your mind at rest, I shall ask around and see what I can discover about him."

"Oh, Mr Weston, could you?" she said, looking so desperately relieved he was glad he'd suggested it. "Like you, I found him rather endearing, but this is Aunt Connie we are talking about, and I cannot bear for her to be hurt or disappointed."

"I will discover what I can," Larkin promised, adding. "On one condition."

She gave him a speculative look. "What condition?"

"Might you dispense with the Mr Weston in private, and call me Larkin?"

A slow smile curved over her lush mouth, sending a sudden shaft of desire lancing through him. Lord, but the need to pull her into his arms was becoming hard to resist, but he did not wish to move too fast and spook her. Yet, since their conversation, all the uncertainties he had felt seemed to be evaporating. Maggie wasn't Elmira, she wasn't keeping secrets from him, and he wasn't being a fool, wasn't viewing her as some perfect version of herself and refusing to see and love the reality of her. She was real and imperfect, stubborn and proud and kind and lovely, and she wanted him as he wanted her. He took a step closer, gazing down at her.

"Larkin," she said, as if trying his name for size.

The soft, slightly breathless way she said it sent heat coursing over his skin.

"Magdelina," he said in return, but she shook her head, smiling to show it was not from disapproval.

"Maggie," she corrected.

"Maggie," he repeated, his heart picking up speed as she took a step closer to him.

They stood toe–to-toe, staring into each other's eyes. The small distance between them seemed to fizz and prickle, tickling his skin and warming it until it burned with the need for her to touch him, yet neither of them moved. Longing filled his chest, a pleasant ache that demanded soothing as his gaze fell to her mouth. He swallowed, his entire body on fire with the knowledge that she was right there, so close he could feel the warm flutter of her breath against his mouth. The moment was entirely perfect, heavy with desire, the anticipation of all that was to come so tantalising that he did not break it. He wasn't a naive boy who rushed in, claiming what he wanted, believing he must seize passion to keep it. Larkin knew well that passion heightened if given time to grow; a period of longing and teasing only made temptation grow, and made the inevitable conclusion burn so much brighter.

So he merely extended one finger, and slid it caressingly down her ungloved hand, once only.

Maggie closed her eyes and shivered, and Larkin smiled, pleased and a little smug at her immediate response.

He leaned in, his lips close but not touching her ear. "I should go," he murmured.

"Y-Yes," she replied, her eyes still closed as her chest rose and fell with increasing speed. "You-You sh-should."

"Maggie?"

"Yes?"

"I will not kiss you here in the hallway, but you ought to know that I want to, very, very badly, and I'm going to be thinking of nothing else for the rest of the day."

Her breath hitched, her colour rising as her eyes fluttered and she gazed up at him, her mouth opening a little. "Oh, you wicked man," she said ruefully.

Larkin chuckled and straightened. "Bye, love. If you need me, you know where I am."

Giving her a wink, he picked up his hat and let himself out.

Maggie stood, staring at the door he'd just closed. Her entire body was taut with longing, vibrating like a plucked violin string for a kiss that had never come. *He* was going to be thinking of nothing else for the rest of the day, she thought crossly. What on earth did the wretched man think she would be doing?

She smiled, still feeling the brush of his finger against her skin and knowing he was playing a game that she had missed out on with her first husband. Their courtship had been short and sweet, two young people who knew nothing, infatuated and getting swept up in the romance of their ideas about each other, about the moment they were living in. This was different, this was considered and deliberate and far, far more powerful.

"Well, Auntie is having a nap. She's quite exhausted the poor darling," Caro announced as she came back down the stairs.

Maggie jumped and turned around, making Caro stop in her tracks.

"Why are you standing there staring at the door?" she asked curiously.

"I'm not," Maggie retorted.

"You were."

"Well, I'm not now, I'm staring at you. Now stop talking nonsense and let's have some tea. I'm afraid I was too on edge to take advantage of all those lovely cakes Mr Thompson provided, and now I'm famished," she said briskly, hurrying into the parlour to ring for Wallace.

Caro followed her and then stopped, the colour draining from her face as she entered the room. Noticing her sudden pallor, Maggie frowned.

"Caro? Whatever is the matter?"

Caro swallowed nervously and glanced at the wall. "Well, I was just wondering, Maggie, if Cecil is still alive… Exactly who is haunting the cuckoo clock?"

Chapter 17

Dear Larkin,

My father had his staff do some digging, and it appears Mr Thompson's story is exactly as he informed you. He did a very lucrative deal with the East India Company and is a wealthy man indeed. Yes, it was precious stones and Indian textiles. From all we can gather, he is a decent fellow who always dealt fairly with everyone. No dirt, no scandal. I hope this is what you wanted.

—Excerpt from a letter from Mr Felix Knight (son of Mr Gabriel and Lady Helena Knight) to The Hon'ble Larkin Weston.

11thNovember 1850, Hyde Park, London.

Mr Thompson was as good as his word and not only called the next day, but every day that followed. Whilst Maggie and Caro chaperoned their aunt over the first few days of this long-awaited courtship, the billing, cooing, and reminiscing soon became more than they could bear. So, they left Wallace outside in the hallway, informing Mr Thompson that the door must be left open, and they expected him to behave as a gentleman.

To be fair, this did not appear to be an issue, for the man was so obviously enamoured of their aunt that he seemed entirely in awe of her. Maggie rather hoped this would wear off in time or Auntie might become entirely unmanageable.

Maggie's own courtship blossomed more slowly however, as with all the excitement over Mr Thompson she had not seen Larkin alone since the day he hadn't kissed her, drat him. However, this morning she was accompanying Caro to Montagu House, where her sister would sit as Larkin painted her. Of course, Aunt Connie was supposed to take turns with her, chaperoning Caro, but Connie was now far too busy getting reacquainted with her beau. Mrs Harris, Miss Barrington's governess, had offered her services as chaperone, though, so Maggie might also spend a little time with the Lady Montagu whilst she was there.

They travelled to Montagu house together with Larkin, after a rather trying morning for Maggie. Between Caro deciding what she ought to wear to be immortalised for posterity and Aunt Connie dithering over the perfect outfit to see her darling Cecil, both Maggie and Sally were at their wits' end by the time everyone was dressed.

Still, it was worth it, for Larkin proclaimed the bonnet Caro was wearing entirely charming and told her he was glad she had worn green, for it brought out the colour of her eyes.

Maggie and Caro went to pay a brief call upon Lady Montagu whilst Larkin prepared his materials for the sitting. They found her reclining with her feet up, a book in hand, and surrounded by flowers.

"Goodness!" Maggie exclaimed as they entered the room, realising on closer inspection that she was surrounded by orchids. Never having ever seen one such bloom before, to see such a profusion of them was stunning.

"Oh, Mrs Finchley, Miss Caroline, how glad I am to see you," Lady Montagu said, smiling warmly as she saw the two women.

"But how beautiful they are," Caro said, moving to look closer at the delicate flowers. "Wherever did they come from?"

"Montagu," she said simply. "They're my punishment."

Maggie and Caro exchanged a look of bewilderment. "They're a punishment?" Maggie repeated, wondering if they'd misheard.

"I wish someone would punish me with flowers," Caro said with a sigh.

Lady Montagu laughed and shook her head. "Indeed, you do not. These little beauties are appallingly temperamental and die at the slightest provocation. Put them in a draught, they die. Too much water, they die. Too little, they die. Too much sun, they die. You get the idea, I trust?" she lamented, putting a hand to her head. "And they're so very lovely, every time one of them dies I feel utterly monstrous."

Maggie and Caro laughed, rather delighted by the Machiavellian punishment.

"Whatever did you do to deserve such torment?" Maggie asked, for as Lady Montagu had brought it up, she did not think it too indelicate to ask.

The marchioness, feet on a low stool, raised her skirt an inch, revealing a heavily bandaged ankle. "I climbed to the top of the library steps when no one was around—something Montagu forbade years ago, fearing I'd break my neck. They are rather high, I will admit. Well, I defied him, naturally, and overreached myself, trying to lean over for a book instead of repositioning the ladder. I slipped several rungs, though I did not fall, mind. But I did twist my ankle. So, this is Montagu's riposte," she said with a sigh. "He was so furious."

"So now you must try not to kill them all?" Maggie asked, grinning.

"Yes. He's far too clever for his own good, though he's done this before, when we were courting. Everyone else sent me beautiful hot house cut flowers that were *supposed* to die in a few days, and he sent me one of these wretched things. I drove myself mad, reading every book I could find about the care of orchids, determined I would not have to confess to having killed it."

"And did you learn to look after it and keep it alive?" Caro asked, her pretty eyes dancing with mirth.

"Of course not!" she exclaimed in annoyance. "The dratted thing died. Not that I admitted it to him until after we were married," she said smugly.

"Oh dear," Maggie said, pressing her fingers to her lips to stop herself from laughing.

Lady Montagu snorted at her expression and shook her head. "Don't you worry, I shall get my own back. Just see if I don't," she said darkly.

At that moment, the butler appeared and announced that Mr Weston was ready for them.

Maggie and Caro got to their feet, promising to see Lady Montagu again later, and followed the butler to where Larkin was waiting.

Maggie met Larkin's eyes as they entered the room, finding such warmth there that her heart did a happy little dance behind her ribs. For the next hour, he was all business, however, as he settled to his work. The time passed pleasantly for Maggie, who enjoyed watching Larkin work far more than the book she was pretending to read. Caro, however, was getting fidgety by the time he called a halt.

"Thank you, ladies. If you'd like to stretch your legs and take tea with Lady Montagu, I shall see you again in an hour for today's last sitting."

Maggie looked up and nodded as Caro got to her feet and smothered a yawn. "Sitting still is so very tiring," she complained as she walked from the room.

"Go ahead, darling, I'll be right there," Maggie told her, taking far longer than she needed to put her bookmark in place and set the book aside.

She wanted desperately to exchange a few private words with Larkin but at that moment the butler entered with a message for him, and she did not feel she could stay. Hurrying from the room to catch up with Caro, she almost collided with a woman walking in the opposite direction.

Mrs Regina Harris stumbled back, having been too lost in her own thoughts to have noticed anyone else was around.

"Oh, I'm so sorry!" the woman she had bumped into said, though Regina did not believe it had been her fault at all.

"No, it was entirely my—" Regina began and then stopped as she noticed the way the woman was staring at her, mouth open, eyes wide with shock. Regina froze and then returned the favour.

"Maggie!" she whispered, appalled as she knew she had been recognised.

"Mmmff!" Maggie said in lieu of the name she'd been about to utter, as Regina clamped her hand over her mouth.

"Hush!" she said desperately, grasping hold of Maggie's hand and dragging her into a lovely room that seemed to be a small, private parlour. She closed the door and leaned back against it as Maggie stared at her in shock.

"What on earth—"

"*Mrs Harris*. My name is Mrs Regina Harris, and you do not know me," she said firmly, glaring at Maggie. "You've never seen me before in your life. Do you understand?"

Maggie opened and closed her mouth, considering, and then gave a decisive nod. "Very well, *Mrs Harris*," she said, before moving closer to her and giving her an impulsive hug.

Regina sighed and hugged her back. Though she had not known Maggie as well as she would have liked, for they had not moved in the same circles, she had warmed to her at once on the occasions they'd met.

"Everyone thinks you're dead!" Maggie exclaimed as she stood back, adding in a strangled voice, "Good lord, another one. Is it an epidemic, I wonder?"

Regina did not know what she meant by that but answered the part of the question she understood. "No, they don't," she said with a smile. "My family—at least those I care to know— are well aware I am very much alive."

"And do they know where you are? What are you even doing here… wait. Mrs Harris? You're the governess!" Maggie all but squealed.

"Keep your voice down!" Regina hissed. "Yes, I am the governess, and I'm most content in my position, and I swear if you give me away, I shall never forgive you, Maggie, you must understand that."

Maggie sobered at once, presumably recalling just why Regina had disappeared. "Of course. Forgive me, only… only it was rather a shock to see you, out of the blue."

Regina nodded. "I understand, and I cannot tell you how happy I am to see you, but I beg you, don't do or say anything to give me away. Please, Maggie. If the Barringtons realise I've been lying all this time, it would be terrible."

Maggie let out a breath and nodded. "You may rely upon me, but won't you come and visit me so we may speak in private? Please, my dear?"

Regina considered this, remembering what she had heard about Maggie's family, and the death of her father. "Very well. Give me your address."

Maggie fumbled in her reticule for a pencil and a notebook and jotted down the address.

"I was so very sorry to hear of what befell Mr Merrivale," Regina said, as he had been a kindly and jovial man who had always made her laugh. "And for what it must have meant for you too, Maggie. My condolences."

Maggie looked up and handed her the scrap of paper. "Thank you. We shall talk more soon, though. Promise me, *Mrs Harris.*"

Regina returned a rueful smile and nodded. "I will come when I am able to, I promise," she replied. Heading to the door, she cracked it open and looked out. "Come on," she said, watching as Maggie walked back out into the elegant hallway.

Maggie turned, raising a hand as she carried on toward Lady Montagu's parlour.

"Goodbye, Maggie," Regina said softly, and turned away.

"Are you all right?" Larkin asked Maggie as the carriage conveyed them home. Caro was dozing, her head resting against the side of the carriage after the exertion of sitting still for several hours.

Maggie jolted and looked up, smiling as she saw the concern in Larkin's eyes.

"I am," she said. "I beg your pardon, I was only wool gathering. How is the painting progressing?"

"Well, it's not a painting yet," he said with a laugh. "I'm just sketching the composition in, making sure everything is balanced, and trying to capture Miss Caroline's likeness. With luck, I might start painting tomorrow and I shan't need her to sit every day."

Maggie nodded, rather disappointed that she would not be in Larkin's company more often.

Larkin glanced over at Caro and grinned as she gave a soft snore. He looked up at Maggie and patted the seat beside him. She shook her head, looking nervously at Caro, who did indeed appear to be fast asleep.

"Coward," Larkin taunted.

Maggie glared at him. Though she hardly knew how she dared, she got to her feet just as the carriage lurched to one side on the uneven road. Maggie gasped, overbalanced, and fell heavily into Larkin's lap.

"Ooof!" he muttered, giving a strangled groan as she wriggled, trying desperately to get up. "Oh, no you don't," he said, sounding a trifle breathless, but holding onto her waist. "I've got you now and I don't intend to let you go."

"Larkin!" Maggie exclaimed in an undertone. "We can't, not with—"

Larkin pressed a finger to her lips, silencing her.

"Now, then. I finally have your undivided attention."

Maggie snorted. "You had that several days ago and did not bother to take advantage of it. So it's hardly my fault."

"Ah, still cross with me for not kissing you, I take it?"

"No," Maggie retorted with dignity. A big fat lie, but she wasn't about to admit to that. "It's no trouble to me whether or not you wish to kiss me."

"It isn't?" Larkin asked innocently. "Oh, well. In that case, I won't bother. I don't go about kissing women who do not sincerely desire me to do so."

"Oh!" Maggie said, indignant. "You are the outside of enough. Now you just listen here," she said crossly, before thinking better of her words and grasping hold of his lapels.

Leaning in, she pressed her mouth hard to his and then pulled back with a gasp, as she realised how horribly bold she was being.

But as she covered her mouth with her hand, she saw the slow grin dawning on Larkin's face, and the delight glittering in his dark eyes.

"Why Mrs Finchley, I do believe you want me to kiss you after all."

"Oh, finally you catch on. I was beginning to think I must take out a notice in the paper to make you—"

Maggie gasped as his mouth covered hers, his arms pulling her close. She melted, only too ready to submit as the feeling of being held close, securely against a man she trusted. He swept away so much of the misery and anxiety of the past months, kissing her deeply, tenderly, one hand cradling her face as though he held something precious.

When he finally pulled back, she was trembling.

"Much as it pains me to say this, you'd better return to your seat. This is Berwick Street," he said with obvious regret.

Maggie smothered a squeak of alarm and flung herself back down on the opposite seat just as the carriage drew to a halt.

Caro stretched and yawned sleepily. "Are we there yet?"

"Yes, dear," Maggie said, smoothing her skirts with agitation and glaring at Larkin for not having warned her sooner.

He winked and she bit back a smile. How she wished the journey had been longer, that Caro had not been with them, that she could have stayed in his arms for the rest of the day. She looked away from him but some of what she felt must have been visible in her expression, for when he handed her down from the carriage, Larkin's eyes were dark and full of unspoken need as he held her gaze, making her blush scarlet.

"Thank you, Mr Weston," Caro said, heading for the front door.

"Yes, thank you, Lar— I mean, Mr Weston," Maggie said, still too flustered to think straight.

"It was my pleasure," he told her with a roguish smile. "And don't forget, I'm just next door if you need anything."

With a devilish wink, he escorted her to her front door and Maggie almost fell up the front step she was so discombobulated by his provocative comment.

Chapter 18

Jenkins is still winning. All three rounds done. I hope you're up to his weight, Lars, for he's a tricky bastard and extremely unpleasant. I want this done so we can get him out of our club. See you Tuesday for the final game.

—Excerpt from a letter from Mr Leo Hunt (Son of Mr Nathanial and Mrs Alice Hunt) to The Hon'ble Larkin Weston.

11th November 1850, Hyde Park, London.

"Af'ernoon, Westie!"

Larkin didn't even blink as he entered his kitchen in search of food to discover Gideon sitting at the table there. Barnes was with him, helping the lad line up a row of tin soldiers. Larkin smiled, pleased at his forethought as he remembered the parcel that had arrived that morning.

"Master Gideon," Larkin replied, giving his valet an amused glance.

"The lad arrived about an hour ago. I went round and squared it with Mrs Moody. Reckon she was glad to have a bit of peace," Barnes said with a grin. "So we played catch in the garden for a bit, didn't we, eh?" said he added, ruffling the boy's hair.

234

"Yes, an' then Sally came, and we played hide and seek. Sally and Barnes are very good at hiding," Gideon added thoughtfully.

Larkin's eyebrows shot up, and he levelled an enquiring look at his now red-faced valet.

"Er, well, we was just larking about, like," he said weakly.

"Hmmm." Larkin said, grinning, for he knew full well Barnes would never dally with the maid if he were not serious.

"Ah, there you are, sir. Thought I heard the door," Mrs Goodall said, bustling into the kitchen. "I just popped next door for a cup of tea with Mrs Moody, seeing as how Master Gideon was being looked after by Mr Barnes. I made some scones earlier. I'll fetch them out with some of that jam you like and make some tea, how's that?"

"Excellent," Larkin replied and then glanced at Gideon, whose eyes had lit up at the mention of scones.

"Bring two plates," he called.

"Well, I'm not daft, now, am I?" Mrs Goodall retorted, and went off to see to it.

Once they'd divested themselves of coats and bonnets, Caro pushed open the door to the parlour ahead of Maggie and stopped in her tracks as she discovered Aunt Connie cuddled up on the sofa with Mr Thompson.

"Auntie!" she cried in shock.

Aunt Connie grinned unrepentantly at Maggie and Caro as they came in, then held out her hand, upon which a magnificent ring glittered. The biggest amethyst Maggie had ever seen in her life was set in gold and surrounded by diamonds, but it still didn't sparkle as brightly as Connie.

"We're getting married!" she exclaimed, surging to her feet to envelop both Caro and Maggie in hugs. "Cecil says he doesn't want to waste another minute, so he's already bought the licence. We shall be married at the weekend!"

"Oh! We're so happy for you, Auntie!" Caro exclaimed, as Maggie kissed Mr Thompson's cheek in congratulation, which made him blush and shuffle his feet.

"What wonderful news!" Maggie said, meaning it, for she believed that Cecil Thompson was everything he purported to be, and that Aunt Connie would be truly happy with him. She certainly deserved to be after so many years of devotion. "I am so glad to have an Uncle Cecil. Welcome to the family."

"Thank you, Maggie," Cecil said gravely. "I know I'm not really good enough, but Connie never seemed to mind it, so I hope you won't neither."

"Dear Cecil, I cannot think of anyone I would rather entrust with my aunt's happiness," Maggie said, as she'd seen the reverence and respect with which Cecil treated his beloved and knew he really would do anything to make her happy.

"Thank you. I'd give her the moon if she wanted it, I'll admit, but we want you to be happy too, and Caro. I want you to know that Connie and I have discussed it, and we want you both to come and live with us in Belgravia."

Maggie's mouth fell open. At once it was everything she had dreamed of, though it had been Caro she had imagined marrying a wealthy man. This was even better, for she did not believe Cecil would begrudge them anything, which meant Caro had time to mature and experience the season, knowing there were more to come. Yet now Maggie found she did not wish to leave the house she had professed to hate. The idea of moving away from Larkin was a wrench she did not need right now. She scrambled for an excuse why they could not possibly do such a thing and realised at once she had the perfect reason.

"Why, that is most wonderfully kind of you, Cecil, and so very thoughtful, and Caro and I will be delighted to do so, only not just yet. Newlyweds need their privacy and, no matter how large the house, you need time to get used to married life. Let us leave things as they are for a few weeks, and then we can discuss it again."

Cecil looked a little crestfallen at having his beneficence refused but Connie patted his arm. "Maggie is right, love. They'll be fine here for a few more weeks. More than fine, by my reckoning," she added in an undertone.

Maggie shot her a sharp glance, wondering what she knew, but Connie only returned an enigmatic smile and returned to her Cecil, standing on tiptoes to kiss his cheek.

Cuckoo, cuckoo, cuckoo, cuckoo!

"Now, now Gerard, don't be jealous!" she scolded, wagging a finger at the cuckoo clock.

"Gerard?" Maggie and Caro said in confusion.

Connie sighed and nodded sadly. "Yes. In my despair over Cecil disappearing, I made a foolish mistake. For Gerard loved me madly the first year I came out, but he died, the poor dear, of tuberculosis. Such a frail, wan little fellow he was, but utterly devoted."

Cuckoo, cuckoo, cuckoo!

"Yes, yes, Gerard. I know. It was a most upsetting mistake, I see that now. You're still very welcome here, I assure you," she said, turning to look at her husband to be, who was glowering at the cuckoo clock with an expression of displeasure. "Now, Cecil, do be reasonable."

"I mean it, Connie, I'll give you anything you want in the world, but I won't have that blasted clock."

"Yes, dear. We'll talk about it later," she said soothingly, giving poor Cecil a comforting pat on the arm. "Do come and sit down again and I'll pour you a nice cup of tea."

Maggie and Caro exchanged glances, trying hard not to laugh as they made their escape and left the two lovebirds to their negotiations.

Maggie took herself off downstairs in search of Gideon, intending to give Mrs Moody the good news and ask her to send a fresh pot of tea up to the parlour. Frankly, she thought Cecil needed something stronger, but she was certain Connie could handle him and would know better than she what to do.

"Well, isn't that the loveliest news!" Mrs Moody exclaimed, putting the kettle back on the range. "A wedding, and so soon. Oh, shall I make a cake?"

Maggie hesitated and, to her credit, Mrs Moody understood at once. "Ah, Mrs Goodall should have the privilege, of course."

"Well, perhaps you could work together?" Maggie suggested, for the two ladies seemed to get along rather well.

"I'd be willing," Mrs Moody said at once. "But I'll not step on anyone's toes."

"I'll speak to her," Maggie promised, and then looked around. "Is Gideon with Priddy?"

Mrs Moody laughed and shook her head. "No, pet. He's next door. Barnes has been looking after him and I don't doubt Mrs Goodall is feeding him too."

"Oh," Maggie said, sidling towards the back door. She had not expected to have an excuse to see Larkin again so soon, but she wasn't about to let it slip by. "In that case, I'd best go and see what he's up to, and I can speak to Mrs Goodall at the same time."

"Right you are, missus," Mrs Moody replied, busy with preparing tea for upstairs.

Maggie hurried out of the door. It was dark now but there was enough moonlight to guide her as she made her way up the garden and across the lawn, hiking up her skirts to keep them off the wet grass. Feeling very naughty, she rapped on the back door, which opened a moment later.

"Mrs Finchley." Barnes smiled at her, not looking the least bit surprised. "Come in out of the cold. Young Master Gideon is taking tea with Mr Weston, if you'd care to join them?"

"I would, thank you, Barnes," she said. "Might I have a quick word with Mrs Goodall first, though?"

"Of course," Barnes said, moving away and busying himself elsewhere in the kitchen to give them some privacy.

"Oh, what lovely news!" Mrs Goodall exclaimed, once Maggie had delivered her message. "I'm so happy for her, and how romantic it is, after all these years. As for the cake, I'd be happy to work with Mrs Moody. Truth be told, from what I've seen, she's far cleverer at fancy icing than I am, though I'd swear my fruitcakes are better, so I'm sure we can come to an arrangement."

"Thank you, dear Mrs Goodall! I knew I could rely upon you," Maggie said, before following Barnes up the stairs to the parlour.

Here she found Larkin and Gideon sprawled on the rug before the fire, arranging a veritable army of tin soldiers. As Gideon only had a half dozen, she thought these must belong to Larkin. Spying the battered tin open beside him, she smiled as she realised he had hunted them out so Gideon could play with them.

Barnes smiled at her and melted away, leaving her to watch Larkin as the two of them enacted a ferocious battle. A sensation rose in Maggie's chest as she saw the trust Gideon had in him, and the easy way they interacted and her heart swelled, feeling as though it might burst as she gazed at two of the people she loved most in the world. *Loved.* Her breath caught as the word lingered in her mind, settling beneath her skin and warming her. Of course. She loved him.

"Mama!"

Gideon jumped to his feet and ran to hug her, crushing her skirts, not that she cared. She bent down to kiss him, but he pushed her off and grabbed her hand instead.

"Look, look. Westie gave me all his soldiers! All of 'em!" he said, looking so overwhelmed by such bounty, Maggie had to laugh.

"Why, what a magnificent gift, darling. I hope you said thank you?"

"I did!" Gideon said solemnly. "Didn't I, Westie?"

"You did indeed, and very well done it was too," Larkin said, getting to his feet before turning to Maggie with a sheepish grin. "I had them sent up from Mitcham for him. It seemed a shame they were all gathering dust when they might be sent back into action."

"That was so very thoughtful of you, and I am sorry to interrupt your battle plans, but I was told there was tea," Maggie said.

Larkin laughed and guided her to the chair nearest the fire. "Indeed, there is, and scones too. I'm afraid we got distracted," he said, gesturing to the half-eaten scones on the table. It was a measure of Gideon's excitement that he had left a scone piled high with jam and cream in favour of playing soldiers with Larkin.

"Well, shall I—? I shall pour myself a cup. Would you like another?" Maggie said hurriedly, changing her words just in time before she asked, '*shall I be mother?*' Though she knew very well what she wanted, and Larkin had promised not to trifle with her, he had also been very clear that he was unsure of his feelings, and of what it was *he* wanted. Despite the now clear overtures he had made, she still did not feel confident enough to presume.

Larkin agreed to another cup and asked her to make herself at home, so she refreshed his drink before pouring her own. Taking the seat opposite her, he accepted the cup as Gideon continued playing on the rug between them, making occasional explosive noises as his soldiers battled on. Larkin met Maggie's eye over her son's head and smiled.

"This is nice," he observed, holding her gaze as he took a sip of his tea.

Maggie's heart skipped, wondering if he intended the words to mean what she wished them to. "Is it?" she asked, knowing she was falling now, and terrified lest she was allowing her feelings to run away with her. Gideon was not his son and, just because Larkin was kind to him, did not mean he wished to be his father.

Larkin held her gaze, his expression growing serious. "I think so. It seems rather perfect to me."

Maggie's breath hitched, and she gave a startled laugh, for the words meant so much and surely, they were unmistakable. "To me too," she replied, though her reply was little more than a whisper.

Larkin smiled at her and set down his cup, getting back to the floor to play with Gideon. Impulsively, for she knew it was well past her son's bedtime, Maggie joined them, which delighted Gideon, and they passed a wonderful hour, eating scones and drinking tea whilst Maggie learned the correct way to play with tin soldiers, though they teased her mercilessly for being unable to make a sound like a gun firing. Exasperated, she simply said '*bang*,' which made the two males fall about laughing.

Finally worn out, Gideon put his head down on his arms, gazing happily at his neatly ranked army as his eyes grew heavy and he fell asleep.

"I should take him home," Maggie said, regretful that their delightful evening was over.

"Yes, but not yet. Come here," Larkin said.

He had returned to the chair by the fire, and now patted his knee, a wicked glint sparkling in his eyes that made her breath catch.

Though she knew she ought not, Maggie did not need asking twice and got to her feet. She stood before Larkin, looking down and hesitating, her courage failing her at the last moment. Larkin laughed and reached up, grasping her waist and pulling her onto his lap. She sat with a flurry of skirts and a smothered gasp, not wanting to disturb Gideon.

"Larkin!" she exclaimed, torn between laughter and scolding him. "You can't keep doing that."

"I certainly can, and I shall," he told her plainly. "Besides, the last time you fell. It wasn't my fault. I merely profited."

Maggie sighed and linked her arms around his neck.

"Magdelina," he said, his voice soft, his handsome face cast in bronze by the flickering firelight. "How beautiful you are."

"Not compared with Caro," she said with a laugh. "My nose is too long, my mouth too wide, and I get freckles the moment the sun comes out."

Larkin shook his head. "You're wrong, you know. True beauty isn't perfect, if you ask me. Your nose gives you character and speaks of a woman with courage and determination. I cannot wait to see your freckles, which sound enchanting, and as for your mouth—" He lifted his hand, tracing the outline of her lips with a fingertip that made her shiver. "Your mouth makes me think wicked things, Maggie."

Maggie swallowed, aware of the tension prickling between them, of the heat that flared inside her at the way his voice had dropped, becoming husky and seductive.

"What kind of things?" she asked breathlessly, knowing she ought not, but then she ought not be here, alone with him, with only her sleeping son as a chaperone.

Larkin nuzzled the skin beneath her ear and inhaled deeply before pressing his mouth to her throat. "I want to kiss your mouth for hours and hours, and I want to feel the touch of your lips upon my skin," he murmured, trailing a damp path of kisses up and along her jawline. He lingered at the corner of her mouth, not quite touching her lips, until Maggie could not stand to wait another moment and turned her head. He kissed her then, his arms tightening around her as his tongue swept in, devouring her with an intensity that made her bones and her mind turn to warm honey, melting in the heat growing between them.

A loud snore filled the room, breaking them apart as Gideon mumbled in his sleep and turned over.

Maggie held a hand to her heart, appalled to think he might have awoken and caught them together. Whilst she did not think Gideon would mind having a new papa, and indeed, would be delighted with his beloved Westie being around all the time, she did not want him to be disappointed if things did not work out, or if they did, to discover their relationship in such a shocking way.

"I must go," she said, trying to get up, but Larkin held her back.

"I know you must, but—I don't want you to. *Either* of you," he said, holding her gaze. "I want you to know that. Do you understand?"

Maggie stared at him, believing she did, but too terrified she wanted it too much to trust her own judgement.

"I hope I do," she said carefully. "But I would like you to be very clear, with no ambiguity."

He smiled at that and nodded, allowing her to get to her feet. "I can do that, and we shall talk seriously very soon, my dearest Mrs Finchley, but for now I had best help you get this sleepy fellow home. Wait there."

Larkin disappeared for a moment and returned with a blanket which he laid over Gideon before scooping the boy up in his arms.

Gideon huffed but laid his head trustingly against Larkin's shoulder. Maggie watched as Larkin smiled fondly down at the lad and felt her hopes soar. Perhaps it really was possible for fortune to shine on their family again.

Perhaps Auntie Connie had broken the mould, and now, anything was possible.

Chapter 19

Everything is ready. We'll see you at the club tonight.

Good Luck, Lars.

—Excerpt from a letter from Mr Leo Hunt (Son of Mr Nathanial and Mrs Alice Hunt) to The Hon'ble Larkin Weston.

12th November 1850, The Sons of Hades, Portman Square, Marylebone, London.

"Evening, my fine fellows. How's tricks?" Larkin slurred, falling heavily against the doorjamb as he arrived on the threshold of Leo's private office at the Sons of Hades. He waved the bottle in his hand, peering blearily at the men awaiting him inside.

"You've got to be joking," Leo said, the colour draining from his face as he surged to his feet.

"Oh, Christ," Pip said, staring at Larkin in horror as he staggered into the room.

"Whassa matter?" Larkin asked, taking a slug from the bottle and swaying gently.

"You're half seas over, that's what!" Jules said furiously, getting up and walking over to glare at him. "Dammit, Larkin, you reek of whisky, and after all the bloody work we've done to—"

Larkin straightened up and grinned at them, having received exactly the reaction he'd hoped for. He'd always excelled at amateur dramatics as a young man at family events, and had been confident he could pull it off. "I'm not drunk," he said, walking over to the desk and setting the bottle down upon it. He sat down in the chair Jules had just vacated, enjoying the bewildered glances his friends were exchanging. "I'm afraid I've had plenty of opportunity to refine my portrayal of a drunken lout. Rather too much personal experience and lived in the full glare of the public too," he added ruefully, gesturing to his rumpled appearance. He'd not shaved that morning and put on the previous day's wrinkled clothes, much to Barnes' distress, who took his dishevelled appearance as a personal affront. He'd deliberately got soap in his eyes to make them bloodshot, which had stung like the devil, and then rubbed glycerine into his face to make it look sweaty. To cap it all, he'd then doused himself liberally with whisky before filling the empty bottle with cold tea.

Leo stared at him and then gave a bark of laughter, returning to his seat. "You're going to make him think you're bidding recklessly because you're foxed," he said, admiration in his eyes now. "Nice. Very nice indeed, and I tell you now, it couldn't happen to a nicer fellow. I want that devil out of the club tonight and never to return."

"Charming chap, is he?" Larkin asked, feeling anger rise in his chest as Leo pulled a face in answer. Larkin remembered the bastard's audacity, the revelation that he had goaded a drunk and desperate man into playing too recklessly and could not wait to give him a taste of his own medicine.

Not only had he fleeced a man on the edge of his sanity of all he owned but had tried to force the grieving family's beautiful young daughter to marry him. Oh, he was going to enjoy tonight and make certain Mr Jenkins rued the day he'd tangled with the Merrivale family. *His* family, he thought, with a sudden swell of protectiveness. For that was what they were now, as far as he was concerned. Aunt Connie might have found love and the protection only a husband could offer, but he knew Maggie. He knew she would not feel comfortable for long living on her aunt and uncle's charity, no matter how pleased they were to offer it.

No. Maggie and Gideon were his to protect and love now, supposing they would allow him that privilege, and Caro too if that's what she preferred. Somehow, Larkin suspected Aunt Connie would throw herself into fashion and the theatre and the excitement of her new world, which would probably appeal to the young lady, having been sheltered for all her life. He did not think that prospect would appeal to Maggie, though. All she wanted was to return to her beloved manor and bring up her son in the place she missed so desperately. Larkin meant to give her that chance, whether or not she wished to live that life with him. At least then, she would be free to choose.

A knock at the door revealed one of the staff who told them Mr Jenkins had arrived and was waiting for them. The game was on.

Larkin waited in the room next door as his friends filed in and greeted Mr Jenkins, congratulating him on winning the chance to play the owners of the Sons of Hades. They explained that membership was as rare as hen's teeth but, if he beat them all, they would give him that privilege. A privilege it was too, for not only did one need to be fabulously wealthy to gain entry, but to meet a set of criteria that no one in the *ton* had yet to fathom. For the sons did not judge upon breeding and who you knew, but upon whether they deemed any man decent, honourable, and a person with whom they would willingly sit down and spend a couple of hours in company. Entry to their elite world would open doors at which Jenkins could not even guess.

Larkin listened, lip curling, as Mr Jenkins tried to ingratiate himself to Jules. As the Marquess of Blackstone, he was the highest ranking of them all, and Larkin did not doubt that Jenkins had done his homework, discovering who was who, and might be of use to him. It was nothing new, of course, and how their world worked, but his toadying only made Larkin itch to get this night over with.

"But we're one short, aren't we?" Jenkins asked. "Mr Weston is still one of you, is he not? Won't he be joining us?"

Larkin smiled as he imagined the worried glances the men were exchanging.

"I believe he will be joining us shortly," Pip drawled, and Larkin heard the sound of a chair being pulled back. "But we may as well start without him, or we might wait all night."

"Ah, yes. I heard he's rather a wild young fellow. Likes a drink, don't he? Comes of hanging about with all those artistic types, I imagine," Jenkins said, his tone amused.

"No doubt," Pip replied dryly. "We're playing Pharo, five hundred guineas a counter. I trust that suits you?"

If it didn't, Jenkins was in no position to complain, though the staggering sum for one counter had to give him pause. He'd won a considerable sum over the past games, according to Larkin's friends, but not enough that he could view bids like that with equanimity. Larkin heard no reply, so assumed the fellow had nodded. Play began and silence reigned for a while, the only sound the occasional chink of the ivory counters and the players making their bets.

Larkin bided his time, though he was climbing the walls with impatience.

"I'm out," Pip said, three games later, during which he'd had managed to lose an eye-watering sum to Jenkins. This was Larkin's cue, so he picked up his bottle, this one a quarter full with actual whisky, took a deep breath, and went out to the corridor.

"Evening, chums," he said, lurching in through the door and allowing the bottle to slip from his fingers. It clattered to the floor, spilling its contents and filling the room with alcohol fumes.

"Bloody hell, Lars!" Pip remonstrated, surging to his feet. "What did we tell you about turning up tap hackled?"

Larkin looked bemusedly at the bottle on the floor and then squinted blearily up at Pip, blinking hard as he pretended to struggle to focus. "Huh?"

"Never mind," Pip said wearily, tugging on the bellpull to rouse someone to come and clear up. "Come along, you're in no fit state to play tonight," he told Larkin, taking hold of his arm.

"Gerroff!" Larkin objected, tugging free. "I can play. I wanna play. Not my mother, damn you."

"Pip's right," Leo said, a warning note to his voice. "We told you the rules."

"Bugger your rules," Larkin replied, pulling out the chair Pip had vacated and thudding down into it. "I'm playing."

"Oh, can we not let Mr Weston play?" Jenkins said with apparent good nature, though Larkin did not miss the shrewd glint in his eyes. "I was told I had won the opportunity to play *all* the Sons. I would be sorely disappointed not to test my mettle against all of you after such a promise."

"S'true!" Larkin said at once. "He won. S'not fair."

"Oh, fine. It's your funeral," Jules said in disgust, apparently having had enough. "Bloody well deal, Leo. I came to play cards, not watch Larkin play the fool. Though if you cast up your accounts again, I'm banning you for life," Jules added savagely, glaring at Larkin.

Larkin winced, wishing Jules had not said that, for it made him recall a particularly awful evening. Well, not that he *did* recall it, having no memory of the night whatsoever, but his friends had filled in the details with excruciating detail, much to his shame.

"Fine, fine," he said, waving a hand and gesturing for Leo, who was banker, to proceed.

A servant hurried in and began mopping up the whisky. Pip ordered a large pot of coffee for Larkin and then bade them a good evening. Larkin made a rude gesture at the door once Pip had gone through it and grinned at Jenkins.

"Bloody old woman," he muttered.

Jenkins laughed indulgently, and they proceeded to play.

Larkin lost extravagantly on the first three rounds, more moderately on the next, all the time watching Jenkins as he played, certain he was cheating. Still, he had to give the man his due, he did it with such skill, it was difficult to be certain. However, Jules and Leo especially were very fine players, yet Jenkins had all the luck tonight, winning time and again until Jules threw down his cards.

"I'm out," he said with a sigh. "Are you satisfied, Mr Jenkins?" he asked, making Larkin look sharply at his friend, furious for giving him an out. Yet Jules had gambled and won this time, for Jenkins shook his head, despite the vast stack of counters at his side. Avarice lit his expression, the fever that gambling could alight blazing in his eyes.

"Oh, no. I'm a long way from done," he said, eyeing Larkin with a speculative smile. "What say you, Mr Weston?"

"Play on," Larkin said dismissively, and then peered owlishly at the diminished stack at his own elbow. "Say, Leo? Loan me, will you?"

Leo pulled a face. "Stow it, Lars. You're done."

"I *ain't!* Loan me, damn you. Ten thousand. Pa will settle it, you know he will," he said, though this was so far from the truth Leo's lips twitched. If Larkin had really lost that much gambling, his father would have murdered him.

Leo looked revolted but relented. The deal was done, with Larkin signing his vowel with an erratic slash of the pen that purported to be his signature.

"What do you say to a thousand pounds a counter?" Jenkins suggested smoothly, looking at Larkin, not Leo.

"Certainly," Larkin said before Leo could object. "Get on with it, Leo."

Leo complied but looked deeply unhappy about it, whilst Jules ordered more coffee, for Larkin had refused the first pot, ordering whisky instead.

"Drink the damned coffee, or I'll pour it down your throat myself," Jules told him.

"Why are you all so *boooring*?" Larkin complained bitterly, but took the cup from Jules and drank it, privately glad to do so. His nerves were jangling now, for not only did he need to beat a fine player, but a cheat too.

Leo began turning up cards, one on the right for the bank, one on the left for the players.

Jenkins lost the next round in spectacular fashion, finding himself five thousand pounds the poorer. Sweating but undaunted, for he still had a hefty stack of counters, he played on.

The next round was a near thing, but Larkin prevailed. Leo sent him a level look that warned him he had best up his game or they might not come out of this in the manner they hoped. Jenkins, however, seemed rattled, perhaps as much by the fact that Jules was no longer playing but watching him with an intensity that would not allow the man to attempt to cheat. Any accusation of foul play by a man like the Marquess of Blackstone would ruin what little reputation Jenkins might lay claim to and could land him in serious trouble. Not being a gentleman in any sense of the word he was unlikely to blow his brains out, but if Jules pressed charges, things could go very wrong for Mr Jenkins. No one would doubt the word of the heir to a dukedom.

With his usual tricks out of his hands, Jenkins began to lose steadily and with speed. He was grey with strain and fatigue by the time Larkin decided enough was enough. Only a few scattered counters lay at Jenkins' elbow, everything else piled beside Larkin. He needed a big win to stay in the game.

"I tell you what," Larkin said, as if suddenly struck by an idea. "Aren't you the fellow old Merrivale blew his brains out for?"

Jenkins stiffened, what little colour remained in his cheeks draining away. "That was no fault of mine. It was a fair game," he said at once, his gaze darting from Larkin to Jules and Leo, who stared back, expressionless.

"Yes, yes," Larkin said dismissively, waving this away as a mere nothing when all he wanted to do was throttle the bastard with his bare hands. "But you won a very tidy little property, didn't you? In Norfolk? It just so happens I have a pretty little lady friend in Norfolk. Could do with a snug little place there. Play you for it," he said with a grin, sliding all his counters across the table.

Jenkins stared at the fortune in counters, looking as though he could hardly believe his luck.

"You want Merrivale's manor?" he said, the relief in his voice audible.

"Said so, didn't I?" Larkin said impatiently. "Are you taking the wager, or no?"

"I am," Jenkins said decisively. "Write me out a vowel. I'll sign it."

Pip came in at that moment. "Ah, I see things are getting interesting," he said with a grin. "Mind if I watch?"

Without waiting for an answer, he sat himself down opposite Mr Jenkins, lounging back in his chair beside Jules, both men turning their attention to the perspiring Jenkins as he laid his vowel on top of the vast stack of counters.

"Proceed," Larkin said to Leo as the cards continued to turn up in his favour, grinning at an increasingly alarmed Jenkins

"Trente à la va!" Larkin said, seeing panic flickering in Jenkin's eyes. This was the tipping point, Larkin knew. If Jenkins had any sense, he would cut his losses, but no.

"Paix," Jenkins said, demanding to continue upon the same course.

The silence rang in Larkin's ears as Leo turned the cards, both Jules and Pip unmoving beside him.

It was Jules who shouted first, a bellow of triumph that made Larkin jump out of his skin, such was his agitation. But there it was, the winning card. *His* card. He'd done it.

"I want to play again," Jenkins said, almost breathless, gazing in disbelief as Larkin pulled the counters and the note for Merrivale Manor towards him.

"Sorry, old man," Larkin said, yawning broadly. "Feeling a trifle bosky, and Jules here forbade me from puking on the cards again. Best call it a night. No hard feelings, eh?"

He got to his feet, allowing Jules to sweep his winnings into his hat. He grinned at his friend, flushed with triumph. "Call me a cab, Jules, there's a good fellow."

"You're a cab," Jules said, for the Marquess of Blackstone was no one's lackey.

"You're a damned cheat!"

The words rang out in the room and the silence was absolute as the four men turned to gaze at Jenkins in appalled astonishment. All of them knew Jenkins was a Captain Sharp and, despite Larkin's ruse, he'd played fair and square, as had everyone else. The only thing they'd done was lose when they needn't have. If Jenkins hadn't been so greedy, he might have left with a considerable fortune in his pocket.

"What did you say?" Larkin spoke softly, mingled fury and delight bursting together in his chest. As much as the accusation made him wild with anger, it gave him the opportunity he wanted. He was not about to meet the bastard at some godforsaken hour of the morning and risk his own neck, but he was very certainly going to break his nose.

"Shouldn't have said that, old man," Leo said, shaking his head sadly. "I should take it back."

Despite this sensible advice, Jenkins squared his shoulders. "You heard."

"So I did," Larkin said mildly, knowing Jenkins thought he'd fall over he was so far gone. Poor fool.

"Come here," Larkin said. "And say that again."

Jenkins did so, but before he could say more than 'You're—' Larkin punched him in the guts. Jenkins doubled up but was swift to strike back. The man was faster than Larkin had expected, and the blow knocked him back a pace, but in his darkest days Larkin had gained a fair bit of experience at barroom brawling, so it hardly registered. The fight was swift and vicious, each man delivering a series of violent blows as Larkin's friends tried to move furniture out of the way with little joy, for the room was not a large one. Jenkins threw a punch that might have broken Larkin's nose, but he dodged back at the last second, the blow only grazing his cheekbone instead. He retaliated with a right hook that connected with Jenkin's nose and almost certainly broke it. The blow sent Jenkins windmilling backwards onto the card table. It was a fine, elegant thing, rather old, and could not withstand the assault, for Jenkins was no lightweight. His heavy frame crashed onto the table, and it split in two, with Jenkins landing heavily on the floor, surrounded by splintered wood. He stared up at the ceiling for a moment, dazed, but Larkin reached down and grasped hold of his shirt, pulling him back to his feet.

Larkin drew back his fist, but Pip intervened, holding him back.

"Leave off, Lars, the fellow's done for," he said, watching as blood dripped steadily from Jenkins' nose as the man swayed and then fell to his knees, groaning.

Larkin let out a breath, annoyed to be interrupted when he had a good deal left to explain to Mr Jenkins about his personal feelings, but Pip was quite correct. It was done. Jenkins was done, and Larkin had won back the manor for Maggie and Gideon. The truth of that suddenly expanded inside him, joy at the gift he could offer the woman who had come to mean the entire world to him, and the little boy who had wormed his way into his heart and made Larkin love him.

He was suddenly full of gratitude towards Elmira, for being strong enough not to allow him to persuade her into a future that would have been wrong for them both. It seemed so obvious now that he had Maggie and Gideon, and he might have missed out if not for her courage. He'd heard from Thorn, who had written to congratulate him, and told him Elmira was walking out with a gentleman farmer who lived close to Gillmont. He had been kind to the women upon discovering what manner of house it was and had offered his services if ever they were needed. They'd been courting for some months now, and Thorn expected an announcement any day. Larkin had been relieved to discover he felt nothing but happiness for Elmira, who deserved everything good in life, and he hoped she would be as happy as he intended to be.

"Well done," Leo said, patting him on the back. Larkin grinned at him. "Leave the clearing up to us. We'll get Jenkins off the premises and escort him home. Don't worry, we won't let him out of our sight until we have the deeds to the manor. You'd best get Barnes to find some steak for that eye. It's going to be a beauty," he said appreciatively.

Larkin laughed, wincing as he touched a finger to the swelling flesh, realising Leo was quite correct. "Thanks, Leo, and you two as well," he added, nodding to Jules and Pip. "Once again, I'm in your debt. I owe you, and I shan't forget it."

"Stow it," Jules said with a snort, winking at Larkin before looking down at Jenkins, his lip curling with distaste. "Come along Leo, held me take out the refuse. We don't want Pip sullying his pretty hands."

"I should think not," Pip replied, apparently having no qualms with this observation. "I'm far too high in the instep for such menial labour, but I shall watch with pleasure," he added, his eyes twinkling.

Laughing, Larkin left them to their bickering. Now it was done he was weary to his bones, his eye, his ribs and his jaw had all begun throbbing in concert, and all he wanted was to have a quiet drink while Barnes attended to his injuries, and then to fall into bed. No, he amended, all he wanted was to see Maggie, to hold her in his arms and explain that everything was going to be all right, but he could not rouse her at this ungodly hour of the morning, and certainly not while he was in this state.

So, with that option out the window, he hailed a cab and made his way home.

Chapter 20

Dear Lord and Lady Montagu,

St Anne's Church, Soho, will host the wedding of Miss Connie Merrivale and Mr Cecil Thompson on November 16th at 11 am, with the reception to be held at Ridgeley House, Belgravia, to which you are cordially invited.

—Excerpt from a letter from Miss Connie Merrivale to The Most Hon'ble Marquess and Marchioness of Montagu.

13th November 1850, Berwick Street, Soho, London.

If Larkin had been under any illusion as to the state of his physiognomy, Maggie's shriek of alarm on finding him waiting for her in her parlour the next day put them to rest.

"Oh dear, is it that bad?" he asked ruefully, watching the colour leave her face.

"What happened?" she demanded, rushing to him and touching gentle fingers to his face, the worry in her eyes warming his heart. "Does it hurt? Who did this to you? Oh, if I get my hands on them—"

Larkin didn't doubt she'd wreak some vengeance if she could; she was far braver and more capable than even she realised.

"Hush, love. It's all right. You should have seen the other fellow!" he added with a laugh.

"How can you joke about it?" she exclaimed crossly. "How did this happen?"

"You've asked me that twice now but still not given me the chance to explain. Why don't we sit down, and I shall explain?"

Hardly soothed but slightly mollified, Maggie allowed him to guide her to the sofa, where he sat close to her and took her hands in his.

"Now, love," he began, seeing her cheeks turn pink with pleasure at the intimate address. He smiled and squeezed her hands. "Before I tell you the whole story, I have a present for you."

Her brow wrinkled in confusion at the sudden switch in topic. "A present?"

"Yes. Are you ready?"

Maggie let out a little huff, clearly believing it was a ruse to distract her from his injuries. "Very well."

Larkin grinned, reached into his coat pocket and withdrew the small bundle of documents he had received in the post earlier that morning with a congratulatory note from Leo. He handed it to Maggie, who gazed down at it in confusion.

"What is this?" she asked, her fair eyebrows drawn together.

"Well, that's the thing with packages and parcels, darling. You must open them to discover what's inside."

Sending him a look of sheer exasperation, she tugged on the ribbon holding the documents together and unfolded them. She stared down at the title page on the deed to her beloved manor for such a long time, he suspected she did not dare to believe what she was seeing. Then her breath caught, and she turned to him, eyes wide, her hand pressed to her heart.

"What—? What does it mean?"

"You know what it is, darling, and yes, it's quite authentic. Those are the deeds to your estate. The manor is yours again, Maggie."

He watched her, his heart swelling with too many emotions as her eyes filled with tears and her throat worked. "H-How? I-I don't understand."

"I won it back last night, for you, love," he said simply. "If you hadn't realised it yet, I'd do anything for you, Maggie, and whilst I might not quite manage the moon and stars, I hoped this might be a good start."

Maggie looked down again at the deeds, and he saw a fat tear plop onto the vellum. She gave a choked laugh and wiped it away, before gazing at him in wonder.

"You won it back," she said unsteadily, disbelieving. "For me?"

He nodded. "For you and for Gideon, and Caro too. Because I love you, Maggie, and I wanted you to have your home back. To know that you had options, and you were under no obligation to say yes."

She stilled, staring at him. "Say yes to what?" she asked, her breathing growing fast and erratic.

"To the question I'm about to ask you," he said with a smile. He got to his knees beside her and raised one hand to his lips, kissing her knuckles tenderly, his heart beating harder than he could ever remember as he put it on the line once more. He did not wish to think of what he might feel if she rejected him, but he would not hold back, risking it all with his eyes wide open this time. "My darling Magdelina, I finally know what it is I want, and who it is I wish to share the rest of my life with. If you will have me, I would be the happiest man alive if you would consent to be my wife, if you would allow me to be a father to Gideon, and to live our days in the beautiful home that means so much to you both."

Maggie's hand flew to her mouth, and she stifled a sob. For a moment, Larkin felt as if his entire life hung in the balance, but he waited, hardly daring to breathe until she gave a strangled laugh and threw her arms about his neck.

"Yes!" she exclaimed, throwing herself at him with such force he fell over backwards, taking her with him. "Yes, yes, yes, a thousand times, yes!" she cried, covering his face with kisses as he laughed and held her to him.

The door flew open then, and Caro stood in the doorway and gave a little scream of shock as she saw Maggie sprawled on top of Larkin in an appearance of complete abandon, skirts and petticoats billowing around her.

"*Maggie!*" she exclaimed, clearly thinking her big sister had taken leave of her senses.

Aunt Connie, appearing a bare second later, looked over her niece's shoulder and didn't so much as blink. She only gave a satisfied nod. "Well done, Maggie, dear. It's about time too," she said with a touch of exasperation. "I already told Cecil to plan for a double wedding and he applied for the licence when he got ours done, so everything will be ready for you."

This startling piece of information stunned everyone into silence, and no one had anything to add except for the clock.

Cuckoo, cuckoo, cuckoo, cuckoo, cuckoo, cuckoo, cuckoo!

"Is Gideon awake yet?" Maggie asked Priddy as she entered the kitchen.

"No, Mrs Finchley, not yet. Shall I wake him?" the little maid asked politely.

"Oh, no, thank you, Priddy. Let him sleep. We had terrible trouble getting him to bed last night," she told Larkin, giving him a pointed look. "For he insisted he could not be expected to go to sleep in the middle of a war with France. So that's two late nights he's had in a row."

Larkin hid a smile and attempted to look sheepish. "I beg your pardon. I will do better in the future, I promise."

"I know you will," Maggie said, her teasing expression turning to one of such adoration Larkin had to clear his throat to remind her they were not alone.

Maggie started and turned back to the kitchen table, where all the staff were assembled at their request having just received their happy news. She blushed a fiery red as everyone grinned indulgently at them. Giving their mistress a moment to gather herself, they returned to their conversation.

"So what's this manor like, then?" Barnes was asking. "I've been hoping Mr Weston would return to the country this age, but he don't listen to me," he added, earning a reproving glance from Larkin, which only made him laugh.

Mrs Goodall immediately launched into a detailed description of the charming old manor house with particular detail about the kitchen, over which Mrs Moody had agreed to preside. Mrs Goodall would return as housekeeper, with Wallace restored to his position as butler. Priddy had decided to remain in town as her family were here, but Larkin had promised to find her a position with one of his friends, so she was satisfied too. Sally would stay on as Maggie's lady's maid, and Barnes, whom Larkin considered as much a part of his life as Maggie did Wallace and Mrs Goodall, would obviously continue as valet.

With everything else settled, all that remained was to inform Larkin's parents, news that he knew would put their minds at rest after his behaviour over the previous years, and to tell Gideon. This last was, he had to admit, giving him more than a little anxiety. It was one thing to befriend a fatherless boy, but quite another to try to be a father to him.

Whilst he was reasonably sure Gideon would be pleased, there was always the chance he might resent Larkin inserting himself so forcefully into his life. Nervously, he reached into his pocket to reassure himself his gift for the child was still there. He hadn't shown it to Maggie yet, and did not know if he was making a horrible mistake, but he didn't think so. His instincts told him this was the right thing to do, and finally he felt his confidence return to him.

"Mama?" said a sleepy voice, and everyone turned to see a rumpled Gideon standing in the doorway, rubbing his eyes.

"There's my darling. Did you have a nice nap, Giddy?" Maggie asked, holding her arms out to her son, who went to her and climbed into her lap.

"Yes, but want my soldiers now."

"In a moment, darling. Mrs Moody has made crumpets for tea. Would you like some?"

"Crumpets? With butter and jam?" he asked, perking up.

"Why, how else would you eat them?" Maggie said with a smile. "Of course with butter and jam."

Having expected the order the moment Gideon appeared, Mrs Moody set a plate with two crumpets, liberally slathered with butter and jam on the table. Picking up a chair, she placed it between Maggie and Larkin, who moved to make space.

"Sit there, Master Gideon, and don't go getting sticky fingers on your mama's skirts."

"Yes, Moody," he said, scrambling onto the seat and taking a bite before she could get the large napkin tucked into his shirtfront.

"There," she said, satisfied. "Would it be all right if we popped next door, missus?" she asked Maggie. "Mr Barnes is opening a bottle of something for us all to celebrate your good news, and I promised to take a couple of bottles of my peapod wine. I'll be back in plenty of time to get dinner done, I promise."

"Of course," Maggie said, smiling. "Go and enjoy yourselves. There's no rush. We won't mind if dinner is a little late."

Thanking her, the staff went out, closing the door behind them.

Left alone with only Gideon, Maggie gave Larkin a conspiratorial smile. "I shouldn't bank on getting any dinner tonight. Mrs Moody's peapod wine is not to be trifled with."

Larkin laughed, but Gideon's ears pricked up.

"Trifle?" he asked hopefully.

"Not tonight, you little rogue," Larkin said, laughing and getting up to fetch a damp cloth. Carefully, he wiped Gideon's sticky hands and took the empty plate away. Despite his earlier confidence, he felt sick with nerves now. "Gideon, could I have a little talk with you?" Gideon nodded, looking expectantly at Larkin as he sat back down again.

"Want to play war?"

Larkin grinned. "I certainly do, but not right now. I need to show you something."

"More soldiers?"

"Not more soldiers, but one very special soldier," Larkin said, reaching into his pocket.

Maggie frowned in confusion and then gasped as Larkin set the little miniature he'd done on the table. He'd never painted a miniature before, and it had been difficult for more reasons that simply the blurry photo that Montagu had secured for him from he knew not where. But there was Gideon's father, looking handsome and proud in his red coat.

"This is a picture of your papa, Gideon," Larkin said softly, aware of Maggie trying not to cry beside him. "He was a very, very brave man, a hero, who went to war to keep us all safe."

Gideon squinted down at the tiny image and looked back at Larkin, eyes wide. "Papa is in heaven," he said eagerly. "Mama said, but… this is Papa too?"

"Yes," Larkin agreed, suddenly finding his throat very tight. "This is a painting of what your papa looked like, and it is for you to keep always, so you can remember him."

"For me?" Gideon repeated, picking up the picture and staring at it very hard. "My papa," he said. "Look, Mama! Look what Westie gave me."

"I see it, darling," Maggie said, her eyes shining as she stared at Larkin in wonder. "And it is a beautiful gift, and you must treasure it always and keep it safe. It… It looks just like him, you know."

Gideon beamed at her and stared down again at the little portrait.

"Fanks, Westie," he said, putting the tiny painting down and getting off his chair.

Larkin had to swallow hard as the child hugged him tightly. He picked Gideon up and settled him on his knee. "There's something else I want to talk to you about, Gideon," he said, as this was the part that made his heart clench with anxiety. "Because you don't have a papa here, as he's in heaven, but I would very, very much like a son like you."

"Like me?" Gideon repeated, eyes wide.

"Just like you," Larkin agreed. "You see, I love your mama very much, and I love you too, and though I'm not a brave soldier like your father, I *am* here, and I would very much like to be here for you every day, if you think you would not mind it?"

"Would you live here with Mama and me?"

"Well, not here, but yes, back at your old house, the manor. We would all live together and see each other every day. You and your mama, and me."

Gideon stared up at him thoughtfully. "All right, then," he said simply. "Can I get my soldiers now?"

Larkin stared at him, a little taken aback. "Er… yes, if you want to."

"Can you read to me tonight then, if you're my papa? And can we play ball? And can we have cake, and can we—"

"Yes!" Larkin said, nodding to all of it. "Yes, and I'll take you fishing, and teach you to ride like an out-an'-outer, and drive a carriage, and do all the things my papa did with me, I promise."

Gideon gave a whoop and ran from the room. "Stay there, I get my soldiers!" he shouted, thundering from the room with all the grace of a small hippopotamus.

"Well," Maggie said, her voice trembling with emotion. "I do hope you've allowed a little time for your wife among all those manly activities," she said with mock indignation, and then burst into tears.

"Darling," Larkin said, pulling her into his arms. "I'm so sorry. Ought I to have warned you? It must have been a shock to see him again like that."

"It was," she said, laughing and crying at once. "But a lovely shock, and you know, I had the strangest feeling when I saw his face, the sense that he was happy for us, that he approved. I think he would have liked you, Larkin. Very much."

"I will do my very best to be a father to Gideon, love, I promise, but you might need to be patient with me. I'm rather new to this, you see."

"No," Maggie said, gazing up at him. "No, you are already perfect, and I love you, Larkin Weston, with all my heart."

Chapter 21

*Lord Bradley scowled at her and Georgette
quailed inwardly but put up her chin. This
vile libertine might be a peer of the realm, but
she would not cower before him. Instead, she
regarded him with the full measure of
contempt she felt blazing in her eyes.*

**—Excerpt from 'His Grace and Disfavour',
by an anonymous author.**

16th November 1850, St Anne's Church, Soho, London.

Larkin wondered if it was the most unusual wedding that St Anne's Church in Soho had ever witnessed. If it was, he had to give the vicar credit, for the man didn't bat an eyelid, even when Aunt Connie, resplendent in bright purple and glittering with the largest display of amethysts and diamonds Larkin had ever seen, floated down the aisle. She called out greetings as she went, waving to Lord and Lady Montagu and the Marquess of Blackstone—who, she had told Larkin in confidence, was a wicked darling—and even blowing a kiss to Ashton Anson.

Maggie, who had insisted Connie walk first up the aisle, appeared a moment later, and Larkin ceased to think of anything else. She wore her thick blonde hair in a simple chignon, and her ivory gown was trimmed with Brussels lace. However, despite his artistic eye and love of detail, he barely noticed the gown, the flowers, or the diamonds lent to her by Lady Montagu, for her face, serene behind the lace veil, was the single most stunning thing he'd ever seen in his life. His heart gave an erratic thud as he realised how terribly lucky he was.

"Mama! Mama!"

Gideon bounced up and down beside Caro, who tried to hush him, to no avail as he spotted his mother.

"Pretty Mama!" Gideon said, his tone approving, clapping as the congregation chuckled indulgently.

Maggie laughed and blew him a kiss before taking her place beside Larkin. Through the lace veil, he saw her beautiful blue-green eyes glittering with happiness and knew the same joy was reflected in his own.

He hardly heard a word of the service, making his replies in a daze, unable to look away from his bride as the rest of the world disappeared. It was just Maggie and him, making each other promises they would be sure to keep, no matter what.

When the vicar finally said the grooms could kiss their brides, the congregation erupted as Cecil swept his wife up into his arms and spun her around before planting a smacking kiss upon her lips. Larkin was barely aware of the furore, too consumed with the lifting of Maggie's veil. The action made him feel strangely reverent, as if he were casting aside their old lives with the removal of the delicate lace, and letting in the future as the sun shone through the stained glass and fell like a blessing upon her lovely face.

She smiled up at him, and he suddenly saw everything he had ever wanted before him, as simple as breathing.

"Thank you," he told her, with all the love and emotion he was feeling, and whilst she might not understand precisely what she was being thanked for, it did not matter, as he lowered his mouth to hers, and kissed his wife.

♡♣◇♠

6th November 1850, Ridgeley House, Belgravia, London.

The wedding breakfast was lavish and, after being presented with a spread of food in both great quantity and exquisite quality, most of the guests had probably hoped for little more than a nice nap. However, the company had quickly come to understand that Mrs Connie Thompson was a force to be reckoned with, so whilst it was most unconventional when she insisted everyone must dance the moment everyone had finished eating, no one thought to deny her and, moreover, they all seemed delighted to join in.

Maggie watched her aunt, finally in her element, and felt almost as overwhelmed by Connie's good fortune and happiness as she was by her own. Aunt Connie's joy was infectious, her desire that everyone be as happy as she quite irresistible, and it had made the day so special it would live in everyone's memory forevermore.

"Look," Larkin said as he danced Maggie around the floor for a second time. He had refused to relinquish her hand to allow the Earl of Ashburton to dance with her, telling his friend in the most amicable of terms to 'sling his hook.'

Far from taking offence, the earl had promised to try again later when her husband was feeling a touch less possessive. Now, however, she looked over to see Lord Montagu guiding Aunt Connie around the ballroom.

"Oh, my lord," she said, suddenly panic struck by what her irrepressible aunt might do or say to the intimidating marquess. However, as Montagu lowered his head to listen to whatever it was Connie was whispering to him, his eyes twinkled with mirth, and he gave a sudden burst of laughter. Connie glanced across to see Maggie watching and smirked, well aware what a coup it was to have made the ice cold marquess laugh in public.

"May I?"

Larkin halted the dance the moment before he moved her into a turn, and Maggie looked around to see Baron Rothborn, her father-in-law, at their side, holding out his hand to her. She glanced at Larkin in surprise, for he had told her his father very rarely danced due to the injury he'd sustained in the war. Larkin sighed.

"I've just sent Ashburton off, must I do so to you too?" Larkin asked, quirking an eyebrow.

The Baron, whose ruggedly handsome features were echoed in his son, mirrored the expression. "You may try," he replied dryly.

Larkin snorted. "No chance," he said with amusement, and reluctantly handed her into his father's care.

"I'm afraid I'm no dancer, but I could not resist stealing you away for a moment or two, which is all I will manage, I'm afraid," the Baron said with a crooked smile.

"I'm honoured," Maggie replied, for though she had only met Larkin's parents briefly the previous day, they had both been so warm and kind she knew she was sincerely welcomed into their family.

"Gideon is a lovely fellow. You must be very proud of him."

"I am, my lord," Maggie said, touched by his kindness, for she had seen him take pains to introduce himself to Gideon, who was still sitting with Lady Rothborn, who seemed equally enchanted.

"Call me Solo. Everyone does," he said. "If I may call you Maggie?"

"Please," she replied at once.

"My daughter, Grace, and her husband, Sterling, were sorry not to be here today, but leaving the farm can't be done at the drop of a hat. They're to be at the Priory for Christmas, however. I have not asked Larkin yet, but I hope you might join us, too."

Maggie considered this and looked ruefully up at the Baron.

"Ah," he said, understanding at once. "You have plans."

"It's to be our first Christmas back at the manor, and there have been so many changes in Gideon's life of late—"

"Say no more. Jemima told me as much, but I'm a stubborn fellow and like things all my own way," he said ruefully.

Maggie laughed and shook her head. "Indeed, I would have loved to join you, but perhaps we might come for Easter?"

He brightened perceptibly at this suggestion. "An excellent notion. I shall look forward to it immensely."

"As shall I," Maggie replied, meaning it.

The dance ended, which she suspected was just as well as the baron's limp was rather more pronounced as he made his way back to his wife.

"Mama! *Grandmama* is almost as good at drawing as Westie. Look!" Gideon brandished the drawing of a pig sitting at a table and wielding a knife and fork, with obvious delight.

Lady Rothborn looked a little sheepish as she regarded her daughter-in-law. "I'm sorry, I'm so used to being 'Grandmama' to my daughter's children I did not stop to think and—"

"I think it's wonderful that Gideon has grandparents. Don't you, Giddy?"

Giddy, who had returned to his drawing, ignored this, instead tugging at Lady Rothborn's sleeve. "Grandmama, do another. A duck," he insisted.

Laughing, Lady Rothborn complied at once.

6th November 1850 Ridgeley House, Belgravia, London.

Though the party looked set to go on long into the night, by late afternoon Larkin was champing at the bit. He had arranged with Barnes and Mrs Goodall that his house be made ready for his wife, and food enough provided for several days, so that they needed no extra staff, though Priddy was waiting to help Maggie prepare for her wedding night before leaving to take up her new position working for Lady Belinda Knight. Whilst Maggie and Larkin remained in town, Caro and Giddy would stay with Lord and Lady Rothborn, who were guests at Montagu House, and the staff would go ahead to the manor to prepare everything for their arrival.

They were to have two blissful nights alone before travelling to Norfolk, and Larkin did not wish to share his wife for another moment. He had already taken action and requested their carriage be readied for them, so when Pip tried once again to dance with Maggie, Larkin once more told him to get lost.

"Larkin!" Maggie protested crossly.

"I know, I know," he said, holding up a hand to forestall her scolding. "I'm a highhanded brute, and at any other time I would not dare, but I want to go *home*, Maggie," he said, his expression meaningful.

Maggie turned pink, the colour flushing down her neck to her décolletage. He wondered just how far it spread, which did not help his impatience.

Ashburton cleared his throat. "Another time, Mrs Weston," he said politely, grinning at Larkin as he went to ask Maggie's aunt to dance instead. Connie, who had just held Ashton Anson to his promise to waltz with her, was so gracious as to accept.

"Do you mind very much?" Larkin asked, frowning as he realised he was a greedy devil. This was her special day and, if she wished to stay, he would endure it.

"Of course not," she said. "If only you'd said so in private instead of in front of the earl, you wicked man! Come along, then, before anyone notices."

So saying, she grasped his hand and hurried out of the ballroom, towing him behind her.

"Gideon?" Larkin asked, rather delighted by this turn of events, but wondering if they ought not say goodbye first.

"He's asleep in your mama's lap," she said with a laugh. "He adores her, and he won't know we've gone. He seems delighted at the prospect at staying with them *and* seeing Miss Barrington again, and he's got Caro too. I'm sure they can manage him."

Relieved, Larkin needed no further persuading and rushed her to their waiting carriage.

The moment the door closed, Larkin pulled down the shutters and drew Maggie into his embrace. She laughed, her breath warm against his lips as he pressed his mouth to hers, and the quarter hour drive back to Berwick Street passed in a blur of increasingly heated kisses.

Though he was frustrated by having to let her go, spending his wedding night in a carriage did not appeal and so Larkin helped Maggie down before sweeping her up into his arms and carrying her over the threshold.

Maggie laughed, delighted, but protested as he continued on up the stairs. "You'll hurt your back! Put me down!"

"I may not be as brawny as Cecil, but I am quite capable of carrying a featherweight like you, love," Larkin reproved.

Still, he set her down as they came face-to-face with a blushing Priddy, who gave a giggle and rushed into the spare room that had been set aside for Maggie to ready herself.

Sending Larkin a look of amused mortification, Maggie scurried after her.

"Don't be too long, love," Larkin called after her, unable to resist.

Maggie gasped, knowing Priddy would have heard that too, and closed the door on him.

Laughing, Larkin went to see to his own preparations and prayed she really wouldn't take too long to punish him for his cheek.

6th November 1850 Berwick Street, Soho, London.

Though Maggie rather regretted having arranged for Priddy to help her, for Larkin was certainly well able to play lady's maid and undress her, she could not deny the sweet-scented bath that awaited her was very welcome. Also, taking a little time to reflect upon the wonderful day, and to prepare herself for the coming night, was not such a bad thing.

She was no blushing virgin, she reminded herself, and though her first marriage had been tragically brief, it had been a happy experience. She had no qualms about the coming night, knowing both she and Larkin were older and wiser and trusting her new husband implicitly.

So, whilst she fizzed with impatience, Maggie enjoyed the momentary respite after the excitement of the day and allowed Priddy to soothe her nerves by brushing out her long hair until it shone. Finally, however, Priddy was done, and she stepped back.

The nightgown was simple but lovely, a sheer fine silk edged with lace and tiny white bows. Maggie had fretted over wearing white on her wedding night until Aunt Connie had scolded her for being such a silly goose and observed she was unlikely to be wearing it for long.

"You look ever so pretty, Mrs Weston," Priddy said, still blushing a fiery red.

Mrs Weston. The sudden change felt at once new and strange and utterly perfect.

"Thank you, Priddy. That will be all, but I should like to thank you for everything you've done for us. We shall miss you."

Priddy grinned. "I'll miss you too, especially that naughty scamp Master Gideon, but I'm that excited to work for Lady Belinda. *Me,* working for a real lady!" she said in awe. "Mr Weston was so kind to arrange it for me, and I'm that grateful. He's a good 'un, missus, and I reckon you'll be happy."

"So do I," Maggie said, giving Priddy an impulsive hug. "And I know you will be too. Good luck to you."

Priddy bobbed a curtsey and left a few minutes later.

Maggie heard the back door close. They were alone.

Steeling her nerves, Maggie padded along the corridor to where she now knew Larkin's bedroom was. With a soft knock, she opened the door, her breath catching as she found Larkin waiting for her. He was standing by the fire that blazed in the hearth, a glass of brandy in his hand, and he wore the magnificent banyan she had seen once before.

Her breath caught. She bit her lip but was unable to hide her smile.

"What are you grinning at, wife?" he asked with amusement, though the words sounded somewhat breathless as he gazed at her. He set down his glass, not taking his eyes from her as they grew dark and hot with emotion.

"I'm so glad you wore that," she admitted, hurrying to him and losing no time in wrapping her arms about him. "I'm afraid I've become a little obsessed with it ever since the day I saw you wearing it in the kitchen."

"Obsessed?" he repeated, his dark eyes glinting wickedly. "I like the sound of that."

"So you should. I've thought about it far too often, about this intriguing triangle of skin I could see here," she added, trailing her long fingers through the hair on his chest as she had dreamed of doing ever since that morning. To her delight, he shivered.

"What else have you thought about?" he asked, his voice becoming pleasantly low and husky.

She pushed her hand beneath the wide sleeve, sliding it up his bare arm and delighting in the feel of hard muscle beneath her palm. "About the brawny arms I saw that day in the garden, when you brought Gideon home, and how it might feel to have them wrapped about me."

His eyes darkened as he gazed down at her and excitement stirred low in Maggie's stomach.

"You mean to say you've been ogling me and thinking wicked things," he accused.

"I'm afraid I have," she admitted, trying her best to look remorseful.

"Thank heavens for that," he said, grinning as he reached for her, sweeping her up into his arms. "It makes me feel a good deal better."

"Why?" she demanded as he carried her to the bed.

"Oh, Maggie," he said, shaking his head. "You would not believe the dreams I have had about you."

"Really?" she said, instantly desperate to know. "Tell me."

"I cannot," he told her, his eyes glinting with mirth. "For then you will realise how very depraved your husband is, and I fear you will be shocked."

"Oh, Larkin," she said with a sigh as he laid her gently down on the bed. "I do hope so."

He stared at her for a moment and then gave a bark of laughter. He tugged at the sash of his banyan and cast it aside with such abandon the sleeve hit the lamp on the bedside table. It wobbled and Larkin lunged, setting it upright again.

"That's a relief. The only fires I want to start tonight are the kind to make you sigh and moan, not run screaming out into the street," he said ruefully.

Maggie snorted, trying not to laugh, but then she noticed just what he'd revealed, and her laughter stopped abruptly. Instead, her heart thudded hard as she stared at him, at the landscape of finely wrought muscle across his chest and abdomen, his broad shoulders and powerful arms, and at the evidence of his love and desire for her. The fire he had promised her burst to life beneath her skin, her blood suddenly hot, her entire body blazing to life. She held out her arms to him, he came to her, and she revelled in the feeling of his flesh burning beneath her palms, of the sensation of hard muscle shifting beneath satiny skin.

He made a sound low in his throat that made her pulse leap as he tugged her nightgown off, over her head.

"Maggie," he murmured. "You've no idea how I've longed for this, dreamed of it. I need you," he told her, pulling her into his embrace and claiming her mouth with such passion it stole her wits.

The feel of his body and his hot skin pressed against hers made the fires blaze higher, and when he pressed himself closer, finding his place between her legs, she cried out in startled surprise. The sensation that rocketed through her was a bright shock of desire that made her forget everything but her need for her husband, the rightness of how it felt to be in his arms.

"I need you too," she gasped, writhing against him impatiently. "So much."

She wrapped her legs around his waist, her hands moving restlessly over him, sinking into his hair and sliding down his back to grasp his buttocks.

"Maggie… Maggie, love, slow down! I meant… I meant…"

But whatever it was he'd meant to do or say, Maggie did not know nor care. He had promised to set her on fire, and she was ablaze, an inferno, out of control.

"Please, please," she gasped.

Larkin had never denied her anything, had always given her everything she could possibly need from the moment they first met, and he did not resist her now. He thrust into her, the sensation so exquisite and powerful she moaned and held on as if she might fly away if she were not anchored to him.

Larkin groaned, burying his face in her hair and breathing deeply for a moment before he began to move, slowly at first and then with increasing fervour as she followed his lead. Dimly she realised that whilst she had known what passion was, what desire felt like, it had only been a shadow of what she felt in this moment. Now she knew what it was to love and be loved, not only with heart and emotion, but with body and soul too. She felt giddy with pleasure, dizzy with the frenetic joy of their union and yet she could not slow it down, could not deny it or try to savour the moment. There would be time enough for that, for slow love making and tender words, but this, this perfect burst of desire and adoration was everything she had ever wanted and needed, though she had never, would never have realised that without the man loving her now.

"Maggie," he rasped, his breath hot and damp against her neck as his movements became erratic and faster. "Maggie."

"Yes," she said simply. She cried out as he shattered too, feeling the powerful shuddering of his big body as he abandoned himself to her, giving himself to her, to *them*, and she gave herself with equal fervour.

She closed her eyes, blinded by the starburst of joy, by the overwhelming pleasure of it as they flew into the skies, and returned to earth, still joined physically and in all other ways that mattered, forever.

8th November 1850 Berwick Street, Soho, London.

"Are you ready?" Larkin asked, walking back into the bedroom as Maggie slid the last pins into her hair.

"I suppose so," she said with a sigh.

"Well, I like that. After all the trouble I went to getting your manor back, now you don't want to go!"

Maggie laughed at his feigned indignation, for she knew he was as loath to leave as she was. "I do!" she protested, getting up and walking into his arms. "I cannot wait to go home, and to show it all to you and have Giddy and everyone I love around me again. But I want you all to myself, too. I'm greedy, you see."

"So you are. Never satisfied," he observed, a glint in his eyes that made her blush.

She gave him a playful smack, huffing at his teasing. "And aren't you lucky," she said wryly.

"I am," he replied, quite serious now. "I am the luckiest fellow that ever lived. Let's go home, Maggie. It's a place I've never been before, but I've been looking for it for such a long time I'm even willing to share it with all the others that live there too."

She reached up and touched his face, staring at him, still astonished by how dramatically and splendidly her life had changed. "Larkin Weston, you are the most wonderful man, and I am so glad Gideon plagued you to death. I suspect you only married me hoping to get some peace and quiet, but whatever the reason… thank you."

He laughed at that and pulled her close. "Strangely, I don't think I'm going to get a second's peace and quiet for the rest of my days, and I'm glad of it, Maggie. For all of it. I love you."

And though the carriage was waiting, and they were already late, he did not miss the opportunity to prove that to her again.

Epilogue

At Lady Andover's ball, it was once again noted that this season's incomparable, the beautiful Miss Merrivale, was very much in demand.

Since the unveiling of her magnificent portrait by the acclaimed Mr Weston, there have been no end to the odes written in her honour, nor to the demands of every other debutante to have their likeness painted by the town's fashionable new master artist.

—Excerpt from an article in The London Morning Star

Sixteen months later...

20th April 1851, Easter at Merrivale's Manor, Cawston, Norfolk.

"Come here, you little rogue," Larkin exclaimed, but Gideon darted out of reach, a marchpane fruit clutched in each fist.

"Can't catch me!" he shrieked, laughing maniacally as Larkin walked out of the kitchen after him.

"Oh, ho! That's what you think," Larkin said, grinning and letting the boy get a head start before giving chase.

"Don't think I'm chasing you pair of lunatics!" he heard Maggie call after them, already breathless as she heaved her bulky form out of the chair at the kitchen table. At almost seven months pregnant, moving with any speed was quite beyond her.

Aunt Connie and Uncle Cecil had come to stay, bringing Caro too, all of whom looked the height of fashion and quite spectacularly glamorous. It was also their turn to host Larkin's parents, as they had spent last Easter at the Priory. But, as much as she loved them all, Larkin knew Maggie was weary. As she'd refused to take a nap, he suggested a quiet moment in the kitchen leaving everyone else chattering noisily as they exchanged gossip.

They'd been having tea and a comfortable coze with their housekeeper and their cook, affectionately named by all, Moody and Goody, when the little thief had swooped in and filched the sweets.

Larkin ran after his adopted son, chasing him outside and into the orchard, which suited him fine, as they had a surprise for the lad.

The trees were full of blossom, drifting down like lazy snowflakes as Larkin ducked under branches and Gideon squealed with laughter.

"Come back, you two reprobates!" Maggie shouted after them, having made it as far as the gate.

As Gideon was red-faced and panting, Larkin decided he'd best catch him before he made himself sick, so he swooped the lad up and threw him over his shoulder.

"Got you," he said smugly. "And if you get that sticky mess in my hair, I shall dunk you in the horse trough."

Gideon snorted and Larkin heard smacking noises which told him the marchpane was being devoured in case his mother confiscated it. She'd already told him he'd had enough.

"I found this in the orchard," he told Maggie as he strode back to her, turning Gideon over and holding him up by his ankles.

Gideon shrieked with delight, thinking this a great game, but Maggie exclaimed in horror.

"Oh, put him down. You'll make him sick after all those sweets."

Obligingly, Larkin deposited the lad on the grass at his mother's feet.

"Pa caught me," Gideon exclaimed, grinning up at them.

Both Maggie and Larkin sucked in a breath, for Gideon had never referred to him as anything other than Westie, and neither of them had thought to force him to do otherwise, feeling it was Gideon's decision.

"So I see," Maggie said, darting a glance at Larkin.

Larkin gazed back at her, a foolish smile curving his mouth. He couldn't have said a word, for his throat seemed strangely tight, his chest full of emotion. Happiness lit him up on this perfect day, in this idyllic place. The manor was every bit as ancient and charming and beautiful as Maggie had told him. Rambling roses climbed everywhere and nowhere was there a straight line to be seen. Age had settled upon the old building, sinking the roofline here, making a wall lean preposterously there, until there was the perfect amount of imperfection, set among a garden that rioted out of control with flowers. It was their own little idyll, their escape from the hurly burly of town life, their home, and nothing could surpass it.

"I've asked Jeb to send everyone else around to the stables," Maggie whispered in an undertone, and Larkin was glad she had flagged down the stable lad and organised everything as she always did, for suddenly he was all at sea. "But I don't think we can show this little thief his surprise until he goes and washes his hands."

"Surprise?" Gideon asked, immediately on alert and scrambling to his feet. "For me?"

"Well, I'm not sure you deserve it now, you naughty boy," Maggie said, folding her arms and looking stern.

Gideon hung his head, kicking at a stone with the toe of his boot. "Sorry, Mama. Sorry, Pa. I like marchpane, but… sorry."

Larkin thought he could probably forgive the boy anything if he called him Pa, for he said it so naturally, as if he didn't need to think about it at all.

Maggie's lips twitched. "Well, run inside and ask Moody to wash your hands and then we'll see."

Gideon, aware he'd been given a reprieve, ran off at once.

Maggie turned back to Larkin who let out an unsteady breath as she held her arms out to him. He pulled her close, smiling as her burgeoning stomach kept them a little apart.

"I told you he'd come to it in time," she said softly.

Larkin nodded, pressing a kiss to her forehead. "You did. And, as ever, you were right. Do you think he will mind having a little brother or sister?"

"No. I think he is excited, and I think his father is clever enough to ensure he never feels left out."

She reached up on tiptoes and pressed her mouth to his, just as Gideon burst out of the house with Mrs Moody not far behind.

"Ready!" he called, running to them. "Ready for my surprise."

Laughing ruefully at the child's terrible timing, he picked Gideon up. "Come along then, my fine fellow."

He grinned at Moody, who was in on the surprise, as was everyone else in the household. If Gideon thought it strange that his Aunt Connie and Uncle Cecil, Caro, Grandpa and Grandma, and Wallace and Barnes and everyone else was gathered in the stable yard, he did not mention it, for he had seen his surprise, and nothing else mattered.

"Bertie!" he exclaimed, wriggling until Larkin put him down. He ran to the fence, where the pony stood chewing placidly next to his mother's pretty mare, Starlight, and swishing its tail. "Pa, Pa! Is it Bertie?"

"It is," Larkin said, crouching down beside Gideon. "He's your pony, Gideon, and I shall teach you to ride him, just like my father taught me."

Gideon stared at him, back at the pony, and then at Larkin again. He hurled himself at Larkin, throwing his arms around his neck and squeezing tightly.

"Thank you! Thank you, Papa. He's wonderful!"

Larkin cleared his throat, afraid he might weep in front of everyone, for he was only holding onto his composure by a thread. "You're wonderful too, Giddy, and I love you. Thank you for being my son."

Giddy pushed away from Larkin, apparently less moved by the moment than Larkin for he began jumping up and down. "Ride him now, Pa? Please?"

"Certainly," Larkin said, nodding. "If you go into the stables and find Jeb, he'll show you Bertie's saddle and bridle, and you may carry them out to me if you are careful.

Gideon gave an excited yip and ran off across the yard. Larkin turned to see his father smiling at him.

"Well done," he said, and gave an approving nod.

Larkin smiled back but found this exceedingly high praise the last straw. Taking a moment for himself, he walked into the paddock, reaching into his pocket for the lump of sugar he'd stowed there earlier. Bertie snuffled at his palm with his velvety muzzle and crunched amiably. The gate creaked, and Larkin looked up to see Maggie had followed him.

"Don't," he said, holding up a hand and grinning ruefully. "If you say anything nice, I shall be quite undone."

She smiled at him, warmth and love shining in her eyes. "Then I shan't say a word," she said, and put her arms around him, holding on tight and resting her head upon his chest.

As ever, she knew exactly what he needed, and Larkin sighed as the emotion settled, changing into something peaceful but unbreakable.

"Can you win at life, like you can at cards, do you think?" he asked, looking down at his wife.

"Of course, silly," she said, gazing up at him with adoration, as if he truly was the hero he had always wanted to be, slaying the dragon and bringing her and Gideon and everyone she loved safely home. "We've been winning from the moment you tripped over that packing case and taught Gideon his first bad word."

He laughed. Much to Maggie's chagrin, he'd taught the lad a couple more in the interim, too.

"So we have," Larkin said, and kissed her, uncaring of the family still gathered in the yard, or Bertie nudging at him, searching hopefully for more sugar.

Gideon would be back any moment and, if Larkin had learnt anything since becoming the boy's pa, it was that such moments ought never to be missed.

independence is something she will not consider. Having tasted success writing under a false name in The Lady's Weekly Review, her alter ego is attaining notoriety and fame, and Prue rather likes it.

A Duty that must be endured

Robert Adolphus, The Duke of Bedwin, is in no hurry to marry, he's done it once and repeating that disaster is the last thing he desires. Yet, an heir is a necessary evil for a duke and one he cannot shirk. A dark reputation precedes him though, his first wife may have died young, but the scandals the beautiful, vivacious and spiteful creature supplied the ton have not. A wife must be found. A wife who is neither beautiful or vivacious but sweet and dull, and certain to stay out of trouble.

Dared to do something drastic

The sudden interest of a certain dastardly duke is as bewildering as it is unwelcome. She'll not throw her ambitions aside to marry a scoundrel just as her plans for self-sufficiency and freedom are coming to fruition. Surely showing the man she's not actually the meek little wallflower he is looking for should be enough to put paid to his intentions? When Prue is dared by her friends to do something drastic, it seems the perfect opportunity to kill two birds.

However, Prue cannot help being intrigued by the rogue who has inspired so many of her romances. Ordinarily, he plays the part of handsome rake, set on destroying her plucky heroine. But is he really the villain of the piece this time, or could he be the hero?

Finding out will be dangerous, but it just might inspire her greatest story yet.

To Dare a Duke

Dare to be Wicked

Daring Daughters Book One

The fashionable image of a meek, weak young lady, prone to swooning at the least provocation, is one that makes them seethe with frustration.

Their handsome childhood friend ...

Cassius Cadogen, Viscount Oakley, is the only child of the Earl and Countess St Clair. Beloved and indulged, he is popular, gloriously handsome, and a talented artist.

Returning from two years of study in France, his friendship with both sisters becomes strained as jealousy raises its head. A situation not helped by the two mysterious Frenchmen who have accompanied him home.

And simmering sibling rivalry ...

Passion, art, and secrets prove to be a combustible combination, and someone will undoubtedly get burned.

Dare to be Wicked

Also check out Emma's regency romance series, Rogues & Gentlemen. Available now!

The Rogue
Rogues & Gentlemen Book 1

The notorious Rogue that began it all.

Set in Cornwall, 1815. Wild, untamed and isolated.

Lawlessness is the order of the day and smuggling is rife.

Henrietta always felt most at home in the wilds of the outdoors but even she had no idea how the mysterious and untamed would sweep her away in a moment.

Bewitched by his wicked blue eyes

Henrietta Morton knows to look the other way when the free trading 'gentlemen' are at work.

Yet when a notorious pirate bursts into her local village shop, she can avert her eyes no more. Bewitched by his wicked blue eyes, a moment of insanity follows as Henrietta hides the handsome fugitive from the Militia.

Her reward is a kiss, lingering and unforgettable.

In his haste to flee, the handsome pirate drops a letter, a letter that lays bare a tale of betrayal. When Henrietta's father gives her hand in marriage to a wealthy and villainous nobleman in return for the payment of his debts, she becomes desperate.

Blackmailing a pirate may be her only hope for freedom.

**** **Warning**: This book contains the most notorious rogue of all of Cornwall and, on occasion, is highly likely to include some mild sweating or descriptive sex scenes. ****

Free to read on *Kindle Unlimited*: The Rogue

Already running from a dark past, his future is becoming increasingly complex as he finds himself caught in a tangled web of jealousy and revenge.

A feisty young maiden

Temptation, in the form of the lovely Miss Clarinda Bow, is a constant threat to his peace of mind, enticing him to be something he isn't. But when the old man dies his will makes a surprising demand, and the fates might just give Harry the chance to have everything he ever desired, including Clara, if only he dares.

And as those close to the Preston family begin to die, Harry may not have any choice.

Order your copy here. A Dog in a Doublet

Lose yourself in Emma's paranormal world with The French Vampire Legend series….

The Key to Erebus

The French Vampire Legend Book 1

The truth can kill you.

Taken away as a small child, from a life where vampires, the Fae, and other mythical creatures are real and treacherous, the beautiful young witch, Jéhenne Corbeaux is totally unprepared when she returns to rural France to live with her eccentric Grandmother.

Thrown headlong into a world she knows nothing about she seeks to learn the truth about herself, uncovering secrets more shocking than anything she could ever have imagined and finding that she is by no means powerless to protect the ones she loves.

Despite her Gran's dire warnings, she is inexorably drawn to the dark and terrifying figure of Corvus, an ancient vampire and master of the vast Albinus family.

Jéhenne is about to find her answers and discover that, not only is Corvus far more dangerous than she could ever imagine, but that he holds much more than the key to her heart …

Now available on Kindle Unlimited and Amazon

The Key to Erebus

Check out Emma's exciting fantasy series with hailed by Kirkus Reviews as "An enchanting fantasy with a likable heroine, romantic intrigue, and clever narrative flourishes."

The Dark Prince
The French Fae Legend Book 1

Two Fae Princes
One Human Woman
And a world ready to tear them all apart

Laen Braed is Prince of the Dark fae, with a temper and reputation to match his black eyes, and a heart that despises the human race. When he is sent back through the forbidden gates between realms to retrieve an ancient fae artifact, he returns home with far more than he bargained for.

Corin Albrecht, the most powerful Elven Prince ever born. His golden eyes are rumoured to be a gift from the gods, and destiny is calling him. With a love for the human world that runs deep, his friendship with Laen is being torn apart by his prejudices.

Océane DeBeauvoir is an artist and bookbinder who has always relied on her lively imagination to get her through an unhappy and uneventful life. A jewelled dagger put on display at a nearby museum hits the headlines with speculation of another race, the Fae. But the discovery also inspires Océane to create an extraordinary piece of art that cannot be confined to the pages of a book.

With two powerful men vying for her attention and their friendship stretched to the breaking point, the only question that remains...who is truly The Dark Prince.

The man of your dreams is coming...or is it your nightmares he visits? Find out in Book One of The French Fae Legend.

Available now to read on Kindle Unlimited and Amazon

The Dark Prince

Want more Emma?

If you enjoyed this book, please support this indie author and take a moment to leave a few words in a review. *Thank you!*

To be kept informed of special offers and free deals (which I do regularly) follow me on *https://www.bookbub.com/authors/emma-v-leech*

To find out more and to get news and sneak peeks of the first chapter of upcoming works, go to my website and sign up for the newsletter.
http://www.emmavleech.com/

Or follow me here......

http://viewauthor.at/EmmaVLeechAmazon